MAGIC REQUIRED

MAGIC REQUIRED

A LOCHLAN ELLYLL NOVEL

BY

HS PAISLEY

Editors:
Dustin Bilyk
Molly Schiever

Second edition

ISBN: 978-1-9995236-1-9 (ebook)
ISBN: 978-1-9995236-0-26 (paperback)

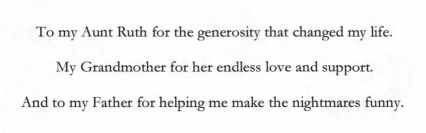

To my Aunt Ruth for the generosity that changed my life.

My Grandmother for her endless love and support.

And to my Father for helping me make the nightmares funny.

CHAPTER ONE

They decided water would be the way I died. But I swam anyway. It was my way of biting my thumb at them. At the Old Gods who made me like this.

To be honest, I hated the water. It scared me. I doubtless hated the fear more than the water itself, because I needed it too. It kept me centered.

I didn't use to swim. I didn't use to need to risk my life to clear my head. There was a time where singing did that for me. It still did . . . sometimes.

But not like it used to.

Not like before my eldest brother died.

My eyes flicked up to the clock on the wall. 5:37 a.m.

Twenty minutes.

The community center pool wasn't huge, but it was long enough for me to pick up some speed. With any luck, I'd have a lane to myself until just after six. Standing at the edge, I looked down at the rippling water and the only other person I ever saw swimming this early.

Tim.

Though he was likely in his early seventies, I could tell he'd been one hell of an athlete in his prime. I suspected a boxer. Or mayhap he reminded me of Muhammad Ali with darker skin.

He was here every day, without fail, right at 5:30, and he had the slowest front crawl I had ever seen.

Looking away from Tim, I positioned my goggles, filled my lungs and dove. Cool liquid engulfed my body and I felt the familiar jump of my heart.

That happened every time I was in the water. Blind panic rose up within me. But this particular brand of panic was familiar. With a practiced progression of thought and movement, I controlled it easily.

Tim and I were soon joined by the 6-a.m.-ers. Sharing the lane slowed my pace. I had no patience to swim slowly.

Not today.

I got out of the pool.

To say I was a little old for nightmares was a cosmic understatement, I thought as I stepped under the lukewarm water of the community center showers. Then again, the longer you live, the more you saw, so perhaps not.

I turned to let the water run over my face. When I closed my eyes, the young girl's lost and tear-stained expression was all I saw. I squeezed my eyes shut tighter, attempting to remember every detail of my nightmare.

I didn't want to remember, but it felt important.

Her crying seemed to flood my ears. She couldn't have been older than five. Why was she alone? The images of her wandering down an abandoned street flashed on the backs of my closed eyelids.

I saw her pass a sign. Fort Totten Park.

Her flushed cream-colored face was covered in blotchy red patches from crying. Dark brown hair stuck to her cheek where it had fallen out of her short ponytail. It was matted with blood from a cut on her forehead. The yellow tie in her hair matched the dress she was wearing. Both were discolored with dirt and grime.

I sighed.

There was nothing I could do for the imaginary girl, lost only to me.

I looked up into the small mirror in the shower. Bright green eyes stared back at me—green eyes that were the exact shape and color as those of my two brothers.

Someone had left a razor on the little shelf beneath the mirror. It reminded me I needed to shave before work. I ran my hand over the roughness on my cheeks and jaw, then through my short black hair that wasn't as short as I'd like.

And a haircut too, I thought as I stepped out of the shower.

"Hey Lochlan!" said the blonde teenager behind the counter on my way out. "How was your swim?"

I adjusted a thin chain under my shirt. The small stone at the end of it settled on my chest before I answered.

"Hi Ella," I said, ignoring her question. At 6:20 a.m., her cheeriness was unsettling.

"I noticed your membership is coming up for renewal," she told me with a bright smile. "Would you like to do that now?"

"No thanks," I answered, pausing briefly at the doors.

"Okay," she said, still beaming. "Have an awesome day!"

"Too late," I said under my breath as I left.

March air hit my face when I stepped outside the community center. The swim hadn't rid my mind of the lost girl as I'd hoped it would, so I tightened the strap of my gym bag and ran home.

I took a slight detour on my way to pass one of my thinking spots. An old oak tree stood tall and proud not far from where I lived, and it reminded me of my homeland and of my brothers. The sight of it brought me peace, short-lived though it was.

Even with the detour, running cut a thirty-minute walk by a third of the time. When I rounded the corner of my block, I saw my elderly neighbor having an argument with the community mailbox. I ran past my house, only slowing once I reached her.

"Mrs. Abernathy," I said pushing my square-rimmed glasses up my nose. The glasses were thick and black. They helped me be less noticeable, more overlooked. I wanted to be invisible.

Society tends to ignore the impoverished, and today, in 2047, laser eye surgery was more affordable than ever, which meant glasses were a sign of poverty. I used this to my advantage and wore them every day, despite my perfect vision.

"How are you this morning?" I asked, waving to the small woman with dark-chocolate skin and grey-streaked curls.

"Oh, Lochlan, better for seeing you," she said, turning to look at me. My face broke into a smile. Mrs. Abernathy's southern drawl and kind face had a way of doing that to me. "You're up early," she said, adjusting her vivid green handbag on her shoulder and tucking a wisp of grey-black hair behind her ear.

"I went for a swim."

She returned my smile before grimacing at the mailbox.

I moved into the neighborhood almost three years ago. On my very first afternoon, while I was unloading the moving van I'd rented, I met Mrs. Abernathy. She called me over, insisted I take a break and offered me some of her homemade sweet tea. Many a hot summer afternoon had been spent thus.

We both carried the accents of our homeland. It made the stories we shared all the better. She would tell me about growing up in the Deep South and I would tell her Celtic folktales. In reality, I was telling her about my childhood too. She just didn't know it.

"I don't know what it is with this darn thing," she said, placing her thumb to the scanner pad beside her mailbox over and over again, receiving nothing but an angry beep in return. "But it's not working."

"Why don't you let me have a look," I said, pulling my phone out of my pocket.

I worked for a technology and security company. That fact alone was usually sufficient explanation as to how I fixed things using my phone.

I didn't need the phone; it was a prop.

I'm a Caster, or at least that's what I call myself. Saying I'm a Demigod, while accurate, would show hubris.

The bottom line was I worked with Magic.

Mrs. Abernathy stepped back, allowing me access to the box. I pretended to fiddle with the scanner pad while I muttered a few words under my breath and brushed the back of my hand over the black square.

"What was that, dear?" she asked from behind me.

"I think it was a glitch, why don't you try it again?"

She beamed at me and took a slow step forward.

Contrary to popular opinion, Magic and technology work brilliantly together if you know what you're doing.

And yes, Magic with a capital M because Magic is a name. Magic is alive.

"Oh!" she cried as the scanner turned green under her thumb. A door

11

popped open to reveal several envelopes. "You fixed it!"

"Hardly," I shrugged. Seeing the multitude of letters she pulled from the small square, I said, "I can't believe you get so much mail. I'm jealous."

"Maybe I'll start writing you, shall I?" she said with a devilish gleam in her eye.

"With the price of postage these days, I wouldn't let you."

"And then you might not ever speak to me again, and you know how much I enjoy that."

"I do," I said.

If only she had heard me speak when I was in school five years ago. There, my thick accent was unremarkable. Here, it would get me noticed. I used to be able to speak without it completely, but for some reason it came back to me at school. I haven't been able to shake it since.

"Can I walk you home?" I asked her, offering my arm. "I'm going that way."

"Why thank you, dear," she said, placing her hand in the crook of my elbow after tucking her mail into her aggressively bright handbag. She walked at a brisk pace I was only prepared for because this exact scene had played itself out several times over the past few years.

Mrs. Abernathy filled me in on her favorite soap operas as we walked the half block to our side-by-side front doors. She lived in 34B and I in 34A.

After going up a few steps, she reached over the little wall that separated our respective porches and waved me towards her. Reaching out, she patted me on the cheek. If the wall were any higher, she wouldn't have managed it.

"You're a good boy," she said with a sad smile. "How come I never see you bringing any girls over?"

"Oh, ummm . . ." I didn't know what to say.

Sorry, Mrs. Abernathy, but any relationship I had would be built on the lie that I was Human. Been there, and I don't want to do it again.

No. I couldn't say that.

"Or boys," Mrs. Abernathy said, misinterpreting my hesitation. "I don't judge dear. In fact, I know of this wonderful bar—"

"No," I laughed. "I don't get out much is all."

"Oh, well try, won't you?" she said, stepping to her front door, punching in the unlock code and laying her palm above the doorknob. "Otherwise, as soon as they come up with some anti-aging technology I'll just keep you for myself."

"If only," I said, putting in my own door code.

φ

"Locherrrrrrr!" The familiar voice carried across the Tjart Tech and Security lobby.

"Jen," I replied to the twenty-something man walking towards me. "How are you?"

"One day I'm going to get here earlier than you," he said as he pulled the drawstring of his zip-up hoodie back and forth.

I gave him a wry grin. It was a bit of a running joke. I always seemed to enter the building steps ahead of him. Even on days when Jenner came in early, somehow, I would come in early too. It was something neither of us could explain.

"I'm good," he said as we walked to the elevators. "Better after I saw this gorgeous blond in the coffee shop around the corner."

"Did you ask for his number?"

"Madre de Dios, with eyes like that? He wouldn't give me the time of day."

Jenner wasn't unattractive. Confidence was his biggest problem. He was tall, only a little shorter than my 6'2". His warm copper skin hinted at his mixed heritage, and his puppy-dog brown eyes made him look nineteen when he was closer to twenty-five.

Jenner was my only friend in the city.

Well, that's not true, I thought. I guess I was friends with his sister, Cam. I made a mental note to call her.

"Anyway," he went on. "I saw him flirting with some skinny little muchacha who was flipping her hair like she had a tick or something." He moved his head back and forth in a jerky robotic imitation of someone brushing long hair over their shoulder.

"That seems like some misplaced anger, my friend," I said, stifling a laugh at the looks Jenner was getting from the people behind us.

The ding of the elevator sounded and we got on. In turn, everyone in the elevator pressed his or her palm to the scanning pad. After a few moments an automated voice told us we were going down.

The elevators are Tjart Tech only allowed five to ride at a time and there were no floor numbers to press. Instead, the system took you where you needed to go after it scanned your palm and looked up your file. No one ever got off on the wrong floor here.

"It's not misplaced anger," Jenner said, his light accent increasing with his irritation. "She was proudly wearing a Right Waters pin on her oh-so-lovely blazer."

I sighed while Jenner swore in Spanish.

Currently making headlines was the Right Waters Party. They were getting coverage because of their strong support of a new immigration bill. Though Jenner and his parents were born in this country, his ancestors had been immigrants.

Long before his mother's grandparents had walked across the border to find new life in "the land of the free," his father's side had been brought over in the belly of a crowded ship. As a result, Jenner kept himself well informed of the goings on in our nation's capital.

"Then she deserves your anger," I said with a serious nod.

"Okay," he said, throwing me a sideways look in exchange for my sarcasm. "Maybe not her specifically but I just, I just . . ." He abruptly switched to Spanish and I tuned him out. After three years of knowing Jenner, I knew once he got going, it was best to let him go.

The rest of my day passed without incident. My job of tech support was busied yet monotonous. It was more often a matter of resetting a system than fixing it. These days everyone and everything had a system. Unless you crossed the river into Lowtown, you'd be hard pressed to find a building that still used keys or a store that still accepted cash. Everything had gone digital.

Tjart Tech and Security took care of all things related to technological systems and private security. From phones to computers, banks to mail boxes, Tjart Tech did it all.

And yet somehow, in this age of technology, "Have you tried turning it off and then on again?" was the phrase I used more than any other.

Eight hours to the second after I had walked into the building, I was walking out. As I headed out of the front doors, I saw my bus nearing the stop at the end of the block.

Like so many times before, I had to make the split-second decision: wait the nine minutes until the next bus came, or sprint down the street in a vain attempt to catch this one. It wasn't cold out, being the warmest

March on record. Waiting wouldn't be so bad.

But who liked to wait?

I clutched my messenger bag and took off down the street. The driver saw me running and, with a vengeful grin, he closed the door and drove off as the light turned green. I got there in time to bang on the tail end of the bus as it passed.

I cursed under my breath and sighed. If there is one lesson a long life will teach you, it's how to let go of the little things.

Sitting down on the bench inside the bus shelter, I looked up at the images flashing across the glass wall to my right. Curious as to the time of the next bus, I stood and approached it.

The bottom half of the glass wall was a 24-hour news station with a ticker tape running across the top. Above that were tiny, flashing squares with rounded edges of blue, red or green. Each square had a number in it signifying a bus route.

I tapped twice on a blue square with a large 16 in the center. It revealed a drop-down list displaying the time of the next buses.

'*Delays*,' an automated voice intoned. '*Next trip: 21 minutes.*'

"Brilliant," I said.

The drop-down list disappeared. As I started to turn away from the screen, something caught my eye. I stared at the image of a smiling young girl with dark brown hair and a rosy complexion that had taken the place of the news anchor.

"I'm sorry." I'd bumped into a man when I took a step backwards to get a better look at the screen. He looked exhausted and made a beeline for the bench in the corner of the bus shelter. He sat so he could lean against two walls at the same time and seemed to immediately fall asleep.

I took another two steps backwards and sat beside him. At this distance I could better read the bold words written beneath the face of the girl who was the focus of my nightmare.

"What? No . . ." I muttered to myself as I read, "Fort Totten Park?"

"Oh, so sad," said the man beside me. I turned to look at him. "They found that poor girl's body."

"What?" I said again, shifting to face him. His skin had grey undertones and dark circles drooped under his eyes.

"Did you not hear?" he said, looking at me through one half-open, very blue eye. "The girl they thought had run away or been kidnapped or got lost or something. Melissa, Melinda?" he said, letting his eye close all the way as he struggled to remember her name.

"Melanie," I supplied, not knowing when I had learned that.

"Oh, so you did hear? Melanie, that's right. Melanie Connor."

"Yes I . . ." I stopped. I could hardly tell this man I had heard the girl's name in a dream. Luckily, he kept speaking and I didn't have to come up with a response.

"Poor girl," he said, his blue eye searching my face. "I feel for her family."

"Remind me of what happened?" I asked.

"She went missing a few days ago and they found her body in Fort Totten Park, oh," he said, peeking down at his watch, "maybe four hours ago. They say if they had found her even an hour earlier, she might have made it. No idea what happened."

"Gods," I said, not knowing what to say. "That's . . ."

"Yeah," the man said.

We sat in silence for a few minutes before he truly fell asleep. It was the snoring that clued me in.

Twenty minutes later when the bus arrived, I shook him awake.

"Thanks," he said, before stumbling onto the bus, finding a seat and falling asleep again.

The ride home was thirty-five minutes with a ten-minute walk on the other end. It took longer than that for my mind to attempt to make sense of my prophetic dream, if that's even what it was.

As soon as I got home, I started towards my office to look into the girl's disappearance. My single-mindedness was interrupted by an angry growl from my stomach. I remembered there was some leftover Chicken Thai soup in the fridge. I heated it in the microwave before taking it to my office.

I set the bowl of hot soup down on my desk, carefully avoiding anything that might make it tip over. Then I started my search.

One of the advantages of working for a tech and security company was there were few systems beyond my reach. And if there was one I couldn't get into, I would ask Jenner to hack it for me. I may be a Caster, but when it came to computers, he's the wiz.

It took me under five minutes to get into the city's police department system. Once inside, a quick search revealed the missing persons file I was looking for.

Melanie Connor, age five, disappeared from a friend's backyard on Saturday afternoon during a birthday party. It took anywhere from five minutes to two hours for the hosts of the party to notice her absence.

It's rare for a child to go missing. In the mid-2030s, it became commonplace for parents to have their children wear locators in the form of a bracelet or a necklace in case they got lost or, for some, broke their curfew.

Melanie's parents had told police she knew how to use the locator and how to set off the panic alarm. The locator bracelet was found on Sunday.

It wasn't working.

Her body was found in a small patch of trees that bordered the southwest side of Fort Totten Park. There was no indication of abuse or sexual assault. The autopsy scan to determine the girl's cause of death was inconclusive and a true autopsy would have to be done.

"Gods below," I said, leaning back in my chair. I looked at the bowl of soup, forgotten. Picking it up, I brought a spoonful to my lips. It was cold. I didn't care. I ate it quickly.

Would I have been able to save this girl's life? Was I supposed to have figured it out somehow? How could I have known it wasn't just a dream?

Was this my fault? I asked myself. Could my soul bear the weight of yet another death if it was?

By the time I was done thinking myself in circles, I was mentally and physically exhausted. I went into the kitchen to wash the bowl and spoon from my soup.

I got ready for bed, thinking of Melanie and what I could have, or perhaps should have, done. It might have been minutes, or mayhap it was hours, before I fell asleep. Either way, I awoke the next morning, tired, blaming myself for the death of a young girl.

CHAPTER TWO

The early morning sun bounced off the pinned-up, professional, black bun at the back of the woman's head. Flawless terracotta skin was pulled together between her perfect eyebrows, frustration clear on her face. Her fingers tapped quickly on her phone as she walked down the busy street. The pale pink of her nails matched the shade on her lips. Lips that were turned down in disapproval at what she was reading.

She slowed and started to turn. Pausing, she looked up at the street signs. Arlington and Metcalfe. Shaking her head, she kept walking straight. Her fingers flashed across the screen of her phone as she cut through the crowd.

The height of her heels didn't slow her brisk pace as she continued down the street. Making an angry sound, she pressed a spot behind her ear to turn on her earpiece. She spoke in an irritated tone. The conversation was over quickly. The woman returned to tapping her screen.

Stopping at a busy intersection, she looked up for the signal to walk. Cars whizzed by until the light turned red. Moments later, after seeing the walk signal light up on the other side of the intersection, the woman hurriedly stepped into the street and—

Breaking glass, a screech of tires, a sickening crunch of bone and the dull thunk-thunk of a skull meeting metal and then the hard asphalt. Blood pooled, people screamed, and I jerked awake.

Another nightmare.

My breath was coming heavy and fast, heart pounding in my chest. I lay still, staring at the imperfections of the white paint above me, waiting for my heart rate to return to normal. I noticed a crack in the corner of my room and the beginnings of water damage before I processed what I had dreamed.

It had been three weeks since Melanie Connor's body was found, and not one day had gone by that I hadn't thought of her. Over that time, I had gone back and forth on what I would do if this happened again.

After the mental tennis match, I decided no matter how stupid I felt or how ridiculous it seemed, if I had another nightmare like that, I would try to find the person.

"Arlington and Metcalfe," I whispered to the damaged ceiling. "The business district. Not far from Parliament."

I waved my hand over my bedside clock. Angry red numbers appeared in the air above the small black rectangle. 5:23.

I had no idea what time the woman was going to be there. I didn't know her name, I didn't know where she worked or even what day this was going to happen. But I did know the cross street, and I knew it was early morning.

I closed my eyes, trying to remember where the sun was as it peeked between the tall buildings. I was certain it had been before nine. I'd go today, and if she wasn't there, I'd go again tomorrow.

I pictured her face in my head, the stern masculine features. She looked familiar. Something to do with the news, but I couldn't put my finger on it.

"Arlington and Metcalfe," I said again, swinging my legs out of bed. "That's a start."

φ

I stood in the alcove of a tall building a few doors down from the corner where I had dreamed the woman would be. My eyes scanned the crowd. The sun was barely up, and the mass of suit-clad pedestrians was not as thick as in my dream. She wouldn't be here yet.

I waited.

After about ten minutes, I saw her. A head of brown hair in a business-like bun and eyes turned down to her phone.

Bright red lips.

Cream-colored skin.

No. Not her.

The woman I was waiting for had terracotta skin and black hair. This one wore a deep-green pea coat to protect against the cool spring morning; the woman in my dream wore black.

Thirty minutes later, I thought I saw her, but this woman with pale pink lips had alabaster skin and didn't attempt to turn down the wrong street. I closed my eyes for a heartbeat to remember the rich red-brown of the woman's skin tone.

The street grew busier as the sun climbed slightly higher in clear sky. Had it been a clear sky in my dream? I wondered.

I was certain it had. I could remember the sun finding the long lines of space between the tall buildings.

I looked down at my watch, not wanting to miss her if she came by at exactly the wrong moment. Within the next half-hour I would not only be late for work, but it would be too late in the morning for the light to match my memory. If she didn't show up soon, I would come back tomorrow.

I walked slowly over to lean against the post that labeled the intersecting streets. Perhaps I was being crazy. Perhaps Melanie Connor was some kind of wild coincidence. I must have seen the newscast about her, forgotten it, then dreamed of her later on. The Fort Totten Park bit was harder to explain. Or mayhap I hadn't dreamed that part at all. My mind could have put it there later.

I crossed my arms as insecurities swirled in my mind. The chill morning air bit through my thin long-sleeved shirt but I didn't mind. I stayed where I was, leaning against the signpost. I had promised myself I would wait for the woman.

"Oh, I'm sorry," said someone, bumping into me. "I should be more aware. This damn thing." She looked down at her phone.

"No problem," I said, still wrapped up in my own misgivings.

"Just one of those mornings." Her pale pink lips gave me a strained smile before going back to her phone and walking away.

I returned to scanning the group of passing people when my eyes caught up with my brain.

I whipped around, trying to find her.

Her.

The woman from my dream.

Pride and triumph rose in my chest. I was right to come. I was right to wait. Could this be my second chance, my redemption, and my opportunity to make up for deeds long done?

I saw the sun gleaming off her dark hair and weaved my way through the crowd to catch up. I followed at a distance of a few feet, glad I hadn't lost her in the melee of people because of my delayed reaction.

She cut through the sea of suits, which only slowed her slightly, but enough to allow me to catch up. Once I was walking behind her, I heard the angry phone conversation.

"I don't care what your excuses are! A deadline is a deadline and if you want to publish that piece on Right Waters on my site and not just on your little blog then you will get it to me in the next ninety minutes."

She paused, listening to the response of whomever she was scolding.

"Yes," she said. "Yes, she went through the same thing you're going through now. Okay . . . yes . . . Well she's gorgeous, what do you expect! That's why she has an interactive video blog attached to the . . . your blog doesn't . . . Because she brings in viewers! You know what? I don't care. Get it done or go back to answering her fan mail." She hung up the phone.

I followed her for another two blocks before she stopped and waited for the walk signal, still tapping on her device.

I noticed there was a small gap between the woman and the people around her. Though the crowd at the light was growing, no one dared move closer to her. When I looked harder, I saw the small sideways glances. The nods to friends and colleagues.

Who is this woman? I thought, before my mind returned to the task at hand.

I tried to move behind her. Close enough to grab her, as if everything would play out as in my dream. My route was blocked by two men in long overcoats.

"No way, no way," one said.

"I swear," the other replied.

"Excuse me?" I said trying to push through. I was ignored.

My heart started beating loud in my ears. What if I couldn't get to her?

24

What if these two linebackers prevented it?

My body tensed as I weighed my options. The light would change any second.

"Nartha," I said under my breath, asking Magic for strength and feeling its consent.

The white light flashed its consent to cross only a breath before the woman stepped into the street.

"Yes, that's her," linebacker one said. "That's Adri—Hey!"

I easily shoved the two of them apart as the woman stepped into the street.

Time seemed to slow.

An engine revved. I stepped towards her. The woman turned her head. I was only a foot away now. A collective gasp rose from behind me at the same time as she realized she was going to be hit. Her face contorted. And she was hit.

But not by the car.

I slammed into her and our bodies flew forward. I managed to turn us in the air so she landed on me and not the hard ground. Better it was my head hitting the concrete.

And it did. Hard.

Everything went black, but only for a moment. When the world came back to me in a rush, I saw a crowd had formed around us. I tried to blink the stars out of my eyes and ignore the beginnings of a massive headache.

Slowly, I loosened my hold on the woman.

"Are you all right?" I asked, talking over the many other voices inquiring the same thing. A few people yelled curses at the driver, now long gone.

"I . . . huh?" she said, trying to focus.

"Are you all right?" I repeated. A few people helped her up and out of the middle of the street. I followed, picking up one of her black high-heeled shoes that must have fallen off when I hit her.

I felt a strong pounding in my head.

Concussion, I thought. No question.

After seeing the woman and I were both okay, the small gathering dispersed.

I placed the shoe at her feet. She kept a hand on my shoulder as she slid her foot in.

"Prince Charming," she said, her breathing returned to normal. "You saved my life and my favorite pair of shoes. I don't know which I'm more indebted to you for."

"I'm just happy I was here to help," I said, standing.

The woman looked up at me. Even in heels, she was several inches shorter than I was. In her mid to late forties, I noted the minute grooves in her face, evidence that she smiled as much as she frowned.

"Thank you," she said in earnest. Then, reaching into her bag, she pulled out a card.

"I don't know what kind of business you're in," she continued, her tone professional and sharp. She was back to all business. "If modeling is a path you're interested in, I know a few people who would like your look. Here." She handed me the black rectangular piece of paper as I shifted uncomfortably.

It was most definitely not a path I was interested in, but I took the card.

Looking down at it I saw her name in silver ink printed neatly above her title.

"I'm Adrienne Jace."

My jaw dropped. I did know her. Everyone in this city knew her. Adrienne Jace, founder of JACE Co. and media magnate. She was not only one of the wealthiest people in the city, but a prominent advocate for indigenous rights on the world stage.

"Wow," I said dumbly.

She smiled. It transformed her face from the gritty businesswoman into someone warm. I imagined this was who she was when she wasn't fighting against misogyny and the stereotypes so often tied to her people.

"Let me know if I can help you out with anything." Turning away from me, she headed across the street. I grinned as she paused and let a few people cross in front of her before turning back to me. "I owe you one."

Then she waved and disappeared into the crowd.

I slid her card into my pocket at the same time as my phone rang.

Danu, I swore. I'm late for work.

φ

"Good Afternoon Mr. Russo, Tjart Tech Division. My name is Lochlan, what can I do for you today?" I said to the image of a middle-aged man with black hair and olive-toned skin. There was a loud beeping in the background.

Can he even hear me? I wondered.

"I can't get this damn alarm to turn off!" he shouted, which answered both of my questions.

"Right, I can hear that. I assume you've tried scanning your thumb and it didn't work?"

"No," he said with awe, like I had given him the secret to the universe. "I hadn't thought of that. What a novel idea."

27

He glared at me.

"I'm sorry, but you would be surprised how many times that works. Can you show me the room to ensure you are alone and not being coerced to de-activate the alarm?" Mr. Russo groaned in response but showed the room. "Thank you, sir. Is the scanning pad malfunctioning?"

"How the hell would I know that?" he yelled.

"Could you scan your thumb and show me what happens? I have put in the request to cancel emergency services."

A 4-by-6-inch panel came into view and it was flashing an angry red. Mr. Russo placed his thumb in a black square outline. For a moment, the panel turned green. There was a second of silence before the panel went back to red and the alarm started again.

"Aye," I said, typing quickly. "I think I can fix the problem easily enough if you give me remote access. It should be all cleared up in a couple minutes."

"Thank God!"

"Can you give me the number on the side of the device we are speaking on?"

"Why do you need that number?" he asked, obviously suspicious. "Don't you have my system numbers on file?"

Danu, I thought. Usually they didn't ask.

I quickly tapped for a few seconds before there was a slight glitch in the video.

"Are you still there?" he asked, even though he could see me.

"If you give me the number on your device, I will be able to use it to turn off the alarm." He opened his mouth, probably to ask why I couldn't do it with just his name and passcode.

"I could do it with your name and passcode," I told him. "But not only would that take longer but this way gives me better access to your security system."

What I didn't tell him was I would hack into his system to do it.

There was another quick glitch on the screen. This time he ignored it and rattled off the number.

All calls are recorded and stored. Forever. I've worked at Tjart Tech and Security for three years, and in the first week I learned it was easier to hack a home system than spend time getting all the clearance information.

The more security questions I asked, and the longer the alarm was on, the angrier the client got. It's not strictly allowed. I cut those bits of conversation out of the recordings.

"Great," I said. "Now scan your thumb . . . perfect. Got it. Just a second."

A replica of his scanning device and security dock was projected in front of me in blue light. Through the rendering, I was able to manipulate the 3D image to see where the damage was.

"There's a crack in the second layer of the scanning screen on your device," I told him.

"What in God's name does that—oh," he had started yelling, but half way through his sentence the alarm turned off.

"You will have to get it replaced. Can I send someone today?"

I used to fight shoulder to shoulder with a God, I thought bitterly as I pulled up the day's schedule. My brain was still foggy from the hit I had taken this morning. I cursed my slow healing. It used to be faster. Back when I was with my brothers.

"They could be there in the next forty-five minutes," I told him.

"Sure," the man said, and he hung up.

I used to fight with Gods. And now I'm hacking home systems.

"Oh, how the mighty have fallen," I muttered to myself. Then I mentally recoiled at my use of the expression.

I had never wanted to be mighty. Not really. I wanted to protect my people, my brother's people. I wanted to protect my family.

An image of three men flooded my mind. The one in the middle was broad-shouldered and strongly build. He carried a sword at his hip and his long dark hair was braided down his back.

To his right, but for the blade, stood his mirror image. And to his left . . . well, even at 6'2", I was dwarfed by my brothers, both in height and breadth. Where my brothers' hair was long, mine was short. Where they wore heavy fur pelts, I wore a thin shirt. I preferred to feel the bite of the chill pre-dawn air.

"But mighty we were," I whispered.

And no longer, I thought.

I knew I had to stay hidden. To do that I had to lead a monotonous life.

I sighed once before ending my pity party. I looked at the timer on the top of the screen.

"That's thirty-seven," I said. Then I tapped a code into the wall on my right and a window slid opened to reveal a man at an identical station.

"No sir," said Jenner from the workstation next to mine. His accented words hinted at his first language.

When Jenner was two, and Cam was a newborn, their older sister Mariana had a seizure and was never the same. She was five at the time. Jenner was sent to live with his maternal grandparents while his mother and father cared for Camile and Mariana. When Cam was two, she followed him. They moved back when Jenner was eleven and Cam was nine. It wasn't an easy transition.

I rested my chin on the sill of the window that opened up between us and listened to Jenner try to talk over a loud alarm going off in the back of his call.

"Now, sir, I am only trying to help. If you could allow me to get a bit more information from you I can—." The line went dead.

"Hey, Jenner," I said to him with a sympathetic look. He gave me a very rude hand gesture.

"I have to call this jerk back and fix his system," he said.

"You know he's already on a call with someone else. Admit defeat."

"Death first," he said.

My eyes flicked down to the tee shirt under his red hoodie. Those same words were printed over an image of a man with a little moustache.

"What did you get today?" I asked.

Jenner and I had a competition: How many calls we could close in under five minutes over the course of an eight-hour shift. Jenner was by far the superior hacker, but he refused to use those skills at the office.

I didn't.

"A million," he said.

I scoffed.

"You were late," he said, upset about his lose. "You're never late. Where were you?"

"Nowhere," I said, trying to sound as uninteresting as possible. "I was just late."

"Yeah, whatever. You don't want to tell me where you were. Fine. Lie to me," he said. "I'm never covering for you again."

"I'm not lying!"

"Uh huh." Jenner could always tell when I was lying.

"How many did you get today?" I asked again, not-so-subtly changing the subject.

"Twenty-seven," he said in a defeated voice. Then he braced for a losing blow. "You?"

"Twenty-seven," I said, trying to look bothered by it.

"Liar," he told me with a crooked smile.

I shrugged.

"I had one person hang up on me today because she said I had taken someone's job. Lady!" Jenner threw his hands in the air. "It's 2047." He followed with a small rant in Spanish.

"Did you call her back?" I asked.

"Madre de Dios, no I didn't call her back! How many people hang up on you because of your accent?" he asked.

I don't think he expected an answer.

We both knew it was zero.

"Sorry." I knew how much he let those calls get to him.

Over the past few days, the majority of news outlets were reporting on the new immigration policy put forward by the Right Waters Party. It would require all third- and fourth-generation immigrants to put their "country of origin" on their personal identification. People were scared. Scared people were stupid.

"Want to go grab a beer after work? On me?" I asked him.

His face brightened immediately. He was so easy. Easy to please, easy to make smile, and it was easy for him to see the good in people.

He made me see the good in people too, even when I was unsure of its existence.

CHAPTER THREE

"Latte. Double the espresso. And no cinnamon." The man's words were sharp. The woman behind the counter hastily tapped on an order sleeve before setting the disposable green cup with its white logo on the slow-moving conveyer belt.

"No cinnamon," the man repeated. He was wearing an expensive navy suit. "Thanks, doll." He gave her an appraising look before turning to glance at the long line behind him. "You guys busy like this all the time?"

"That will be 15.50, please, and we usually quiet down around ten."

"Uh huh," he said. He wasn't listening. His eyes were locked on a young woman a few people behind him in line.

"Fifteen fifty?" the woman behind the counter said as she offered the pay pad. The man absent-mindedly placed his thumb on the pad before walking towards the young woman he had been eyeing.

"Hello," he said, giving her a well-rehearsed half-smile. She looked up at him brightly. "If I had seen you sooner, I'd have offered to buy your morning coffee."

Her bright expression faded.

"Thanks, maybe next time," she said in a polite attempt to shut him down.

"Sure." He winked at her, not taking the hint and looking at her up and down. "How about tomorrow? Do you come here every morning before work?"

"Latte, double shot of espresso, no cinnamon!" called a barista as she placed a cup on an open space of counter.

"Call me," he said, giving the girl his card. He flashed the exact same half-smile at her again before turning to get his drink. He bumped into someone on the way to the pick-up counter. "Watch it, man!" he said.

The man muttered something before walking away.

"No cinnamon?" he asked, examining the contents of the cup before putting on the lid. "Hey." He snapped his fingers at one of the women working behind the bar. "I'm allergic to cinnamon. Gives me hives. Is there cinnamon in this?"

The woman shook her head and he nodded before leaving the café.

He stood outside the coffee shop and took a sip of his drink. "Nice," he said. The comment was directed at a pair of women walking past as much as it was to his coffee.

Beep beep beep

He coughed a little and loosened the navy-blue tie.

Beep beep beep

After walking only a few steps, he coughed again. Harder this time.

Beep beep beep

Bending over, he placed his hands on his knees. He tried to breathe. His latte fell to the ground at his feet. He fell beside it.

I gasped and bolted upright. A loud beeping filled my bedroom.

My alarm clock.

Looking over, I saw the spilled water glass beside my bed. I must have knocked it over at some point during my . . . what? Vision? Nightmare?

I rubbed my eyes and thought hard.

Another one.

Looking over at the clock, I waved my hand to silence the alarm and reveal the time. 7:30.

How many times had I hit snooze?

Mourning the loss of the swim I'd wanted to get in before I went to work, I sat up. Not only had I slept in, but now I had to find some random coffee shop.

I was going to be late for work.

Pulling my watch off my bedside table, and adjusting the chain around my neck, I pressed a button on the side of the watch. "Call Jenner."

"*Calling Jenner,*" an automated voice echoed. After a few moments of ringing, he picked up.

"Locherrrrr," he said, dragging out the "r" in the nickname. His face filled the square space of my watch for a moment before I was looking at a sidewall of his home office.

"Let me guess, let me guess." He was chipper and sounded like he'd been up for hours.

"Yes Jenner, I will let you guess," I waited and heard the dull thunking sound of his nail-less fingers hitting the key screen with more force than necessary.

"You are going to be late and you want me to cover for you."

"Why else would I call you this early?" I asked, getting out of bed and walking to the bathroom.

"No reason, Locher, no reason at all."

"I—"

"No," he interrupted. "Still my turn."

"Apologies," I said. I put my watch on the counter beside the sink before grabbing my toothbrush.

"You slept through your alarm, hmm, because you . . ."

"Am I allowed to speak now?" I asked before starting to brush my teeth.

"No, shut up!" he said sharply. "I'm thinking. Because you had a vision—"

My chest tightened, and I almost choked on the toothbrush. How the hell did he know that?

"—of yourself getting murdered and now you're afraid to leave your pathetic excuse for a house," he finished with less accuracy.

"My house is not pathetic," I said, spitting and rinsing.

"Well, I wouldn't know since you've never invited me over."

"True enough, friend," I said. "I'll make you a trade." I paused deliberately to pique his interest.

"I'm listening."

"I'll have you over for pizza and beer if you cover for me today."

"That's twice in as many weeks, Locher." He was right. It was only last week I had been late because I was waiting for Adrienne Jace. "I'm going to want a reason as well as pizza . . . and beer," he added as an afterthought.

"You will be content with pizza."

"And beer!" he repeated.

"And beer, and any video game you would like to attempt to beat me at," I said, scooping up my watch and heading to the kitchen.

"Deal!" he said with enthusiasm. "You are so going down! RG just came out with a new system and, of course, I have it."

"The gFlat 760?" I asked. I'd wanted to try that system. "Don't they look like the old laptops from thirty years ago?"

"Si, except they don't open and if you get through a certain level of *War Games,* it projects a scene through the entire room!"

"I hate *War Games,*" I said, pulling a French press out of a high cupboard in my kitchen.

The image of my brothers and I preparing for battle invaded my mind. I missed them. I missed having a purpose in my life other than staying off the radar.

And I had been through too many real wars to enjoy the idea of a simulated one.

"You know I like the vintage games," I said.

"I'll think of something for you. Any idea of what time you'll be in?"

"After 9:30, I hope no later than 10." I looked at the clock that now read 7:35 and remembered what the barista had said.

"I hope it's a sexy chick keeping you up so late that you have to sleep in till ten," he said, excited. "And I want to hear all about her!"

"You wish," I said, filling my kettle with water.

"There's a chick?!" he practically shouted. The dull rhythmic thunking stopped as his face filled the square space of my watch.

"Goodbye, Jenner, see you in a couple hours." I clicked off, shaking my head at the shrinking image of my friend's face before the ticking hands of a clock replaced it.

φ

It took some time to figure out where the guy would be, but I did. I also named him Douche. Anyone who winks that much should be called by no other name.

Perhaps I was being harsh. I had a good friend from my school years

37

who was a winker. I mentally cringed as I remembered my dislike upon meeting him for the first time. It didn't help that he had classic good looks and charmed everyone he met. Perhaps this man too was all right . . . once you got to know him.

There were no street signs in my dream and I hadn't seen the name of the café Douche was in, but the distinctive cup helped narrow it down.

There were three RidgeBean Coffeehouses in the city and their cups were solid green with a white logo. They were a local chain and only one of them was located in the business district. I assumed it was the business district because of the way the people in line were dressed.

By 8:30, I was back downtown. Only a few blocks away from Arlington and Metcalfe as chance would have it. Waiting outside the RidgeBean, I searched the faces of the passers-by. Anyone who was tall, blond and handsome caught my eye as a potential candidate. I even followed one into the store, but he was so polite to the woman behind the counter I knew it couldn't be him.

As I stood waiting, I reflected on the scene I'd dreamed.

There was no reason someone who was deathly allergic to cinnamon would chance going into a coffee shop with so much cross-contamination.

"Gives me hives," I remembered Douche saying. Couldn't have been the cinnamon that killed him.

Then he turned away with his cup and bumped into someone before leaving. He drank his coffee and collapsed.

Perhaps he had already been poisoned before entering the coffee shop and I was too late? But then why would I have dreamed it?

Maybe the man who bumped into him had done something?

I made a mental note to try and see who that man was and prevent the collision.

I looked down at my watch and saw it was almost 9:30. The server had said they slowed down by ten. He should be here any minute. Or mayhap it wouldn't happen today.

"Nice," I heard from behind me.

Bingo.

A woman with a confident stride passed me, trailed by a tall, blond man whom I followed into RidgeBean. I thought I had gone in right behind him but there were four people between us in line.

In front of me was a smallish woman in a pencil skirt and heels. Looking at her more closely than I was able to in my dream, I saw she was hardly older than eighteen, where Douche looked about thirty.

What a creep.

"No cinnamon," I heard him say for the second time. "Thanks, doll." He practically leaned over the counter to check the server out before saying, "You guys busy like this all the time?"

"That will be 15.50 please, and we usually quiet down around ten."

"Uh huh," he said. I could see his eyes light up when they fell on the girl ahead of me in line.

"Fifteen fifty?" she asked again. Douche pressed his thumb on the pad and walked away.

"Excuse me," I said to the girl, thinking I'd save her the trouble of Douche's attentions. I waved a finger over my watch before lifting it to eye level.

"My watch has been glitching all morning." I showed her the small screen flickering between a clock and static blue-green. "Can I bother you for the time?"

"Hello," Douche said, giving her a half-smile.

Yep, he worked on that in the mirror.

She looked up at him with confusion before turning back to me to give me the time.

She opened her mouth to speak. He interrupted her.

"If I had seen you sooner," Douche said, stepping closer to her. "I'd have offered to buy your morning coffee."

"I'm sure," she said a little coldly, before she pointedly turned away from him. "Sorry, it's about 9:40, 9:42 if you're able to set that thing." She glanced sympathetically at my flickering watch.

"I hope it's fixable," I said, looking down at it.

"How about tomorrow?" said Douche. "Do you come here every morning before work?"

"Latte, double shot of espresso, no cinnamon!" called the barista as she placed a cup on an open space of counter.

"Call me," he said, giving her his card and a wink. He flashed the exact same half-smile at her again before turning away. The girl looked uncomfortable.

"What a creep," I said.

Her face softened when she turned to me.

"I don't even know why I took the card," she said, looking at it as if confused.

"Do you want me to go talk to him?" I asked as I saw someone walk in and make a beeline for Douche.

I moved quickly before she could give me an answer.

"No cinnamon?" he asked, examining the contents of the cup before putting on the lid. "Hey." He snapped his fingers at one of the women working. "I'm allergic to cinnamon. Gives me hives. Is there cinnamon in this?"

"Hey, man," I said, deliberately standing between him and his would-be attacker. Douche turned right into me.

Scalding milk and coffee spilled down my front, but at the same time I felt something like a pinprick in my back. I gritted my teeth to keep any sound from escaping my lips as my skin burned and a numb sensation started to spread across my side.

I turned to see the attacker, but he was already gone.

"Nasgadh," I whispered with a hand on my side, performing a small cast. I immediately felt the slow-spreading numbness in my side cease. I would deal with it more thoroughly later.

"What the hell, man!" Douche said angrily, shaking his latte-covered hands in my face. "What is your problem?"

"I'm so sorry," I said, not meaning it. "Let me buy you another drink."

"Damnit!" he said loud enough to quiet the coffee shop. "I don't have time to wait in line! Thanks, klutz." He bumped his shoulder into me as he left the café.

You're welcome, I thought.

The words sounded bitter, even in my head. Just because he's a jerk doesn't mean I should have let him die. Right?

"Are you okay?" said the young woman who'd taken his card.

"You lost your spot," I said gesturing to the long line. She handed me some napkins.

"Thanks for trying to say something," she said, shaking her head. "I should be able to do it myself. I'm sorry it turned out so bad for you."

"That's all right," I answered. "I just happen to have a change of clothes in my bag."

"Happens that often, huh?" She laughed a little.

"Coincidence," I said. "I was hoping to get a swim in after work."

"In your clothes?" she asked.

Touché, I thought.

"Go change," she ordered. "I'll get back in line and get something for the both of us. What would you like?"

"Coffee," I said. "Black."

She nodded and turned away.

This redemption thing is great, I thought. Free coffee.

A wave of pain stopped that cheery thought and nearly took me to the ground as I hurried into the bathroom. The cast binding whatever I had been stuck with was wearing off. I hurried into a stall to cast a more permanent cure.

Then again, maybe not so great after all.

CHAPTER FOUR

I sang one of my favorites from some seventy years ago as I slid the pizza into the oven. It had been a long time since I'd used the kitchen. I missed making pizza from scratch.

"It was long ago and it was far away and it was so much better than it is today," I sang as I ran upstairs to change out of my white t-shirt, now spotted with tomato sauce. In moments of self-doubt, I wondered if this new purpose of saving lives was worth potential exposure. As if my life, my secret, was so valuable people should die for it.

"More people," I said bitterly as I thought of the things I had done to keep myself safe. I stripped off my red-speckled t-shirt and pulled on a black one before heading back to check on the food.

Pizza is my go-to home-cooked meal and I am very good at it. I wasn't always.

Over the years, I'd had several culinary teachers who, by the end, had taught me more about the world than the kitchen. They had all saved my life in their own ways.

When my eldest brother died—no, when he was drowned and murdered—I retreated from the world. I lived off the land for a long time, but eventually made my way back into society. Eternally twenty-three, I had to move constantly so the few people I saw regularly wouldn't notice I wasn't aging. It was a lonely existence. Then I met Helena.

Gods, I loved her. We met around the turn of the millennia. Not this one, the one before. I went by Loïc then. She had the kindest heart I have ever known and taught me how to cook, among other things. I cast a bonding spell, attaching myself to her life force. That way I aged as she did.

We married. Tried to have children. She miscarried five times. She decided it wasn't the will of the Gods. When she died, the spell was broken. I became a young man again and had to move on.

After centuries of wandering, I met Rosamund. I told her my name was Lawrence. When you live as long as I have, sometimes you start to lose sight of the things that make you human. Rosamund reminded me. That woman was fiery.

She was older than I was, too old to have children, but we were happy. I cast my bonding spell and aged with her. When she died, I was a young man again and forced to leave the home I'd made.

Again, there was the emptiness of lonely years, until Phillip, the father I never had. He was the first person I told the truth to, after my brother died. I told him everything. I was fully myself with him.

We traveled the world together, never staying anywhere long enough to cause suspicion as to why I wasn't aging. His death hurt the most, perhaps because I was more myself with him than anyone else in centuries. I was honest. It made for a nice change.

Helena may have started my cooking lessons, but Phillip completed them. He was the one who taught me how to make the perfect pizza.

I tapped on the oven light and looked in the little window. Most ovens today would monitor your food for you and turn off when whatever you were cooking was done. When I bought this house, part of the appeal was its lack of modernization.

This was the first time I had tried Phillip's recipe without him hovering over my shoulder. I looked behind me as though he was there. In a way, he still was.

I heard the beep of the security system that told me when someone other than Mrs. Abernathy was walking up the path to my house. The system was one of my home's few upgrades.

Standing up from my hunched position over the oven, I walked to the front door. An automated voice said, "*Locator Identification: Jencilvadonner Hernandez.*"

What the—

"What?" I repeated aloud as I opened the door to let Jenner in. "What exactly is your first name? Jencilver..."

"Jencilvadonner, thank you very much. And no, my parents did not love me," he said.

"Come on in," I gestured to the living room, visible from the front door. "Does Cam have an equally extensive full name? I thought it was Camile."

"It is," he said, disgruntled. "She's their favorite."

"Ha," I said dryly, closing the door behind him.

"It smells amazing in here," Jenner said. "You didn't make the pizza, did you?"

"Was I not supposed to?" I asked. "I hope it's all right, I haven't done it in a while." Making the dough had always been my favorite part. I think after Phillip died I didn't have it in me to do it without him.

"I didn't imagine you knew how! Do they even have pizza in Ireland?"

"No," I said, laying on an accent as thick as I could, while still ensuring he would be able to understand me. "We live on a liquid diet over there! We don't have food a-tall," I linked the last two words together for effect. "The pizza is for you, and the beer is for me."

"Yeah, yeah," Jenner said as he stripped off his coat and hung it on the coat tree by the door. Removing his shoes, he stepped out of the front vestibule and looked around. "Nice place."

He couldn't see much from where he was standing, just the living room, the stairs up to the second floor, and the hallway that led to my eat-in kitchen. He walked down the hall, sniffing as he went.

"How long before it's done?" he asked.

"Perhaps fifteen minutes. Beer?"

"Sure." He extended his hand after I took two cold bottles out of the freezer. "Is that where they keep beer where you come from?"

"These were room temperature thirty minutes ago," I explained.

"Isn't that how you all like it over there? I went to England once. The server asked me if I wanted my beer extra cold. I asked if there was another way. She wasn't impressed."

"I don't imagine so." I brought the bottle to my lips. "We have time for a game before the pizza's done."

Jenner gave me a crooked smile before heading into the living room.

φ

"*Timer expired,*" the disembodied voice said as the game paused. "*Oven temperature lowering to 170 degrees.*"

I was lucky the timer went off when it did. I was about to get my head blown off. The game started up again as soon as the voice finished speaking.

"This is as good a time as any to stop," I said, hitting pause.

46

"What? I was about to win!" Jenner said.

"Exactly." I stripped off the gloves linking me to the gFlat.

"*Player Two, forfeit,*" the game called after me as I walked into the kitchen.

"I can handle it," I said. "I hate war games." I muttered the last part under my breath so Jenner couldn't hear.

I pulled the pizza out of the oven and set it to cool on the granite countertop. Pulling out two large mismatched plates from a cupboard, I started to set the kitchen table. Jenner sat in one of the light-wood chairs that matched the cupboards. It was only by chance that they matched. I had gotten them second-hand.

"Make yourself useful and grab a couple more beers from the fridge," I said, searching a drawer for my pizza cutter. Did I have a pizza cutter?

"This looks great. What's on it?" Jenner ignored me and got up to examine the pizza.

"Beer," I said again.

"There is beer on the pizza?" He turned to me in amazement.

"There is beer in the fridge," I said. "And yes, there's a little in the dough."

"Mmmm," he said, turning to the fridge and reappearing with two dark glass bottles in hand. He leaned over the hot mass of cheese and meat on the counter and breathed deeply through his nose. "Mmmm," he repeated.

"There are a few different cheeses," I said. "Some sausage and bacon, pepperoni. Is that acceptable?"

"I'm drooling. Si, it's acceptable." He took the beer to the table.

I found a pair of scissors and shrugged.

These'll do, I thought, and dished us each a couple pieces.

Seconds after sitting down across from each other, I got the question I thought Jenner would ask me the second he walked through the door.

"So, Locher," he said through a mouth full of pizza. "What have you been up to these days?"

All right, so perhaps he didn't ask the exact question I thought he would.

"Who's the chica keeping you up so late at night?" he added.

There it was!

"There is no chica," I said honestly. Perhaps I should have lied. Sometimes it's easier that way, but I was sick of lying and he could always tell. "I've slept through my alarm a few times." I took a bite of pizza. It was sinfully good.

"You called me at 7:30 and you live forty-five minutes away from the office, he said. "You can't tell me sleeping in was the reason you got to work at 10. Plus, you haven't been late in three years."

Shoot, what could I tell him? The truth?

"Please tell me she's hot? You got a picture? What's her name?" He tapped his watch, no doubt opening the latest form of social media to search for her.

"There is no girl!" I said again.

"You know what," he said, looking at me right in the eye. "I've never told you this, but I have a gift. I can always tell when someone is lying to me."

No, I thought. There's no way Jenner was a Gifter.

I would have noticed if his Spark was bright enough to manifest in an extra ability. His inner power was as bright as any human's and nothing more. He just thought he knew when people were lying to him.

"Now, I know there is no girl," he said. "Or at least if there is, she isn't the reason you have been coming late to work."

He's right so far, I thought.

"Just eat," I said, trying to deflect.

"You know what? I will," he took a large bite, mumbling the rest through dough, cheese and meat. "Not because you told me to, but because this is the best pizza I have ever had."

For the next twenty minutes we ate and talked of other things. Politics mostly. Jenner was well-informed. I was less so. I used to keep up with current affairs but that was a lifetime ago. Now I had Jenner to tell me what was happening in the world.

"No, no," I said sarcastically when Jenner finished his rant about the blatant homophobia still surrounding blood and organ donation. "Don't get up. After making the pizza and providing the booze, I'll wash the dishes alone."

"I am a guest," Jenner said raising his thick eyebrows at me. "And I will sit here like the royalty I deserve to be treated as."

"Uh huh," I said, smiling as I took the plates off the table. "So what's there to do?" I asked in reference to the previous conversation.

"Some countries are better than others. I think we are one of the last ones to still permanently differ, but," he sighed, "it floats in and out of the spotlight. Right Waters is doing their fear-mongering song and dance... hey, is there dessert?"

"You're still hungry?" I said in shock. The pizza was big. I was hoping to have a slice left over for tomorrow's lunch. No. Chance. Jenner had eaten nearly three quarters of it. If he had a gift, that was it.

"No dessert? Well then," Jenner said, putting his feet on my kitchen table. I knocked them off; they found a home on a chair. "Instead you can tell me why you've been late."

"I have nothing to tell." I turned my back to him, putting dishes in the sink.

"Liar," Jenner said, without a hint of question. "There is something to tell."

"Fine, there is," I admitted. Hot water ran out of the faucet and the soap started sudsing.

"But you're not going to tell me."

"That was more of a statement than a question," I said, avoiding the not-quite-a-question.

"Is it going to happen again?" he asked. Before I had a chance to answer he added, "because if it is, we will need to come up with a better system than calling and bribing me with food and drink."

"What else should I bribe you with? Sexual favors?" I joked.

"You are so not my type," he said with a shudder as he picked at the label on his beer.

"Ouch," I said. The label peeled off Jenner's bottle in tiny strips that I was certain I would have to clean up later.

"Tall with dark hair, si," he looked me up and down. "Don't take it too personally, but I don't go for lying pretty-boys."

"You think I'm pretty?"

"Actually no," he said, rising from the table and coming to stand beside me.

I leaned away from him as he inspected my face.

"Your features are too angular to be pretty. Those huge glasses do nothing to help your nose which kind of ruins the whole cheekbones and jaw line thing you got going on."

"I'm truly heartbroken you think so," I said as I searched for the dishcloth I'd lost somewhere in the soapy water. "Please, stop describing me."

He shrugged and sat back down, taking another beer from the fridge on his way.

"Is there a girl at all?" he asked.

"You don't quit, do you?"

"Dude!" he said, settling into his seat. "I have no life. All I have is living vicariously through you and that's going terribly. Could you suck a little less please?"

"I'm sorry I can't be of more help. Pass me that mug, would you?"

"There is still coffee in it," Jenner said as he obliged. Just as I went to take it, he paused. "Wait." He searched my face. "And keep my gift of truth-seeking in mind here huh? Is there a girl?"

"No?" I said it more as a question. Big mistake. After that, the questions came hard and fast.

"Who is she?" he demanded.

"No." I grabbed the cup out of his hand and almost sloshed cold coffee all over the floor when I turned away from him.

"Are you with her now?"

"No."

"She's an old girlfriend?"

"No!"

"She broke your heart."

"No!"

"The one that got away."

"No…"

"And she didn't even know."

"Screw off!" There was suddenly a spot on the pizza sheet that needed my full attention.

"I told you, man," he said smugly, walking back over to the kitchen table. "It's a gift. What's her name?"

I gave in.

"Zemila," I said. "But I haven't seen her in a long time."

"She hot?" he asked.

"She…" I paused my scrubbing before answering. "She's the most beautiful being I have ever seen in my entire life."

It was true. Not just physical beauty, which she had in spades. Full lips, high cheekbones and bright brown eyes you could get lost in. She had long dark hair that fell like a curtain down to her mid-back, and a body built for sin.

But it wasn't just that.

She was kind when no one was looking. Compassionate to her friends. She was fiercely loyal and smart. Man, she was smart.

"Woooow," Jenner said, dragging out the "oooo."

"You got it bad, huh?"

"How long was I out?" I asked, smiling a little sheepishly over my shoulder.

"You mean, how long were you gazing out the window like a total idiot while thinking about a girl who barely knows you exist?"

"Shut it! She knows."

Or she knew, I thought.

"But yes," I asked. "How long?"

"About a minute," he said. "So, what happened?"

"Unrequited love," I told him. "What do you think happened? Nothing."

CHAPTER FIVE

I filled my lungs with air before pushing off the edge of the pool. The cool water covered my hands first, then my head and the rest of me. I stayed under water, dolphin-kicking my legs, with my arms still extended, for as long as I could. When my head finally broke the surface, I gulped in air.

It felt good, familiar. Panic. Measured breathing. Relief.

It had been too long since I'd had the opportunity for a swim. I needed to make more of an effort to find time. I started with an easy breaststroke. A warm-up. My head moved slightly up and down with my nose staying above water. I had always been able to think here.

No, that's not true. Not always. There was a time when I was too terrified. It was all I could do not to run out of the water screaming and crying in my early years.

Then, after I had learned to swim but hadn't fully conquered my fear of the water, I'd leave it, shaking from head to foot, near paralyzed from the fear.

Fear of death. Fear of disappointing my brothers. My brother.

There was only one still living. Llowellyn. I wish I knew where he was. We were told to split up. I never understood why. It wasn't long after our oldest brother died that I started down a dangerous path.

Llowellyn saved me.

Then we were told it wasn't safe for us to be together anymore. The Old Gods would be looking for us now. We had to separate and flee.

I changed my stroke to front crawl, slowly working up to full speed.

I thought about what I would do, if given the same choice again. I would do things differently. We were vulnerable then, and we didn't ask questions. We said our goodbyes and left.

My hands cut through the water, faster and faster. As usual, it was early enough that I had the lane to myself.

My greatest fear, even greater than my fear of water, was that I would be like my grandfather, power drunk and evil. The Demon King. Cutting down anything and everything to reach his goals. I was set on that path of darkness and had almost been taken by it.

I thought it was inevitable I would turn into him. That alone was my destiny. But I had a new destiny now. A second chance. A chance to save lives rather than take them. And I wouldn't waste it.

Thirty minutes later, I was standing in the shower with the water as hot as I could take it. I might be immortal, but I still needed to stretch. I changed at the gym to be certain I was on time for work. After having Jenner over for pizza last week, I made sure I was always on time or early. If I needed to ask for another cover because of a dream, I wanted it to be the only one.

I waved goodbye to Ella at the front desk, walking quickly so she wouldn't try to start a conversation.

The bus that would take me to work was about a ten-minute walk away. Time enough to lose myself in thought.

These dreams were a chance for me to do something good in the world. I forced myself to believe that. I forced myself to not think of the potential risks. I was not so important. Saving these people, that was what I needed to focus on. It was a message from the Gods . . . the ones who hadn't tried to kill me. They were telling me I was not just the grandson of a Demon King, but that I was meant for so much more.

It had to be.

I hadn't dreamed of anyone in danger since the man in the coffee shop, but I'd seen a hit and run on the news yesterday. If I had only known, I could have helped.

No, I thought. I need to be thankful for the lives I do get to save, and not ask for more. I know what happens when people get more power than they are ready for.

What would happen if I started getting those dreams every night, and every day I had to find a new person to help?

I could quit my job. I just did it to stay busy. It's not like I needed the money. With some handy maneuvering, I had been able to pass my wealth down to myself through the years and my investment portfolio was healthy, to say the very least.

Thoughts of what the future held chased each other around my mind all the way to the bus stop. There was only one other person waiting. It was the tired guy from a few weeks ago, the day they found that girl I'd been too stupid to save.

This morning, Tired Guy was leaning up against the pole marking the area as a bus stop. And yes, he appeared to be fast asleep. He was so deeply asleep that, when the bus arrived, he didn't move. I asked the driver to wait a moment so I could wake him up.

"Thanks," he said before hurrying onto the bus with an apologetic look at the driver.

"That was nice of you," the bus driver said in a smooth baritone that didn't match his thin frame.

"Thanks for waiting," I said.

"My good Samaritan act for the day," he told me with a chuckle.

"Me too, right?" I asked before turning to find a seat.

I was half a bus length away from Tired Guy, but even so, after he yawned and went back to sleep, I yawned and a wave of tiredness came over me.

Yawns are contagious, I thought. This is his fault.

I let my head fall forward and my eyes close.

"Fisher here," said a burly man. He pressed his palm to a scanning pad before his eyes flicked to the clock beside him. "Montgomery Fisher and we are all clear."

The man was in a small room lit up by panels and dials. There was a large window to his left showing a nearly empty platform. A small girl in the arms of her mother waved at someone on board.

A few cars down from Fisher, most of the passengers were silent, though some chatted quietly. The train started to move and pick up speed as it left the station. A woman with a baby in her arms stood to get something from the overhead compartment. There was a jolt and she almost lost her footing. A man in the seat across from her caught her.

"Thank you," she said as her baby started to cry.

"That was close," the man said.

Another jolt. Another cry. A screech of metal on metal. A horn bellowing one low note. A thousand more voices crying out in vain.

"Gods . . ." I jerked awake. My hand automatically found the necklace I always wore under my shirt. I had actually fallen asleep on the bus. I'd never done that before. I looked around to see if Tired Guy was still here. I could blame him, right?

"Danu," I swore as I looked outside. I missed my stop. Luckily not by much.

The bus pulled over and I got off, backtracking its route and thinking of what I saw while I slept.

"Buey," Jenner said when I walked into the kitchenette.

I looked at him quizzically. I was certain "buey" meant "ox," but the way he said it made it sound like he meant "friend."

"You look terrible," he continued. "Coffee? I can make another pot if you want it to be disgustingly strong. This is the stuff for mere mortals."

"What did you—" I looked up at him sharply. "What?"

"New pot it is," he spoke in a sing-song voice. "Someone's cranky."

"I'm sorry, Jenner," I said, realizing he'd been making a joke. "My mind is off on another planet."

"That's all right, man. It just means I'll be kicking your butt today on closed calls under five." He smiled broadly.

"Not likely. Actually, yes you will. Can you cover for me?" I asked. "I have to leave a little early today."

I knew I would make it with enough time if I stayed till the end of the day, but I didn't want the fate of everyone on that train to depend on the timeliness of my bus.

"Are you kidding me, buey?" Jenner said, looking around and taking a step closer.

Aye, I thought. That time he might have called me an ox.

"Boss man has already been snooping. She noticed you were late last time."

"All right," I said. I would make it work.

Our boss, Evette Mutombo, was a no-nonsense, organizational master who kept this place running like a well-oiled machine. I was lucky she had decided to overlook my late days. She saw everything. But usually if the work got done, she didn't look too closely.

By the end of the day, Jenner had closed his record high of thirty-five calls. He was still two shy of my thirty-seven. It had been busy. So busy, I barely had time to think about the dream, but as soon as the clock read 4 p.m., I rushed off to Union Station.

φ

I felt panic rise in me as I stepped off the bus at North Capitol and Massachusetts. "What do I do? What do I do?" I said under my breath over and over again. "Slow down," I told myself. "First I have to slow down."

Though my mind was slowing, I still walked into Union Station at a brisk pace.

I thought through the problem. What do I know? I know mag trains run on their own. The trains have a conductor but only for emergencies.

I squeezed my eyes shut trying to remember exactly how it had happened in my dream. Trying to remember exactly how the train had crashed.

The conductor messed up and then there was a warning signal. Or was there a warning signal before the conductor messed up? If the trains drive themselves, then it would be the signal first, right?

I broke into a run down the station stairs. I let out a hurried stream of excuse me's and sorry's as I pushed my way through the crowd of people headed to and from the many platforms. I hadn't taken a train here in a while and I didn't know my way around the station very well. I paused before rounding a corner. Did I see the number of the train that crashed? No, I only saw the conductor. I tried to hack the station computer to find the schedule.

"Ugh," I grunted in frustration when I was firewalled. "How does a train station have more security than the Senate?"

Thinking fast, I pushed a button on the side of my watch.

"Call Jenner," I said. It rang, once, twice, three times.

I heard the loud beeping and the unisex automated voice telling passengers to board their trains. Three different trains were leaving in the next few minutes and I didn't know which one to stop. If it came down to it, I might have to stop all of them.

"Locherrrrrr," I heard Jenner say. "You left in such a rush, I didn't have time to tell you I kicked your—"

"Jenner!" I said frantically.

"Where are you, man? I can barely hear you."

"Hang on," I said.

My hands shook slightly as I went to push a second button on the side of my watch. Two small transparent discs popped out of the side. I placed one behind my ear and the other on the curve of my throat, just above where someone would feel for a pulse, if anyone felt for a pulse anymore. Taking a scan was faster and more accurate.

"Jen, I need your help," I said, once the headset was in place. When Jenner responded, it sounded like he was standing right beside me.

"You're going to be late for work again tomorrow? You better tell—"

"No," I cut him off. "I need you to get into the Union Station system and tell me the number of the train being conducted by Montgomery Fisher."

"What?" he asked.

"Jenner this is time sensitive!" I yelled. It was loud around me. The strange looks that came my way were few. "What train is Montgomery Fisher driving today?"

"Those trains drive themselves you know," he said in a taunting voice. "And if you want me to commit a felony and risk jail time, then you are going to have to tell me why."

"Jenner, this is not the time!" Even if I wanted to explain it to him, which I didn't, I couldn't now. My frustration mixed with a dangerous anger I was too anxious to suppress. A crackle of excess power surged between my fingers. As the final boarding call for one of the trains was being broadcasted throughout the station, I clenched my fists, trying to hold in the Magic.

"What are you doing at Union?" he asked.

"Jenner!" I yelled again, as my fury at the situation and his lack of cooperation broke through and took over. It made my next words sharp and my accent thick. "I swear to the Gods Below, if you do not tell me what train Fisher is on I will curse you within an inch of your life!" Power crackled over my skin and the connection glitched for a moment.

"Oh, curse me, would you?" His accent equally increased.

"Fine, you don't want to help me? Fine."

I would have to disable all three trains. But how to do that without drawing attention to myself? And not just from the humans here. Magic attracts Magic. Especially the kind of cast it would take to pull off stopping three trains at once. I had to get a move on.

"Thanks for nothing," I said and started to hang up.

"Train 42 to Toronto," Jenner said. "You're a real piece of work, you know that." And he hung up.

I looked down at the square on my wrist that had displayed the face of one of the only friends I had left in the world.

The watch setting reappeared.

I'll make it up to him later, I thought.

The train pulling out of the station was not the 42 to Toronto. A wave of relief washed over me. I had a little time.

I looked up at the nearest display board to see which trains were leaving from where and when. Walking over to an open space of wall, I double-tapped the glass panel and the image of a microphone appeared.

"Direct to train 42," I said in a loud voice.

The number 42 popped up with a small map beneath. I looked at the directions it gave me. They weaved through the massive station and over to Platform 17 where Train 42 would be departing in eight minutes. It would take me at least half that time to get there.

Clutching my messenger bag to my side, I ran through the crowd. After doubling back more than once, five minutes later, I was on the flight of stairs that would take me to an overpass and then down to Platform 17.

If the problem was not the conductor, would I have to stop the train entirely?

The gleaming silver tube hovered inches off the magnetic track. The final boarding call went out as I finished my descent onto the platform. The doors were about to close.

I still had no idea what I should do. I was running out of time. Magic crackled in my fist. I tried to think of a solution. A bell chimed. The doors started to close. I rushed onto the train.

There was an announcement from the driver. I recognized Fisher's voice. My panic rose. I shoved my hands in my pockets to hide the blue sparks flashing between my fingers.

Most of the passengers were silent. Some chatted quietly as the train started to move and pick up speed as it left the station.

I saw a woman with a baby in her arms retrieve something from the overhead compartment. I recognized her. She seemed to stand in slow motion. Horror filled me as I realized I could do nothing to stop this, that I would have to watch all these people die.

There was a jolt. The woman almost lost her footing. A man in the seat across from her caught her.

No, I thought, as the woman's baby started to cry.

"That was close," the man said.

"No," I said aloud.

I would not allow this. I could not. I couldn't watch all these people die.

I pulled my hands out of my pockets and called Magic to me.

I stood with my eyes closed and fists clenched at my side as there was another jolt that rocked the train.

The baby kept crying, there was a collective intake of breath. And I exhaled a single word.

"Fanaidh," I said as I threw the power that had been gathering in my core. My open hands sent sparks of blue Magic from my fingertips through the floor of the train. There was a screech of metal on metal. A horn bellowing one low note.

And Time stopped.

I collapsed where I stood. I felt the power of the spell draining me. Every second that passed, every moment that I held Time in place, Time took something from me . . . just like Magic did.

Flat on the ground, I lay my hand on the dirty linoleum floor. I inhaled and sent a silent prayer to the old Gods before whispering, "Tothaim."

Time regained its normal pace. A thousand voices cried out. Everything went black.

φ

"Slap him."

"Don't slap him."

"I saw it in a movie once—it worked."

"Don't slap him! Call 911."

"I'm gonna slap him."

"Please don't slap me," I said quietly.

"Thank God you're awake!" said a woman.

My eyes flicked open. I was still on the train floor. Emergency lighting lit both the passengers slowly exiting the train and the figures huddled around me.

"Ahh, man," said a teenaged boy. "I really wanted to slap you."

"Hush," said the woman. I think she was his mother. Then to me she said, "Are you all right?"

"What happened?" I asked, sitting up.

"Dude, you fainted!" The boy laughed. "The train malfunctioned. Started moving, then stopped real sudden for no reason. And you totally passed out."

"Oh," I said.

It worked. Thank Danu and the Gods it worked.

"Can I call someone for you?" the woman asked.

"Thank you, no," I said, getting to my feet.

Concern filled her eyes.

"Maybe we shouldn't leave you alone," she suggested.

"Really," I said, as I swayed on the spot. "I'm okay."

"You don't look okay," said the teenager. "I could still slap you?" he added with a hopeful look.

"Thanks, but no," I said to the kid. "I'll be all right," I said to his mom.

Then I pushed through the crowd, leaving the train behind me.

Jenner had sent me a profile of Montgomery Fisher with a note reading, "You're an asshole." Pushing the thought of Jenner's hurt feelings aside, I tried to process what happened.

A male voice announced that trains would be delayed or cancelled for the rest of the day. Ignoring the many groans and complaints of the station patrons, I silently thanked the Gods. I hadn't used that much power in centuries. Millennia even. It should have killed me.

It would have, I thought as I nearly fell, stumbling up the stairs. If I could die that way, I would have.

I clutched the railing for support, my legs weak beneath me. I had to take a breather next to a young man chatting animatedly to someone about how his train was cancelled and it was a sign he should quit his soul-sucking job.

Another life saved, I thought jokingly before moving on.

A few minutes later I was making my way out of Union. The train was disabled, at least temporarily, and I hoped the Magic I used wasn't enough to attract anything nasty.

Except something felt different. Something was off, yet it was also familiar.

Sure, I feel weak, but something is missing, I thought as I exited the station. I'm missing something. What could it—

"Lochlan?" said a familiar voice behind me.

I froze and my heart started to pound in my chest.

"Lochlan, is that you?"

The eastern European accent was gone, but then again, my accent was gone too . . . well, for the most part. All the same, I would have known her voice anywhere.

I turned slowly on the spot. Full lips broke into a smile that reached all the way to her bright brown eyes. Long dark hair cascaded over her shoulders. It was longer than the last time I'd seen her. But that had been five years ago.

"Zemila," I said.

CHAPTER SIX

My voice hitched when I said her name and heat ran through my body. I felt a flush rise to my cheeks. I cursed my pale skin. I coughed to clear my throat and tried to regain my composure as my heart slammed a rapid rhythm in my chest.

"Hi," I said, relieved my voice sounded normal. My green eyes met her brown ones and I felt my heart beat faster, if that was possible. "It's, ahhh, it's been a long time."

"It is you!" she said, closing the distance between us in a few long strides. She threw her arms around me and laughed. Then she whispered into my ear, "God, it's good to see you. How long has it been? Five years?"

I was stunned at first. I couldn't believe she was here . . . with her arms wrapped around me. After a moment, I closed my arms around her too. She smelled earthy and sweet and something else I seemed to associate only with her.

It felt good to hold her, too good. I released her and stepped back, though she kept hold of my hand. My previous weakness seemed to ebb away as I looked at her. My memory had dulled her beauty. There was a pink flush in her olive-toned skin.

Regardless of my true age, Zemila made me feel like I really was twenty-three years old.

No, I thought. At this moment, I'm a clumsy sixteen-year-old who just had a growth spurt at the same time as my voice started to drop. Awkward and totally, one hundred percent, in love.

I first met Zemila in 2037 at Erroin Academy. I left in 2042. It was hard to believe it was ten years ago I first saw her. Time usually feels different for me. It used to feel like it moved quickly. There was a time ten years was nothing. It would pass in the blink of an eye.

When I met Zemila Alkevic, everything seemed to slow down.

"Should I give you two a moment?" inquired a female voice. "Or maybe I should get you guys a room?"

"Oh! Tiffany, I'm so sorry." Zemila laughed and dropped my hand. The sound of her laugh filled me with warmth.

"Hello," I said, extending my hand to Tiffany. She took it.

"Lochlan, this is my roommate Tiffany Spencer. Tiffany this is Lochlan Ellyll, an old friend from school."

"Nice to meet you," Tiffany said, giving me an appraising look.

"You too," I told her.

Tiffany was very pretty and very blonde. She smiled at me in a flirtatious way. As we stood there, I could see passing men giving Tiffany a longer-than-needed look. She wasn't my type, but I gave her a polite smile all the same.

"Nifty accent. British?" she asked, wide blue eyes looking up at me.

My expression faded.

"Irish," I said, which was kind of true. I was older than the Ireland Tiffany knew. But I had made it my home again in the years since.

"Did you grow up there?" she asked.

"It feels like it's been a few lifetimes since I was a boy there," I answered.

"Okay," Zemila said after a moment of silence. "Now that we all know each other, let's get out of here before someone starts a brawl."

We had created a bit of a traffic jam at the exit of the station. Once we were out of the way, we walked shoulder-to-shoulder.

I saw Tiffany roll her eyes at a man who wolf-whistled softly at the pair of them. It made me like her more than I had a moment ago.

"So, what are you doing here?" I asked, turning to look at Zemila.

"It's my day off so I thought I'd go with Tiff and see her to her train. It was canceled. She was boarded and everything, can you believe it? What a disaster."

"No, I mean . . . yes, a disaster," I stammered.

I was amazed, and a little distracted, by how well Zemila covered her accent. I listened for it but there was no trace. When I met her, she could barely speak English, and when I left Erroin, her accent was still strong. How had she gotten rid of it in only five years?

"What are you doing here?" Zemila asked.

"I work in the city," I answered loudly, speaking over the passing traffic of the busy downtown street. "For Tjart Tech and Security."

"We use them sometimes. But that's not what I meant. Were you taking a train somewhere?"

"I was looking into something for work in mid-town," I lied.

"I was supposed to be headed to Toronto right now," Tiffany grumbled. I was unsure if she was trying to draw attention to herself or just venting her frustrations. "A big deal that could have made my name at Simon and Shore."

"You work for the evil SS?" I asked in jest, looking over at her.

"Ohhh," she said sarcastically, "I've never heard that one before."

"Sorry," I said, only half meaning it.

"They're not so bad," Tiffany continued, showing me a dazzling smile. "I've been working there for a few years now. It's a good job."

"Hmm." I was not convinced.

Simon and Shore was one of those law firms you always heard about on the news, defending wealthy tax evaders and the reckless sons and daughters of powerful politicians.

Tiffany stopped walking at the corner.

"I have to head back to the office and call Toronto," Tiffany said, looking right up the busy street at the many skyscrapers.

"Where are you headed?" I asked Zemila.

"Just home," she said. "We don't live too far, maybe a twenty-five-minute walk."

Tiffany coughed but it sounded suspiciously like laughter. Then she turned to her roommate and said, "I hate to ask, even if it's just a twenty-five-minute walk."

"No problem," Zemila said, taking the small bag from Tiffany and giving her a look I couldn't decipher.

"Thanks girl. And I think I left my slippers out. Can you put them away if Oriole hasn't eaten them yet?"

Zemila nodded.

"I owe you. Gotta run!" Tiffany waved at the both of us before walking briskly down the street, her long hair flowing behind her.

"Mind if I walk with you?" I asked. "I can carry that if you like?"

"I am perfectly capable of—"

"I know," I said, shaking my head and raising my hands in a gesture of surrender. "I wasn't thinking."

I had forgotten how sensitive Zemila could get when someone tried to do things for her. It might have been a product of society thinking that because she was beautiful, she was also weak and an idiot. I thought it more likely that she was deeply insecure and felt the need to prove she was capable at all times.

"We can switch halfway," she smiled at me.

I thought my heart would beat out of my chest. I said a silent prayer of thanks that Zemila's gift had nothing to do with mind reading or enhanced hearing.

Zemila was an Earth Driver. She had the ability to manipulate soil, sand and stone, moving the earth with her mind.

"I'm hoping Oriole is your dog and not a shoe-eating third roommate," I said as we walked.

"She's my fur baby," Zemila said. "I got her when I first moved to Baltimore."

I looked at her curiously and she answered my unasked question.

"I lived there for a couple years before moving here. You know," she said, looking at me sideways. "You haven't aged a day in five years."

"Good genes I guess," I said with a nervous laugh. "So what do you do these days?" I was trying to move the subject away from my lack of aging.

Everyone who went to Erroin was Luman. That meant the Spark powering their souls was a little brighter than a Human's. That extra light manifested in a gift. I told everyone at Erroin I was a half-witch, half-demon, which, while accurate, was a little misleading. Like I said, I tried to stay as close to the truth as possible.

They didn't know I was immortal.

"I'm a journalist," Zemila said, continuing across the street when the walk signal flashed at us.

"Huh?" I asked.

"What I do these days?" she repeated my question back to me.

"Oh right," I said.

"I'm a journalist. It's mostly freelance, but I have a pretty popular video blog that got picked up recently."

"That sounds exciting," I said.

"Yes, it is. I love my work," she said, excitement lighting her face.

She seemed so happy. I didn't think I had ever seen her like that before. At Erroin, she was always a little sullen, like she was upset with the world for the life it had given her.

"Is that why you, ahhh," I put on my best Zemila impression. "Changed your voice?"

"If that was supposed to be me, it was terrible," she said, bumping her shoulder into mine.

"I regretted it as soon as it happened," I said, apologetic.

"But yes," she said in her old and heavy Eastern European accent. "People in dis country don't vant to be told dat dey are stupid from an immigrant."

"I see. What's your secret? I can't seem to shake the last of mine."

"I'll trade you for your skin care regiment. Seriously," she said, all trace of her accent gone again. She pulled me to a halt and leaned closer. "Your skin is amazing. You should market whatever you do."

She released me. My breathing, which had momentarily picked up at her touch, returned to normal.

"Anyway," she started walking again. "When people learn I wasn't born here, it's easier for them to believe I've lived here long enough to be acceptable because I don't have an accent. If I still spoke the way I used to, that wouldn't work."

I mentally breathed a silent sigh of relief that she wasn't digging too much into the fact I hadn't aged.

"How long have you been in town? I had no idea you were in the city," I said, before realizing my mistake. Of course, I didn't know. I left Erroin without a word to any of my friends. That doesn't promote ongoing relationships. Especially when you're trying to stay hidden.

"I did an undergrad in Political Science in Baltimore after I left Erroin, then moved here. Maybe two years ago now. You?"

"I was living with Dyson for about a year after I left. I moved out here almost three years ago."

"You still talk to Dyson?" Zemila asked.

"You don't?" I asked with surprise. I'd thought the two had been close.

"Wouldn't she have told you if we did?" she asked.

"I suppose." Dyson knew why I left Erroin. And she knew it wouldn't be good for me to hear about Zemila. "I talk to her every once in a while."

"How is she? Are she and Sahrias—"

"No," I said, frowning. Dyson and her maker, Sahrias, had had a falling out right before she left Erroin. To my knowledge, they hadn't spoken since. "She's happy though. She met someone. I think mayhap, they live together now. I haven't heard from her in a while."

"Oh," Zemila said, surprised. "I always thought, because you two left together . . ." her words trailed off.

"Me and Dys?" I laughed. "No, no, we were never like that."

"I should call her," Zemila thought aloud. "We trained together a lot back at school, remember?"

"I do. Duncan kept trying to get me to spar with him."

Duncan 'Duke' James was another classmate and friend. He and

Dyson would spar and we all would watch. It was quite the show.

One day, Zemila wanted to learn. Dyson taught her.

"Nemo is coming to visit me soon," Zemila said, snapping me back to the present. "He'll be happy to see you. Do you guys keep in contact much?" she asked, before adding, "We're going to take a left up here at these lights."

It had taken a while for Nemo and me to warm up to each other when we were first roommates, but by the time I left, he was like a brother.

"I wish I did," I lied. I hadn't spoken to him in five years. It was intentional. Pointlessly it seemed, as I was chatting up the main reason I left Erroin. "When is he coming? And from where?"

"He's flying in from South Africa in a couple weeks. I haven't seen him in about a year. I miss him. This city," she looked around at the tall buildings and busy streets, "so many people but . . ."

"Lonely at the same time."

"Exactly."

Zemila told me about her work, but we spent most of the walk to her place reminiscing. We asked each other who we had stayed in contact with from school and who was doing what. Two of our friends had had a baby. Zemila had met the little boy, who was named Duncan James II after his father.

I had no information on anyone except Dyson, and that was limited. I made a mental note to check in with her.

We walked to the edge of downtown before crossing a bridge shuttling traffic in opposing directions. This was the bridge my bus crossed every day. We were headed to my neighborhood too it seemed.

I looked down at my watch. Zemila was wrong; it was almost a forty-five-minute walk. I thought of Tiffany's laugh-turned-cough when she had said it was twenty-five minutes away.

I didn't mind.

There was a lull in the conversation as we turned down a side street into a residential neighborhood.

"Hey," Zemila said. "Do you like baseball?"

"I don't really know," I said. "Playing or watching?"

"Do you do either?" she asked, eyebrows raised.

"No," I said sheepishly. "Do you?"

"My dog's name is Oriole," she said and looked at me expectantly.

"Is that supposed to mean something to me?" I asked.

"Wow," she said.

"What?"

"The Baltimore Orioles?"

"That's a baseball team," I said, attempting to state a fact. It came out as more of a question.

"Yes," Zemila said through a laugh. "That's a baseball team."

"I guess I don't know if I like baseball," I said self-consciously.

"Well, the new season just started, and I've been trying to find someone to go with me to Ace and Oakley's."

"Ace and Oakley's?" I asked, feeling dumber by the minute.

"Yeah," her eyes were bright with excitement. "It's pretty cool. It's a small place with two lanes for batting and two lanes for pitching."

"Huh?" I said.

"Batting cages," she explained. "I go there a lot. I've kind of been wanting to go with a friend recently."

"Okay," I said. "But I'll be terrible."

"That's okay. This is me," she said, stopping and looking up at eight stories of peeling balcony railings and an unkempt lawn.

"Nice place," I said.

"Don't lie." She grinned and took the small bag from my hand. True to her word, about halfway through the walk, we had switched. "It's nicer on the inside. Do you want to see?"

"Ahhh," I said stupidly. I felt my mouth open and close like a fish out of water, as my brain seemed to malfunction. "I better get home," I said, and took a step away from her.

"Oh, okay."

The bubble of easy laughter and comfortable conversation that surrounded us had popped.

"I've got to, umm, it was great seeing you," I said, still backing away.

"You too, Lochlan."

She smiled when she said my name and my heart rate picked up again. She said my name the same way everyone else did, but coming from her, somehow it sounded better.

"I'll message you about going to A&O's?" she asked, pulling out her phone.

"Yes," I said in a slightly higher voice than normal.

I cleared my throat as she tapped the screen a few times and turned it to me. A black screen with white words stared up from her palm. I stepped towards her and pressed my thumb to the square under the words "input contact." My fingers brushed hers and my breath caught.

"Okay," I said, backing away after the screen flashed and read 'New Contact: Lochlan Ellyll'. I tripped on an uneven bit of concrete in my haste. "Fine, fine," I reassured her before she asked.

"Do you live far from here?"

"No, just one bus actually. Mayhap, sixteen minutes on the 10."

She looked at me, confused. "Mayhap?"

"Maybe," I corrected. "Maybe ten on the 16." I gave a nervous laugh. "About ten minutes on the 16, that bus really goes everywhere, ha, ha."

Oh Gods, I was going to pieces. I looked wildly around, searching for a savior.

"Okay," she laughed a little. "See you soon?"

"Yes," I saw the bus coming and sent a silent prayer to the Gods. "I, bus, run."

I pointed like an idiot at the oncoming red and blue monstrosity barreling down the street.

"Bye," I said before running away.

Seriously, I ran.

Luckily, the bus driver saw me and waited.

"Thank you," I said, meaning it. "You are a life saver."

After my dead sprint away from her, the only way the situation could have been more embarrassing was if I had missed the bus.

"Just doing my job, son," the old and semi-toothless driver said.

I found an empty seat and flopped down. I leaned my head back and let it press against the glass that seemed to vibrate with every pebble and crack the bus ran over.

I bus run? Gods, what was wrong with me? We were talking normally. She asked if I wanted to see her apartment and I turned into a hot mess.

I groaned loudly and threw my head into my hands. A few looks came my way. I ignored them.

What was I thinking? I mentally chided myself. That she was going to jump me when I went upstairs?

I allowed myself to wallow in self-pity for a few minutes before I remembered the conversation I'd had with Jenner. I'd make things right with him. If nothing else, it would give me something to think of other than Zemila. Then I thought of Nemo. I should give him a call too.

Five years, I thought. Five years since I had woken up in cold sweats with scenes of death haunting me. And the dreams had started again, first with the little girl, then the business woman in the street, then the man in the coffee shop, and finally an entire train of passengers bound for Toronto. But the scenes of death were different this time.

This time the dreams showed me how I could help people, not how I could kill them.

CHAPTER SEVEN

It was just starting to get dark when I walked from the bus stop to my front door. I was in a bit of a daze. Absent-mindedly, I nodded at a few passing neighbors as the last hour played on a loop in my mind.

This wasn't the first time Zemila had taken over my thoughts. The main reason I left Erroin was to escape this exact thing, and now we were well-nigh neighbors. Though a part of me was ecstatic to see her again, I knew I needed to mentally prepare for the other dreams to return.

And if they do, I thought, I'll leave.

Again.

Before I was home, my watched buzzed to tell me I had a message. I waited until I stepped through my front door to check it. Placing my hand on the scanning lock, I waited for the corresponding beep before walking in.

I dropped my brown leather messenger bag by the door and kicked off my shoes. Seconds later I was flopping down into one of the mismatched couches in my living room. They were second-hand.

I had money, but that didn't mean I was going to spend it recklessly.

I checked my watch. The message was from Zemila.

GREAT SEEING YOU TODAY, LOCH, it read. HOW'S TOMORROW EVENING AT 7

FOR BATTING PRACTICE?

I replied right away that seven would work. My mind raced at the thought of what a disaster tomorrow night could be. What a disaster this whole thing could be.

Life seemed so much simpler yesterday. Granted, I was having bizarre visions yesterday, but Zemila wasn't complicating things. Now she was.

The only other time I'd experienced something similar was when I was around her. That was why I left. But that didn't mean I should have expected this, did it?

No. No, I couldn't have expected her.

For a moment, I was lost in past visions, past dreams, past thoughts my mind hadn't created. Thoughts that seemed to be put there . . . just like these ones. But in these dreams, I was helping people, not hurting them. Not hurting her.

I shook my head to clear it. I had an opportunity for redemption here. These new visions allowed me to undo wrongs. This was my salvation.

A memory flooded to my mind: of my hands clasped around the throat of a man in a home lost to time many thousand years ago. Fluidly the image changed, replaced with a field of slain men I had cut down for no greater reason than I could.

I closed my eyes and turned my head away as if that would help. I tried to fight the onslaught of vicious images bombarding me. I had to try and focus on something else.

Zemila had said her brother was coming to visit her. That should be interesting.

The more I thought about my long silence with Nemo, the worse I felt. Since I knew I would be seeing more of the both of them, it would doubtless be better to do my apologizing before he got here.

I sat up straighter on my couch and pressed a button on the side of my watch that connected to my home system. After taking a deep breath, I said, "Call Nemo Alkevic."

"*Calling Nemo Alkevic,*" my home system responded.

A ringing filled the room, and with a two-finger swipe, I moved the call from my watch to the home system and the blank white wall in front of me. I waited, looking up at the pin-sized camera on the wall.

"Hi!" Nemo said, distracted and looking in the opposite direction. I only saw his profile.

He must have been expecting someone, I thought.

Dark hair fell over his eyes and he pushed it back with one hand. Then he turned to look at his screen and his face filled the space on my wall.

"Oh," he paused for a moment. "Wow, Lochlan, it's been a while."

"Hey, Nemo. Sorry."

"Yeah," he said, looking at me with a mixture of confusion and something else. Another awkward moment of silence passed between us before I spoke.

"How are you?" I asked. "I know it's been a long while and—"

He cut me off. "I tried to get in contact with you a few years back. You just disappeared."

"Yes," I said, looking away from the screen. "I wasn't in the best place back then."

"No kidding. You just vanished."

"I'm sorry," I said again. "I shouldn't have left like that."

I looked at him and there was another pause. Then something happened I wasn't expecting.

He smiled at me. It reached all the way to his dark eyes, crinkling them at the corners. "It's really good to see you, man," he said. "I'm happy you called . . . finally."

I smiled too. I was happy to see him. I shouldn't have waited this long, though I felt I had my reasons.

"So, you and Dyson," Nemo said, with a quick raise of his eyebrows. "Did you guys run away together or something?"

"No," I said, more defensive than I needed to be. I was a mirror of Nemo's ear-to-ear grin, so I don't think he noticed. "Everybody thinks that."

"I thought that'd be a weird pairing," he said with a laugh. "And what do you mean everybody? Who did you call before me, after being gone for five years?"

"I saw your sister," I said.

"Oh." His expression turned icy as he looked away from the screen. "Oh," he repeated with a bitter laugh. There was no humor to it. "I should have known."

"What?" I asked, though I had a pretty good idea.

He rolled his eyes at me.

"You know," he said angrily. "For a second there, I was just happy to talk to you. I thought, hey, how awesome would it be to have my best friend back, but no. This call wasn't about me."

"Oh, come on Nemo, I'm calling you because I want to talk to you," I said, meaning it. I did want to talk to him. I missed him.

"You haven't spoken to me in over five years, Lochlan. Five years."

"I . . ." I coughed to clear my throat. What could I say?

"And I could forgive that, you know? People deal with their baggage in different ways. But you had five years to call me and you only do it after you talk to my sister?"

"Nemo—"

"I guess trying to get in Zemila's pants is reason enough. Nice,

Lochlan."

Then he hung up, and I was left staring at a blank wall.

φ

I got out of the pool at seven the next morning. It was a mark of how rattled I was that I had stayed in the water once the lanes got crowded. When the third person joined the fast lane I was in, I switched to my slowest stroke and tried to swim at the same speed as everyone else. When the fifth person joined, I got out of the water.

After speaking with Nemo last night, I decided to wait and talk to Jenner at work instead of calling. It's much harder to hang up on someone in person. After a quick stretch, I jogged home from the community center. Then I got in the shower and got ready for work.

I didn't have to wait long for the bus and wasn't at all surprised when Tired Guy stumbled onto it. He wore dark sunglasses, though there was heavy cloud cover, and gloves, though the air was warm today. He went to the first open seat he could find, one of the ones that faced the middle of the bus instead of forward. Once in, he let his head fall onto the bus window.

Smiling a little and shaking my head, I found a seat at the back.

As usual, Jenner came in to work just after I did. Unlike our usual routine, he walked right past me without stopping. When he got to his workspace, he locked the drop-down window. I missed him at lunch and it wasn't until the end of the day I caught up with him.

"Jenner," I called, jogging to catch him as he left the building. "Wait up!"

He stopped and turned to face me but didn't speak.

"Look," I said. "I'm sorry about yesterday, I needed your help and it was urgent."

"What was urgent?" he asked.

"Huh?" I said, playing for time.

"What exactly was I helping you with that was so urgent?" His expression was stony.

"What do you mean? I needed help finding that conductor."

"Why?"

I readjusted my messenger bag as I tried to think of something plausible. Nothing came to mind.

"I, umm, I just needed to find him." I shrugged, trying hopelessly to make the situation casual.

"Right," Jenner said, turning away.

"Wait," I reached out and caught his arm. He wrenched it out of my grip.

"You know what, Lochlan?" he said angrily. "When you feel like telling me the truth, let me know. Until then, don't talk to me." He turned on his heel and walked away.

Walking to the bus station, I wondered what it would be like to tell Jenner the truth. To be able to talk about what was happening to me with someone. But trust had never come easily, and you never knew how someone would react to learning their friend was related to an ancient god.

No. I couldn't tell him.

Getting off the bus thirty minutes later, I felt my watch vibrate. Looking down I saw a message from my only other friend in the city: Jenner's sister, Camile.

SOMEONE'S IN TROUBLE, the message read. Flicking my fingers over my watch, I projected a keyboard over my wrist and typed one-handed as I walked.

WHAT DID HE SAY? I wrote back. Within seconds she responded.

SOMETHING ABOUT A TRAIN AND YOU BEING A PINCHE MENTIROSO. WHAT DID YOU DO?

I ASKED FOR A FAVOR AND DIDN'T TELL HIM WHY, I responded honestly.

ARE YOU GOING TO TELL ME? she messaged back.

NO.

I CAN'T SAY I'M SURPRISED. OH WELL, HOW ARE YOU? she asked. OTHER THAN BEING A PINCHE MENTIROSO.

I grinned.

I'M GOOD. I'M GOING TO ACE AND OAKLEY'S TONIGHT TO TRY THE BATTING CAGES. HAVE YOU BEEN?

NO, she responded. WHO ARE YOU GOING WITH? NO OFFENCE, BUT I DIDN'T KNOW YOU HAD FRIENDS OTHER THAN JENNER.

THANKS, I responded. She never did pull her punches. That's part of the reason I liked her so much.

I'M ASSUMING IT'S A DATE. WHO IS SHE?

GODS! I responded. DO YOU AND YOUR BROTHER SHARE A BRAIN?

WOW, she sent back. THAT'S JUST MEAN.

CHAPTER EIGHT

Crack! The ball soared down the length of the mesh cage.

Crack! Another followed a similar flight path before getting caught in the back mesh.

Crack! This time the ball nearly hit the man working the machine.

"Easy, ZeeZee," he called.

"Sorry, Mike," Zemila called back.

"That was twenty," Mike told her, moving towards the pitching machine. "Do you want the next twenty faster?"

"Sure," she said. She looked over at me as Mike adjusted the speed. "We can slow it down for you," she said with a wink.

Crack!

Ace and Oakley's was exactly as she'd described. It had two batting cages and two pitching lanes, each running the length of the warehouse, perhaps twenty meters long and five meters wide.

I liked the old-school feel of the place. There were life-sized cardboard cutouts of baseball heroes from seasons long past. Zemila fit right in.

She wore yoga pants and a loose-fitting baseball t-shirt with the A&O logo on it. Greeted as ZeeZee upon arrival, she chatted briefly with Ken behind the desk before getting equipment for me. She had her own.

"You're up," she said to me, stepping out of the mesh cage after what looked like twenty home runs in a row.

"I, umm," I stammered.

"You'll be fine," she insisted, picking my helmet up off the turf and handing it to me.

"All right," I said, putting it on and stepping into the cage.

"Righty or lefty?" I heard a voice call from behind the pitching machine.

"Huh?" I said.

Mike stared at me. I felt like an idiot. "ZeeZee?" Mike asked with exasperation.

"Lochlan," Zemila said. "Swing the bat."

"But where's the ball?" I asked stupidly.

She giggled.

"Put the bat up like you're getting ready to hit," she said.

"Oh." My humiliation increased, but I raised the bat. "Can you tell this is my first time?"

"Yes," Mike called.

"Well, I'm happy to take your baseball virginity," Zemila said with a wicked grin.

I flushed. "Keep it the same side, Mike, but slow it right down."

Fourteen pitches later I hadn't hit a single one, and Zemila had stopped trying to hide her laughter.

"All right," I said after missing the fifteenth. "Keep laughing, don't help me."

"Your swing looks good," Zemila said through her fingers. "Line up your knuckles and kind of push the bat."

I did. I still missed.

"That was much better," she said.

I scoffed and didn't bother to swing at seventeen.

"Mayhap, if I . . ." I trailed off and squatted down, holding the bat parallel to the ground where I thought the ball might hit it. Zemila threw her head back and laughed.

"I just want some form of contact," I said, as ball eighteen flew three inches over my bat. I rose out of my squat three inches, trying to hold the bat steady and waiting for nineteen.

When it too missed, low this time, I gave up and dropped the bat.

"Oh, come on," Zemila said, still smiling. I looked down the lane at Mike, who was laughing too.

"Any advice from the peanut gallery?" I called to him.

"You're just missing," he called back.

"Thank you," I said. "That was most helpful."

"Your swing looks good—you're just missing. Hang on," he said, "I'll adjust the height."

While Mike was adjusting the pitching machine, I turned to Zemila. "How did you get into this?" I asked. "You weren't into baseball at Erroin were you?"

"I played tennis growing up," she told me. "I used to do it a lot actually. It sort of lead me to this."

"Really," I said. I hadn't known that.

"Ready?" called Mike. I gave him a thumbs-up and he started the next cycle of pitches.

Zemila and I went back and forth for the rest of the hour, forty pitches at a time. By the end of it I wasn't bad. I could hit fifteen of every twenty pitches. Sometimes not very well, but I was looking for small victories after my abysmal start.

We returned my gear to Ken at the front desk and he asked how I had done.

"He wasn't bad," Zemila told him. "For his first time."

"It's nice you're lying for me," I said with a sideways look. She stuck out her tongue.

Gods, she's cute, I thought.

"It couldn't have been that bad," Ken said, turning to Mike, who had come out front to say goodbye to Zemila.

"He was on the lowest speed," Mike said.

"Thanks, Peanuts," I told him.

"Off to The Draft?" Ken asked.

"You know it," Zemila said. "See you next week."

φ

The Draft was your typical sports bar. Deep red, blue and purple booths matched the jerseys and logos of varying sports teams covering the walls.

"My team is playing," Zemila said after asking for a table with a TV in view.

"The Orioles," I said, remembering the name of her dog.

"Right!"

The hostess seated us and left us with a couple menus.

We were silent for a few moments. Zemila was watching the screen with intensity. I was watching her.

Her long dark hair was tied back in a ponytail and she had thrown a large zip-up hoodie with the city basketball team logo over her baseball tee. Even with her casual dress, I couldn't help but notice the eyes following her as we walked in. It was hard to dim a light like hers.

"Come on, come on, come on," she muttered as she watched. Even if I had been watching the game, I wouldn't have known what was going on. "Oh, come on!" she said louder.

I looked up at the screen to see the replay of a man with thick arms striking out.

"What are you having?" she asked, drawing my attention back to her.

"Oh, ahhh," I quickly looked over the menu. "A burger I guess. Are they good here?"

"I've been searching for the best fish and chips in the city," Zemila told me. "But I haven't had them here because I always get a burger. They are good here."

I quickly found the burgers on the menu and picked one out just as the server came over to us.

"Hi, my name is Cynthia and I'll be your server today," she spoke with a hard, southern twang. It reminded me of an old friend from school. "Can I get y'all anything to drink?"

Zemila ordered us each a bottle of Keil's.

"Uh huh," Cynthia said before she turned away.

I watched her retreating back for a moment. She looked over her shoulder at me and smiled just as I was returning my gaze to the burger section of the menu.

Feeling eyes on me, I looked up. Zemila was staring at me with a grin.

"What?" I asked, feeling immediately self-conscious. I ran my hand through my hair.

"Nothing," she said, shaking her head. "You're just . . ." She sighed. "Have you decided?"

"Burger," I said. "There is one with hot sauce and pineapple on it."

"I didn't know you liked it spicy," she said.

I felt a flush rise to my cheeks.

She laughed.

"I'd apologize for making you squirm, but you're such an easy mark," Zemila said, putting her menu down.

In response, and inspired by her earlier childishness, I stuck my tongue out at her. The easy smile her laughter had left on her face slipped into a look that made my pulse race. Her gaze held mine in a spell that had nothing to do with Magic.

Someone cleared her throat. I looked up to see Cynthia with our drinks.

With an irritated look, she placed the beers and waters on the table. I wondered how long she had been standing there before making her presence known.

"Have you decided on anything?" she asked, pointing a small black rectangle in our direction.

We ordered and, when Cynthia left, I raised my bottle to Zemila. "To old friends."

"Old friends," Zemila echoed as she tapped hers to mine. We both sipped our beer.

There was a cheer from a table not far from us. In response, Zemila's eyes looked up to the screen showing the game. We watched in amiable silence before I asked her to start explaining things to me. The strike zone for example, was something I never understood.

"You know," she told me after explaining a foul ball counts as a strike, but you can't strike out on a foul ball, "if you watched a few games on TV, you'd learn a lot from the commentators."

"I may do that," I said.

"Liar," she scoffed.

"Burger," Cynthia said, sliding a plate in front of me. "And fish and chips."

"Thank you," I said.

"Y'all need anything else?" she asked.

"No thanks, this is great," Zemila said, and Cynthia left.

"I haven't heard a drawl that thick since Duncan," Zemila said. She squeezed a thick slice of lemon over her fish before dropping the slice in her glass of water.

"That's who I thought of too," I said.

The burger was good, not the best I'd had in the city, but close.

The next twenty minutes were spent eating and reminiscing.

"This is little Duke?" I asked, excited. Zemila nodded vigorously, taking her phone back from me.

"Looks just like his Dad, doesn't he?"

"Yes, he does," I said. "But I can see Agatha in him too. Got any more?"

Agatha had been a good friend of Dyson's. Duke loved Agatha the moment he saw her. Dyson had set them up and the rest is history.

Zemila told me they got married not long after they left school. She said the wedding had been small but nice, and Dyson and I were missed.

There was another awkward pause. I was sure Zemila was going to ask for the real reason I had left so suddenly. Instead, she gave me an assessing look.

"What?" I asked, looking down to see if I had dripped anything onto my shirt.

"I'm just trying to think of a question that I'll get a real answer for," she said.

"What does that mean?"

"If I asked you why you left school, I don't think you would be honest," she said. "And I don't want to put you in a position to lie to me."

"I wouldn't—"

She cut off my words with a stern look.

"I'll trade you," I said.

She raised an eyebrow at me.

"But all I'll tell you about leaving is I was in a bad place and I needed a change. I lived at Erroin for nigh ten years. That was long enough."

Niloc Erroin, founder of Erroin Peritia Academy, was a very powerful being. I would almost say he was a God. He not only accepted me into his school, but he spelled me upon arrival. He de-aged me. I looked fourteen again and aged normally until I left.

"Ten years," she said. "I didn't know that. How old were you when you got there?"

I opened my mouth to respond.

"No, no," she said quickly. "That's not my question. I want you to ask first."

"Really?" I said.

"You wouldn't have suggested a trade if you didn't have a question in mind. I'm curious." She speared her last bite of fish on her fork and ate it while she waited for my response.

"All right," I said, impressed.

I did have a question in mind. In truth, I had many. I wanted to know everything about her—her hopes and fears, her aspirations and her regrets—and I wanted to know what she wanted to be when she was a child and when she had changed her mind. Or if she had changed her mind at all.

But that was a dangerous road. The more I asked about her, the more she would expect from me. I didn't know how much truth I was willing to give tonight. How much truth I thought she could take.

"How did you end up at Erroin?" I asked. The answer could be simple, or complex. I left the choice to her.

"Nemo never told you?" she asked, dipping a chip in mayonnaise, then ketchup, and popped it into her mouth.

"He was always pretty tight-lipped about his past."

"You're one to talk."

"Touché."

She was right, of course. And although I had never told her about my past, she told me about hers.

"Nemo and I were pretty well off as kids," she said, picking up another chip and considering it. "We were happy, or at least I was. Maybe Nemo wasn't. He was older; he saw more." She paused and ate the chip before continuing.

"I was my daddy's little girl," her voice held a bitterness that surprised me. "I was too young to see how he treated our mother. Too young to notice he left the house almost every night after tucking me in. Too young to realize what it meant that he was 'gone on business trips' every other weekend. Then Mom got sick. Terminal."

"I'm so sorry," I said.

"Thanks." She took a breath. "It was rough."

"How old were you?" I asked.

"I was twelve, Nemo was fourteen. That's when the scales fell from my eyes. I realized how much my father was sleeping around. I got mad at him. I wasn't his perfect little girl anymore. When Mom died, he left."

I didn't know what to say. Silence stretched between us for a few seconds before she continued.

"He didn't just leave." She brought her fingers to her lips and blew on them, throwing her fingers apart as if performing a Magic trick. "He disappeared."

She looked up at me and I saw the hurt in her eyes. Hurt clouded with anger.

"You never saw him again?" I asked.

"I did, once, years later," she said. "But that's another story."

I nodded.

"When he left me and Nemo, he left his debt. Our house was seized and since we had no other family, we were put into state care. No one wanted a pair of teenagers, so we were separated. I think it was harder on Nemo then on me."

"How so?" I asked.

"You know him." She rolled her eyes then held out her arms and puffed up her chest like she was flexing. "The protector."

I nodded.

"I think he felt guilty that he couldn't take care of me. He tried though. When Nemo was sixteen, they released him, and he got a job. It wasn't going to be enough for the two of us. He fell in with the wrong crowd.

"Some representative from Erroin went to visit Nemo shortly after he was arrested for some gang-related thing. He was given a choice: go to Erroin or stay where he was. He agreed, but only on the condition that I could go with him."

"But he was my roommate for two years before you showed up," I said.

"I was released at sixteen. He was waiting for me outside the state home I was living in. He was so happy," she said, getting lost in the memory. "I cried."

"I remember how excited he was the week before," I told her.

"Yeah?" she asked.

"Yeah," I echoed. "He wouldn't shut up about it actually."

She smiled, and her eyes seemed to glisten with unshed tears.

"Well, anyway," she said, going back to what was left of her fish and chips. They were probably cold now. "Your turn."

"Okay." I tried to hide my discomfort. "What's your question?"

"Same one," she said through the chip she had just put in her mouth. "What led to you ending up at Erroin? Do you have any family? Where did you grow up?"

"That is considerably more than one question," I observed.

"You can tell me as much or as little as you want, Lochlan," she said. "No pressure."

Heat ran through me at the sound of my name on her lips.

"I have two brothers. I had," I amended. "I had two brothers. We were triplets. One died, the first born of the three of us. He was kind of the protector too."

"Oh my God," she said, "Lochlan, I had no idea. I'm so sorry, what happened?"

"He drowned," I said. "It was a long time ago. Afterwards, my second brother and I were separated too. I bounced around from place to place until I found Erroin."

"You found Erroin?" she asked. "Or Erroin found you?"

"A bit of both I guess, I followed some rumors and was approached."

She nodded. "And your brother, he didn't follow you?" I shook my head. "Are you two in contact now? Since you got out of the system, I mean?"

I didn't correct her assumption that I had also been a ward of the state.

"I haven't seen my brother in centuries," I whispered.

Zemila stared at me.

I realized my mistake.

"Feels like," I corrected. "It feels like it has been centuries."

"Have you ever tried to find him?" she asked.

I smiled, but it wasn't a happy one. "He doesn't want to be found," And truth be told, neither did I.

"I'm so sorry," Zemila said. She placed her hand over mine and gave it a squeeze. My eyes snapped up to hers at her touch and my heart rate picked up.

Can she feel that? I wondered. The sound of my pulse beating loud in my ears.

"Can I get y'all a refill?"

Our hands flew apart as Cynthia loomed over us with a fake smile. Zemila shot me a knowing look and I rolled my eyes before declining Cynthia's offer and asked for the bill.

"Separate?" she asked almost hopefully.

"Together," Zemila and I said in unison. I looked at her and grinned.

"I asked you out," Zemila said, "I'm paying."

I could have sworn Cynthia scoffed as she turned away.

CHAPTER NINE

Zemila insisted on driving me home. I'd taken the bus to Ace and Oakley's.

"You don't have a car?" she said in horror.

"It's not a long bus to work," I told her.

We spent the ride talking about mundane things in each other's lives. She complained about work. I called her out for lying. Her face lit up when she talked about some of her projects. In particular, she was excited about a series of pieces she had done on youth rights.

"Why shouldn't the kids in Lowtown get a say in how their neighborhood is rebuilt? Why shouldn't the kids in the Flats have a say in their curriculum?" she said, her heart in her voice. I made a mental note to look up her work.

Just as we were pulling up in front of my house, she broached the topic of her brother.

"It's just here," I told her as we passed the post box Mrs. Abernathy always had trouble with.

"Sure," she said, and slowed. "So, have you spoken to Nemo recently?" Her tone was innocent, but the question wasn't.

"Have you?" I asked, worried at what he might have said to her.

She pulled up to the sidewalk and parked before she answered.

"Yes," she said.

"And?"

"Well, I know you called him."

"Then why did you ask?" I said with a short laugh.

"I don't know. I think it would go a long way if you just made an effort with him. He took it pretty hard when you left." Then, more to herself than to me, she said, "We both have our issues with abandonment."

"I didn't mean to abandon you, him," I corrected and flushed. "Anyone." I unbuckled my seatbelt and opened the passenger side door. "I didn't mean to abandon anyone."

"No one sets out to abandon the people they care about, Lochlan," she said.

I knew she wasn't talking about me anymore.

"I had fun today," I said. "Thanks for dinner."

"No problem. I had fun too."

I moved to get out of the car, but she stopped me with a hand on my shoulder.

"He was your best friend," she said. Then she leaned forward and kissed me on the cheek. "He misses you."

I got out of the car and watched her drive off down the street. The spot on my cheek burned long after her lips broke contact with my skin.

φ

A haze lifted from my vision to reveal a nighttime scene. I remembered this place. Looking at the familiar home of dark stone with sand beneath my feet.

This dream was different. I knew where I was. I knew exactly what was going to happen.

I was dreaming a memory.

I look down at my feet. They are clad in leather boots and my legs are bare to my knees. It's hot. The linen shirt I wear is soaked through with sweat. A wave of blinding rage washes over me.

I remember, I thought. I'd run here.

I hear something from inside the small stone dwelling. Anger boils in me. A spark of excess power shoots between my fingers.

Yes, I think, and I let my head fall back as the blood-red sparks run over me; blood-red sparks that were usually a vibrant blue.

I remembered feeling that. The simplicity of it. That fury was bliss at a time of agony.

I start towards the door and my hand finds its usual home on the hilt of the short blade at my hip.

I will have no need of this today, I think. The idea of my brother's spear comes to me. Yes, I think. That would have been better. That would have been poetic.

But he would not want the weapon tainted, I think. Not by my hands. Not when I might . . . go over.

I kick open the door and call for Magic. It answers, flowing around me, dark and powerful. It is strongest when I am angry.

A man runs towards the sound of his door splintering. One of three, he will be the first to die this night.

I pull my dagger from my belt and drive it into his stomach, twisting it when I feel it hit bone. I hear the splinter of his spine, and I whisper an incantation under my breath. He crumples forwards on to me as his Spark is pulled into my blade.

I throw him off.

I feel a nagging remorse in the back of my mind. I ignore it. I wish to be rid of it. I feel a presence at my side. This distracts me.

It's the second brother.

I duck down low out of the path of his fist. I bring my knife around to slash his shins. The cut is shallow, but I am just getting started.

The third brother joins the fight with a bellow of rage at the sight of his fallen kin. I'd come ready for a three-on-one fight, ready to avenge my brother and kill the men who drowned him.

Rising quickly as the second brother jerks forward from the pain of his slashed legs, I drive my blade through the soft flesh under his jaw. I kick his legs out from under him and pull back before driving my dagger into his heart.

He falls. Another whisper escapes my lips. His life force joins his brother's.

A tingling sensation flows up the arm that holds my dagger. It is still buried to the hilt in the man's chest. The color of dark grey stone tints my skin. In my mind, the soft call of remorse grows faint.

I am dancing with Dark Magic. I do not care. I am stronger this way. It is easier this way. I am better able to punish them this way. This is the way I was destined to be.

Sharp, hot pain slices through my body. It starts at my back and continues through me. I see the tip of a blade appear in my belly. I stop its advance with my palm.

My hand is moving stone. Though it wasn't before. I am turning. Turning into… I don't care. It is easier this way. It was destined.

"Nartha," I say, and press my hand against the blade. "Gada," I say, and a surge of energy forces the blade out of my body.

The last living brother stumbles back with the force of my Magic.

I turn to him.

Slowly.

He is speaking to me. I hear not what he says. I care not what he says.

"Tothaim," I say to him. He trips over nothing.

It isn't fair, using Magic now. But I was taught there is no such thing as a fair fight if you want to survive.

This was not survival.

Easy. Destined.

I care not.

I throw myself on top of him. No need for my dagger now. I could eat his Spark now. We hit, scratch, claw, bite, punch.

I feel my hands close around his throat.

I squeeze and feel the life slowly begin to leave his body. The power in him, his life force, I feel it flow into me. I close my eyes. I relish the sensation.

Opening my eyes again, I look down at him. Blonde hair covers his face, and blood covers my hands.

No . . .

That was wrong, the dream flickered.

His hair had been short a moment ago.

The memory flickered again.

He hadn't been bleeding like this, had he? That's not how it happened? He'd had brown hair, I knew that.

My hands closed tighter now, tighter than they had been a moment ago. His neck had felt larger beneath my grip before. Now it was thin. His body seemed to shrink.

I looked around, removing my hands from his throat.

I was in an apartment. A glass coffee table was broken, a white couch splattered with blood. When I stood, I saw a mirror to my left.

Instead of the version of myself as I had been when I committed these acts of murder, I saw the current me. Short black hair and modern clothing with thick, black-rimmed glasses.

I looked back at the body confused.

Where was I?

The form on the ground seemed to ghost between a large brown-haired man, a man I knew to have participated in my brother's death, and a thin blonde woman who looked oddly familiar.

I looked back at myself in the mirror, still trying to figure out what was going on. Instead of two bright green eyes looking back at me, one was the dark grey of stone. I looked down at my arm. My skin had changed to match the color of my eye. I looked at the third brother, who was just the blonde woman now.

The door of the apartment opened.

Someone screamed.

I woke up in my bed, drenched in sweat and panting.

"Tiffany," I breathed heavily, realizing who the blonde woman was. "Zemila."

CHAPTER TEN

"Call Jenner," I cried frantically.

The clock on my table read 3:20 a.m. I pulled on a pair of black sweat pants and a thin navy knit hoodie from the chair beside my bed. A ringing filled my ear as I stuck the small mic and speaker attachments behind my ear and under my jaw. I ran down the stairs and hurriedly put on my boots.

"Hi, you've reached Jenner," I heard through my earpiece as I grabbed a jacket. He'd sent me to voicemail. I called again. "Hi, you've reached Jenner—"

"Danu!" I swore.

I opened the phone with a flick of my fingers over my watch in the direction of the wall of my front vestibule. I had no time to get to a better spot and the bad wallpaper didn't bother me enough to move. A virtual keyboard hovered in the air and I typed quickly.

First, I ordered a cab, and with a quick hack, bumped myself to the front of the line by redirecting one that was only five minutes away. Next, I tapped into Jenner's system, calling on a small bit of Magic to aid me. I could never hack it otherwise. I picked up the call I sent him.

"Jenner, I know you're pissed but I need your help," I said, when the image of his bedroom ceiling filled my screen.

"Are you kidding me?" said a very tired, very annoyed Jenner. He followed up with a few choice words in Spanish. "It's three in the morning! When someone doesn't answer their phone, that isn't an invitation to break into their system, you—" more Spanish.

"Jenner, please,"

"Please what?" he said, and his face appeared on the peeling wallpaper before disappearing again.

I closed the screen, putting the image of his bedroom ceiling back onto my watch before hurrying out my front door.

"I need you to hack into a couple cameras," I told him as I pulled on my jacket and headed out to the street to wait for the cab.

"Right." He tried to hang up the call. "Balls," he said, when he realized it wouldn't work. "Right, right, you want me to help you and you won't even tell me what's going on. Just call and demand things. No, I will not help you, you—" more profanity.

"I think someone was murdered," I said.

He wanted to know? Fine, I'd tell him.

"What?" he said.

"I think someone was murdered and I want you to tell me who was on the street outside the apartment building where it happened." I could hear my accent thickening. I sounded a little more desperate than I'd intended. Perhaps it would help. Bouncing on the balls of my feet, I waited on the street for the cab. Only silence met my ears. "Jenner?"

"Fine," he said. I looked down at my wrist. His face filled the screen. "What's the address?"

I finished telling him as a cab turned down my street.

"When you learn anything, call me," I said.

"No," he said. "You're headed there now?"

"Yes."

"I will meet you. You'll tell me everything. That, or no deal."

"Yes," I half-shouted as I rushed out to the cab.

"I'll see you soon," he said and hung up.

I got into the back quickly and told the driver where I needed to go. The cab was spacious and there was a clean white panel on the back of the driver and the passenger seats.

"Perfect," I said under my breath. I had forgotten cabs had these now.

With a flick of my fingers, I projected the screen of my watch onto the white panel and started flipping through the breaking news. It was a few minutes before I found what I was looking for. Someone had posted video of Zemila's apartment building. It looked like it was taken with a phone. It was shaky and went in and out of focus.

"Come on," I said, frustrated with the low quality.

"What's that?" the cabby asked.

"Sorry, just talking to myself. I'll actually get out here."

Zemila's apartment was only a few minutes' walk from where we were, and I didn't want to roll up to the scene of a murder, seconds after it happened.

More and more images of her building appeared on my screen, some from legitimate news stations. In a few minutes, I would be able to walk by and not stand out.

"Sure thing," said the cabby and he pulled over.

I closed my screen, and then pressed my thumb to the pay pad on the back seat.

"Have a good night!" I said. Hopping out, I started to walk briskly down the street.

Five minutes of hurried footfalls later I was outside Zemila's apartment. It was crawling with police and reporters. I immediately saw Zemila sitting in the back of an ambulance getting assessed. Her skin, usually warm and brown, was the pale color of someone in shock.

My heart ached for her.

Had I done this?

No, I had just dreamed it. It couldn't have actually been me. Right?

"Young man." I felt a hand restraining me. "Young man this is an active crime scene; please stay behind the barrier."

I looked up into the face of a rather large uniformed police officer standing in front of a glowing yellow beam of light displaying the boundaries of the crime scene.

"I'm sorry, officer," I said. The officer's hand fell from my shoulder.

I needed the contact. That's not exactly true. I didn't need it, but it would be easier that way.

"I'll head back," I said with a fake smile and a friendly clap on the shoulder. As soon as the officer made eye contact with me, I dropped my expression and said, "obey-ordu."

The officer's shoulders softened, and his face formed a neutral mask.

"What happened here?" I asked him.

"A woman was murdered. Her name was Tiffany Spencer," he said in a flat, obedient tone.

The image of my hands around her throat flashed before my eyes.

"Where was her roommate?" I asked.

"The roommate found her. She wasn't in at the time."

"Any identification on the killer?"

"I don't know," the officer said with a pained look on his face.

"That's all right," I told him, and his expression went back to neutral. "How was she killed?"

106

"Brutally. She was beaten and stabbed. Some of the guys couldn't hold it together."

"Did you hold it together, Officer Garner?" I asked, seeing his name on his vest.

"I didn't go in. One guy said it looked like she had been killed more than once. Overkill. That it was so violent. Unnecessary violence."

"What does that mean?" I asked.

"Unnecessary violence is—"

"No," I cut him off. "In this case, what does that mean? Give me a specific example."

"She was stabbed multiple times, once through her chin, a mortal wound. She was also choked. And there was a slash mark across her shins, along with multiple cuts and bruises showing she was beaten. The coroner hasn't said much yet. That's just preliminary information from some of the uniforms."

My stomach dropped.

It was me. I had done this. Somehow, some way, it was me.

Images of that night flashed in my mind. The night I had murdered those who had murdered my kin. I remembered the way I'd killed them. I remembered how it had brought me pleasure.

A scream broke my reverie.

Zemila.

I saw her fighting off someone trying to speak to her, or mayhap, treat her.

"You are a good officer and will continue to perform your job admirably," I told Officer Garner. Then I paused. "You will let me pass, forget this conversation and never smoke another cigarette again. Cagair," I whispered, letting my hand touch his arm as I passed.

"Excuse me," I heard him say, rushing off to stop someone trying to cross the line.

"Zemila," I said when I approached her. She was still screaming at the paramedic trying to treat her and at the officer trying to question her. "Zemila!" I pushed passed them both.

"You can't be here," said the officer, grabbing my shoulder.

I shook him off easily before placing my hands lightly on Zemila's shoulders as she squirmed away from me.

"Cagair," I whispered. She slowed her movements. "That's it, Mila, it's all right. Just breathe."

"Lochlan?" she said, her eyes seemed to clear, and she saw me for the first time. "Oh my God, Lochlan." She threw her arms around me, pushing me back out of my semi-crouched position. I stood to regain my balance, her arms still tight around my neck.

Her earthy sweet scent surrounded me as I looked up at the paramedic.

"How is she?" I asked as she cried into my shoulder.

"Just in shock. Honestly, she'll be better off with friends right now."

I stood, pulling Zemila with me as I listened.

"There is a twenty-four-hour coffee shop around the corner," a nearby officer said to me. "We have her information. Why don't you take her there? She'll need to come down to the station, but it can wait until after a cup of something hot."

"Thank you, officer," I said. I noticed Zemila was on her tiptoes to allow her head to rest in the crook of my neck. I bent to place one arm under her knees and kept the other around her back. I scooped her up and walked her away from the noise and chaos of her former life.

"I can walk," said a small voice in my ear once we had left the noise and lights of the crime scene behind us.

"Aye," I said, my heart pounding in my chest.

I put her down slowly, keeping my arm around her shoulders just in case. I felt my heart rate slow, but it started up again when she placed both her hands on my shoulders and looked up at me.

Sadness pulled her full lips down and her large brown eyes were brimming with tears. I couldn't help thinking how beautiful she was, even in the midst of such tragedy.

"What are you doing here?" she asked me, placing a hand on my cheek. I turned my face into her touch.

"It was on the news," I lied, my lips feathering her palm as I spoke.

She nodded and dropped her hand.

"Everything happened so fast. I think someone had already called the police before I found . . . they said my name on the news?"

"No," I replied, doing some quick thinking. "I recognized the building. They said a woman was, well . . ." I trailed off as panic and horror at the memory flashing across Zemila's face. "And they said she was found by her roommate. I don't know, I just thought, two women, roommates. I was worried."

She blinked once. The tears she was trying to contain slid down her face.

"Thank you," she said, kissing me on the cheek and pulling me into a tight embrace.

I didn't deserve her thanks. Somehow this was my past, my mind, and my fault. But I held her as she cried and greedily accepted her gratitude. When she finally pulled away from me, I felt a piece of me go with her.

She didn't release me entirely. Holding hands, we walked to the nearby café. I knew better than to think she needed or even wanted me there.

She just needed someone. It was more than I deserved.

The café was small, with a few oddly matched tables surrounded by chairs with uneven legs, but the tea was hot and the service friendly. We sat by the window in silence for a long while.

"Are you cold?" I asked her. She had started to shiver. "Do you want to move away from the window?"

"No. I like the window." She eyed my jacket. "I hate to be that girl but—"

"No problem," I said as I stripped off the coat. I had a long-sleeved shirt on anyway.

"Thank you."

Her shoulders visibly relaxed as my jacket fell around her. I took a sip of my tea to stop myself from staring. She didn't need me making her feel any more uncomfortable. All the same, when I looked out the window, I saw her pull the jacket tightly around her and dip her nose to take in its scent before relaxing into the chair.

I burned the roof of my mouth on a big gulp of tea. It hurt, but effectively rerouted my thought processes.

"Do you want me to call anyone for you?" I asked. "Do you have a place to stay tonight?"

I selfishly wanted her to stay with me, but I knew that was wrong.

"Yes," she said in a quiet voice. She had both hands on her mug of steaming tea. Staring into its depths, she continued. "My boyfriend, Tyler. He should be here any minute now. I'll stay with him. I guess he'll have to take me to the station first."

My heart plummeted. Of course. Of course, she was with someone. I should have known. I tried to shake the thoughts from my mind. Isn't this exactly why I left Erroin? My attraction was becoming an obsession.

But it would be different this time; I'd make sure of it. She needed a friend right now. I could do that.

"All right," I said, trying not to let my disappointment show.

"I just can't believe it," Zemila said as the tears fell down her cheeks again. "First Patricia, and now this?"

"Who's Patricia?" I asked.

"Huh?" She looked up at me as though she had forgotten I was there. "Oh, it's so terrible. My friend's daughter ran away or got lost, we don't really know. Anyways, they found her body in a park a few days later."

Her words were a slap in the face. My heart rate picked up and I tried to control my breathing. This couldn't be. This was not possible.

"That's tragic," I said, panic and confusion warring inside me. "How old was she?"

"Only five, it was all over the news. Her name was Melanie. Melanie Connor."

The name, though I knew it was coming, was still a blow. Before I could react, I heard the door open behind me.

"Tyler," she said, standing up and breaking down again. Still processing, I didn't turn to introduce myself or to see her throw her arms around her boyfriend.

I dreamed of Melanie. I dreamed of Tiffany. What was going on?

"Lochlan," I heard Zemila say. I stood and fixed an appropriate expression on my face. "Lochlan, this is my boyfriend, Tyler Price. Tyler, this is Lochlan Ellyll."

The fixed expression fell.

"Hi," he said, giving me the same practiced smile he had given the girl in RidgeBean Coffee House and extending his hand. "Hey," he changed the offered hand into a pointed finger. "I know you."

His other arm was wrapped possessively around Zemila's waist, pressing her to him. Images of Zemila with past boyfriends at Erroin flashed through my mind. They had all been possessive. She'd liked it. Somewhere in the back of my overwhelmed brain, I wondered if that had any relation to how her father treated her. Or maybe growing up in the system, feeling unwanted. Regardless, I took a savage, irrational pleasure in the fact the she was still wearing my jacket.

"You know him?" Zemila asked, looking up at Tyler with one hand placed on his well-muscled chest.

"You're the klutz that ruined my suit," he said. Rage flashed across his face. It was brief. Zemila didn't see it. She was too busy hiding a laugh in my jacket.

She was so exhausted I think she would have laughed at anything.

"Babe, it's not funny. That was my favorite suit," Douche Tyler said.

"You have three of each one," she smiled up at him out of eyes rimmed red from tears.

"You're right," he said, placing a kiss on her forehead. She closed her eyes at his touch and sadness took over her face again.

Tyler's eyes remained open, glaring at me. Then he turned his attention to Zemila. "Let's get out of here," he said. "We need to go to the station and you need a good night's sleep, if that's even possible. Tomorrow is a big night for your little blog."

"Urg," she groaned into his shoulder, obviously not hearing the condescending tone in his remark. "I don't want to go to the gala," Panic laced her words as tears filled her eyes again. "Especially not alone."

"Do you have to go?" I asked.

"It would look very bad on my employers if I didn't show."

"I'm certain they would understand," I insisted.

"The news never sleeps," she said before looking up at Douche Tyler. "You really can't come?"

"Babe, I got a big business meeting. Huge client. I told you," he said, kissing her on the forehead again.

"Please Ty, I'm going to need you there," she pleaded.

I felt like I was intruding on a personal moment. It was uncomfortable watching Zemila beg for something I would die to give her.

"Babe," he said again. "Big business meeting. Very important. Can't someone else go with you?"

Her eyes flicked to me then back to Tyler.

"Hey, Bockan," Douche Tyler said, snapping his fingers at me.

"It's Lochlan," I said, hoping he wasn't going to suggest what I thought he was going to suggest. I didn't want to get more tangled in this situation than I already was, but I never could say no to Zemila.

"Sure," he said dismissively. "What are you doing tomorrow night?"

"Ty, I'm sure he has something," Zemila said in an unconvincing protest. She looked at me with hope in her eyes.

I melted under her gaze.

"I didn't have anything planned," I said.

"Perfect. Lochson can go with you." He smiled down at her as though he had solved a difficult problem.

"Lochlan," I said through gritted teeth.

"Huh? Okay, whatever. She'll call you." He started pulling her towards the door, despite her continued protests.

"I'll call you tomorrow morning, Loch, okay?" she said over her shoulder. "Thanks again."

I raised a hand to wave goodbye at the same time as my phone rang. It was Jenner.

CHAPTER ELEVEN

"Where are you?" Jenner's accent was heavy, a surefire sign his attitude towards me hadn't changed.

"I'm around the corner at a coffee shop. I'm assuming you're in front of Mila's building?" I asked.

Seeing a cab through the café window, I ran out and flagged it down.

"Who?"

"Zemila, the building that—never mind. Where are you?" I demanded, getting into the taxi. "Just around this corner up here, please," I told the cabby.

"At the address you asked me to get the footage for," Jenner said.

"Stand still. I'll be right there."

A minute later my cab pulled up in front of the building, now nearly cleared of news vans and police cars.

"Jenner," I called out the cab window. He was wearing sweat pants and an old hoodie. I felt a small pang of guilt for getting him up and out of bed at what was now almost five in the morning.

"Get in," I called to him. He jogged over.

"You get out and tell me what the hell is going on?" he countered.

"This isn't the place. Get in."

I would spell him if I had to, but I didn't want to start down that road again. I was saved the dilemma when he submitted and got in. I told the cabby where I lived, and we were on our way.

"I got the footage for the—" Jenner started. I gave him a sharp look.

"Not the place," I said again.

Remarkably, he didn't try to push it and we sat in silence for the remainder of the short trip.

Ten minutes later I scanned my thumb on the pay pad before thanking the cab driver and getting out. As soon as Jenner closed the door behind him, he started in on me.

"What is going on, Lochlan? I think I've been pretty good about all this and I want answers."

I didn't respond. Instead, I walked up to my front door, assuming he would follow me. He did.

"You're just not going to speak to me now?" he said, his anger and accent growing. "Well if you think that's going to get you out of this then, amigo, you are dead wrong."

I scanned my hand on the lock pad and walked in, Jenner right on my heels. Ignoring his stream of questions and complaints, I tried to organize what I was going to tell him and, more importantly, how. I needed him to believe me. I couldn't bear telling him the truth and losing his friendship.

I walked into the kitchen and put the kettle on. After getting out the French press and coffee, I noticed Jenner had stopped speaking. He sat at my kitchen table and waited.

"Tell me—" I stopped.

No, that wasn't the right way to start.

"Did you ever read Shakespeare?" I asked him.

"What?" Jenner said.

I took two mugs out of the cupboard.

"What does this have to do with why you have been running around like a—"

"Just humor me," I said. "I'll tell you what's going on, but I have to do it my own way."

"No," he said.

"No?" What did he mean by "no"? Now he didn't want me to tell him?

"No, I haven't read any Shakespeare," he continued.

"Oh," I said. He was answering my question. I had to get my head on straight if I was going to tell him everything.

"Aye," I said, taking a deep breath. "Well in one of his plays, *Hamlet*, there is a line I think you may have heard before. 'There are more things in heaven and earth, Horatio, than dreamt of in your philosophy.' "

"Who is Horatio?" Jenner asked.

"Not the point, have you heard that quote before?"

"Did you add this random Horatio guy? Si, I've heard it but not with your boy's name in there." Jenner looked daggers at me as the kettle started to whistle.

"What do you think it means?" I asked, pouring the hot water over the grounds.

"Does it mean Shakespeare is going to tell me what has been going on?"

"No, Jen, please. Tell me what it means to you." He leaned back in the chair and looked at me seriously.

"It means God is real," he said.

Of course that's how he would interpret it. Jenner was a devout

Catholic.

"Aye," I said. "Yes."

"Wait, what?" He leaned forward. "Are you telling me that after three years of trying to convince you the Lord exists, now you believe?"

"I have always believed, just not in your God. Well, not in the same way you do."

"What's that supposed to mean?" he asked.

"There isn't just one God, God with a capital 'G', God. They are all real, or were at one time or another."

"Uh huh," he said, not believing me for an instant. "Well, let me tell you, the Lord does not look kindly on those who lie to their friends and then ask for favors. What does this have to do with you anyway?"

"I don't know if you'll believe me if I don't start from the beginning."

"Then start from the beginning," he said.

"It's a long story."

Jenner looked down at his watch and with a flick of his fingers, projected a screen onto the wall beside my kitchen table. A keyboard appeared, and he typed furiously for a few seconds before closing the projection.

"Both of our shifts are covered. We have nothing but time."

"All right," I said, getting cream out of the fridge and setting it on the table. "But let me tell it all, then you can ask questions."

"Si," Jenner said.

Well, here goes nothing . . . here goes everything.

"There was once a young boy, the son of a Druid king." I heard my accent grow stronger and my voice deepen as I spoke. It was a struggle not to fall into the old language. No one alive would understand it. No

Human would, at any rate.

"One day," I continued. "The young boy wandered through the castle he called home. Finding his father's Druids practicing, he looked in on their work. Not having the proper protection spells cast to allow him to see without harm, harm came his way.

"The boy grew one massive and poisonous eye, so huge it took four men to lift the lid. When the lid was lifted, the poisonous eye killed everything in its gaze. The boy's name was Balor."

I sat down opposite Jenner and slid him a cup of hot coffee. He poured in the smallest drop of cream. The dark liquid barely changed color.

"As a man, Balor Béimnech, Balor the Strong Smiter, Balor of the Evil Eye, Balor King of Demons, led an army called the Famorians. The Famorians were an ancient race of semi-divine demons once thought of as the Gods of Chaos and Wild Nature. They were known on sight by their one stone arm, one stone leg and one stone eye.

"One day, a prophecy came to the attention of Balor, the Famorian King. It said he would be slain by his own flesh and blood. His grandson. Balor only had one daughter, Ethinn, and, fearing his own death, he locked her in a tower. The Crystal Tower.

"There he placed twelve women on guard to protect Ethinn and keep her away from male attention."

Jenner opened his mouth, no doubt to ask me what this had to do with anything, but I silenced him with a look and went on.

"One day Balor angered a man, Cian of the Tuatha Dé Danann. The Tuatha Dé Danann were said to be the reverse of Balor's demon army. Where the Famorians brought chaos, the Tuatha brought order.

"Balor had murdered Cian's mother. In retaliation, and with the help of the Druid priestess Birog, Cian snuck into the crystal tower and seduced the Demon King's daughter. Ethinn bore three sons. Triplets."

My voice caught on the last word. It seemed like it had been so long since I had told anyone this story. The last time had been only five years ago, but before that, almost never.

"Of course," I coughed to clear my throat. "Balor learned of his grandsons and ordered the babes drowned in the sea. He gave them to one of the women who had failed to protect his daughter and commanded she do the deed.

"She did as told, save one. One child she saved from a watery death and gave to the sea God Manannan Mac Lir, to raise as his own."

I looked at Jenner then. His expression was unreadable.

"The child was called Lugh," I said.

"I know that character from a video game," Jenner said. "He's a Celtic God and has a huge sword called 'The Answerer'."

I nodded, impressed.

"Lugh of Many Talents, Lugh of the Long Arm, Lugh Master of All Arts, grew up to lead the Tuatha Dé Danann like his father before him. He led them to battle against his grandfather's Famorian army.

"In the Second Battle of Magh Tuireadh, the Tuatha Dé suffered massive losses at the hands of the Famorians. Finally, Balor decided to destroy his grandson, along with his remaining Tuatha Dé forces, with his evil eye.

"Four men were called to lift the lid and unleash its heinous power. When they did, Lugh threw a stone, hitting the eye. The eye fell from the head of Balor, who perished without it. It rolled, then settled, creating a hole that grew deeper and deeper. Filling quickly, that hole became the deepest body of water for miles around.

"Lugh was a hero, a king, a God. He lived to do many great deeds, craft many fine weapons and rule his people with a firm but just hand. He had several wives, numerous children, and lived happily for many years."

I felt the hot sting of tears threatening to spill from my eyes. I blinked them back. This was not the time.

"Three brothers killed Lugh. They were the sons of a man Lugh himself had murdered for having an affair with one of his wives. Lugh of the Long Hand met his end, drowned in the waters of Loch Lugborta, showing one can never truly escape one's fate."

There was a beat of silence where I tried to hold back the tears the memory of my brother brought me.

"That is a nice story, Lochlan," Jenner said sarcastically. "Now can you please tell me what the hell an old myth has to do with the woman who was murdered tonight?"

"It doesn't have to do with the woman," I told him.

"Then why the hell—"

"It has to do with me," I said, cutting him off.

"What?"

"It's not a myth, well, not entirely. To me, it's history. It's my family."

"History," Jenner said flatly. "What does that mean?"

"The story, no, the myth that I just told you. It isn't true."

"Si, that's why it is called a myth," he said sarcastically.

"I'm going to tell you the real story, and you are going to wait until the end to ask questions."

Jenner leaned back in the wooden kitchen chair, crossed his arms and stared impatiently at me.

"The beginning of the true story is almost the same as the myth. There was a young boy and he was the son of a Druid King. He did look into a spell, and though the boy attempted to shield his eyes when he realized what he had done, he only accomplished the protection of one eye. The other, exposed to Magic, became as grey as stone and a death sentence for everything in its path.

"The boy grew to be the man of legend; Balor of his many titles. He did indeed rule over the Famorians and it is also true a prophecy was foretold. Balor would meet his death by his grandson.

"In response, he locked his daughter away in a tower where she was seduced by a man Balor had wronged. Cian. Ethinn gave birth to triplets and Balor commanded they be drowned in the sea. He handed them off to one of the twelve women who had failed him, and this is where the story takes its biggest turn."

I looked up from my now empty coffee cup to Jenner's cold and unimpressed face.

"The woman who took the three newborn sons of Ethinn was no mere handmaiden," I said. "Not only was she Ethinn's midwife, she was also Birog, Druid priestess, member of the Tuatha Dé and friend to the warrior Cian.

"When she took the babes to meet their fate, she gave each son of Ethinn and Cian three gifts. The first gift was the same for each child, survival of their death by water. She merely pretended to drown them before hiding them from Balor. Her next gifts were as follows . . .

"To the first-born son of Cian, named by Ethinn as Lugh, she gave the gifts of leadership and strength."

I took a deep but shaky breath before continuing.

"To the second-born son of Cian, named by Ethinn as Llowellyn, she gave the gifts of compassion and reason.

"To the third-born son of Cian, named by Ethinn as Lochlan..."

Jenner sat up when I said my name. I looked at him, willing him to believe me, willing him to understand.

"She gave... well... let's just say she didn't set me up for success the way she did my brothers."

CHAPTER TWELVE

Moments after I finished telling Jenner the truth of my history, he stood and announced he was going to bed. Without another word, he walked into my guest bedroom and closed the door. It wasn't the reaction I had expected, but I could appreciate Jenner needed time.

At least he was still here.

Before I fell asleep, I called Nemo. There was no answer. I texted him to get in contact with me as soon as possible.

Sleep came quickly, and I was thankful I didn't dream. In what felt like too short a time, the smell of coffee woke me. I looked at my phone. Nemo had yet to respond. I rolled out of bed and went to the bathroom before heading downstairs.

"Good morning," Jenner said as he finished pressing the French press. A pot of oatmeal sat on the stove and there were two bowls on the counter.

"Good morning," I said, feeling like I was in his kitchen and intruding. I went to the stove to fill one bowl with oatmeal.

"Thanks," I said.

"I thought about what you told me." Jenner filled two mugs of coffee as he smoothly ignored my gratitude. "And I have decided to believe you while you tell me the rest."

"The rest?" I asked.

"Si, the rest," he said. "To be clear, I do not believe you. The idea of what you said makes me want to—" He finished the sentence in rapid Spanish.

"All right," I said.

"But because you came up with this fantastic story, I will listen to the rest." He sat down across from me with his own bowl of oatmeal and slid me a mug of coffee. The way he had carried both mugs, the bowl of oatmeal and the cream, told me he had been a server at some point in his life.

"A while ago I was having this recurring nightmare," I said, starting where I thought "the rest" began.

I took a bite of the hot cereal. It was good. Better than mine. He must have gone out for nutmeg. I didn't think I had any, but I could taste it in the oatmeal.

"I dreamt of this little girl; she was lost and crying," I said.

"That's creepy," he told me, eating slowly.

"I dreamt of her wandering through Fort Totten Park," I said.

"That was sad," Jenner nodded. "I read about it too."

"No," I told him. "I dreamt of the girl before she went missing."

A heavy silence filled the room. Jenner stared at me in disbelief. Could I blame him? I didn't know what else to do but keep talking. So that's what I did.

I told him I had dreamed about the girl over and over, not knowing what it meant. Then I told him of how I had seen her face on the news.

"It was torture," I said, as the image of Melanie Connor flashed in my mind. "For weeks I thought if I had just gone to the park, I could have saved her. I could have helped."

Next, I told him about the woman in the street and the man in the coffee shop. Then I told him about the train. That got his attention.

"The train," he said flatly.

"Yes. I didn't know which one it was, but I knew the driver. I needed help."

"That's a nice story, Loch, but—"

"It's not a story!" I said, standing abruptly. My knee hit the leg of the table and coffee sloshed from my full cup. I started to pace back and forth in my kitchen. "Last night I dreamed again. This one truly was a nightmare. I dreamed a memory, I dreamed I was—" I stopped.

How could I tell him the next part? How could I tell him that not only did I murder three men, but also, because of me, Tiffany was dead the same way?

"What?" he asked. "You dreamt you were doing what?"

"I saw that woman being murdered," I said. "What did the video show? Was I there?"

I turned away from him and gripped the edges of my teal countertop so hard my knuckles turned white.

"Why would you have been there?" he asked.

"I dreamed that," I swallowed, "that it was I who killed her."

There was another heavy silence before Jenner broke it.

"I don't believe this," he said. "I don't know how to believe what you're telling me."

"What time did I call you last night?" I said, turning to face him.

I was growing impatient. I needed to know if I had been there. If it was my fault. If the redemption I thought I had been offered was false.

"What time did the police start showing up?" I asked. "What time did the news hit the web?"

I waited while he scanned the log on his phone and a few online news pages. He found what he was looking for.

"Lochlan," he said with awe. His expression changed as his mind slowly wrapped around the fact that, unless I was telling the truth, I couldn't possibly have known what had happened as early as I did.

"More things in heaven and earth," I said with an awkward chuckle.

"It is a gift from God. You saved the woman and the man. You stopped the train crash. God is working through you," he said and crossed himself.

"I don't know, Jen," I said. I sat down again, but this time I was careful not to spill anything. There was a roll of paper towels on the table and I used a few to mop up the coffee. "I don't think so. It doesn't much feel like a gift right now."

"What else?" he asked, his eyes lighting up.

"What do you mean?" I asked.

"What else can you do?"

"I don't—"

"You're right. You called me before the attack hit the web. There was no record of any call to the police or anyone else about it until eight minutes after you called me. And you weren't there."

"I wasn't?" I asked, hope and relief flooding through me.

"No. You weren't there. You were here, at home. I checked."

I sighed and let my head fall into my hands. "Oh Gods, I thought it was me."

"This is forcing me to consider the ridiculous story you told me last night was true. So, I'm asking, what else can you do?"

I stared at him. He believed me. He really believed me. He wasn't running scared or screaming. He wasn't gathering a mob or calling me an abomination.

"I can cast."

"Like a wizard?" he asked.

"Not really, but it's the same idea."

"Show me," he demanded, excitement sneaking through his disbelief.

"What do you want to see?" I asked, hoping he didn't ask for too much.

"Can I have a car?"

"No," I said with a small laugh. "It doesn't work like that. I mean it does, but I'd be pulling the car from somewhere, from someone's driveway. I can't make a car."

"You could pull a car from someone's driveway?" he said in awe.

I chuckled.

"How's your coffee?" I asked.

Jenner took a sip.

"A little on the cool side," he said.

I placed my hand on the side of his mug.

"Ignis," I whispered, calling for a small amount of Magic. I felt heat move through me and into the cup. In seconds, steam lifted from the dark liquid. Jenner sipped his coffee again, his face alight with wonder.

"Madre de Dios, do it again!"

"Gelum," I said and I felt the cool flow of energy from my core.

"No way," he turned the cup upside down. The liquid remained frozen inside. "I wanted to drink that!"

"Ignis," I said again.

"That is awesome," Jenner said, when the liquid had melted.

Just as I was about to tell Jenner how happy I was that he thought it was awesome and not terrifying, my phone rang.

"Your message said it was an emergency," Nemo said in a flat tone.

His deadpan expression on my kitchen wall told me he was still sore about our last conversation. I propped my watch, which had a pin-sized camera, on the table so I wasn't talking to my wrist.

"Has Zemila been in contact with you today?" I asked. Nemo groaned and rolled his eyes. When he took a breath to speak, I cut him off. "Her roommate was murdered in their apartment last night."

"What?" he said, his expression changing.

"Mila told me you were coming in a few weeks, but I think she needs you here now. She was the one who found Tiffany and it was . . . it was pretty brutal."

A shiver went down my spine. Despite the fact I hadn't been at the apartment, I still felt responsible. This was about me somehow. It had to be.

"Yes," Nemo said. I could tell he was a little dazed. "I have to be there. I'll change my flight. I don't know if I can do that. I got the ticket cheap."

"I can do that for you," Jenner said, popping his head into the frame. My watch camera had a wide lens, but even so, he had to be right beside me to fit on the screen. I stepped out of the frame.

"Who the hell are you?" Nemo said, voice hostile.

"My name is Jenner. I work with Lochlan. I see you're in Johannesburg?" he said as he tapped furiously at his own system projected beside Nemo's image.

"How the hell do you know that?" he nearly shouted.

Jenner ignored him.

"Okay, your flight has been changed to this afternoon. You have three hours before you need to be at the airport. I am arranging a cab for you now."

I tuned out as Nemo and Jenner made arrangements. My mind drifted back to what Zemila had said about her friend's daughter. About Melanie Connor. It was too strange. Now that I had Jenner, perhaps I could talk about it with him, to try and make sense of this.

"Lochlan?" I heard Nemo say as I sat down in front of my watch.

"Yes?" I thought I knew what was coming and it was entirely unnecessary.

"Thanks for calling," he told me.

"You're welcome," I answered, knowing I still had much to make up for. "I—" I started but paused. I didn't know what to say. Sorry for disappearing? But I wasn't sorry. I had to. Sorry for not calling?

"I've got to call Mila and then start packing," Nemo said. "I'll see you tomorrow?"

"Yes," I said, relieved I had another day to figure out how to make things right. "We'll come get you with Mila tomorrow."

"Okay. I owe you one, Loch." He ended the call.

You really don't, I thought as I closed the now empty window where Nemo's image had been. I put the watch back on my wrist still thinking.

"Okay," Jenner said, taking a deep breath and letting it out slowly. "I am trying not to be insensitive here."

I looked at him, puzzled.

"I want you to understand that I understand the gravity of all this, but—"

"What is it, Jen?" I said. Worry crept into my words.

"I know, you know? I know how traumatic this all must be for you and I get it. I do. Well not really, but . . . but—"

"Spit it out, Jenner!"

"That was the most beautiful man I have ever seen in my entire life and I think I need a cold shower."

I stared at him for a moment, slack-jawed and stunned. Mayhap, it was everything that going on, mayhap, it was the lack of sleep. It could have been the relief I felt at Jenner's acceptance, but whatever it was, it manifested itself in uncontrollable, unstoppable, hysterical laughter.

"What? I'm serious," Jenner said, fanning his face with his hand.

Doubled over in my chair, I clutched at my stomach as I howled with laughter. Jenner swore a little in Spanish before he started to laugh too.

CHAPTER THIRTEEN

After recovering from our outburst, Jenner and I discussed theories on my visions and the connections to Zemila. Jenner suggested it might be God trying to be my wingman. I couldn't tell if he was joking. As much as I would have liked to believe there was a divine plan for Zemila and me, the morbid nature of the dreams had me fearing a more sinister reason.

Some time between talking about why Tiffany was murdered the way she was, and Jenner crossing himself for what felt like the hundredth time today, Zemila called.

"Tonight?" My mind went blank when she asked me if I was still free. "My gala?"

Right, I thought. Douche had other plans.

"Of course I'm free," I told her.

"Are you sure?" she asked.

I wasn't. I was wary of stepping into her boyfriend's shoes even for just one night. But she needed a friend. I could do that for her.

"Yes," I said. We made arrangements to meet at the gala and get Nemo from the airport afterward, as his flight got in later that night.

"Do you have a tux?" she asked. "It's black tie."

A small smile played at the corners of her mouth. She knew I didn't.

"Umm," I said, smiling too.

"See you tonight," she said, before hanging up.

"So," Jenner said casually as the screen with Zemila's face shrank to nothing. "That was Zemila." He raised his eyebrows and let them fall twice in rapid succession. "The most beautiful being you've ever seen, si?" he said, quoting me. "Can you tell me the real story now?"

"I did tell you the real story," I said. "I met her when I was at Erroin and she—"

"Erroin?" he asked.

"Yes. It's a Luman school and—"

"Luman?"

"For people with brighter Spark and—"

"Spark?"

"Okay," I said, thinking of how best to explain this. "Everything that is alive has something inside called Spark. It's an energy source."

"Like a soul?" Jenner asked.

"Not precisely, but the two are comparable. There is Spark in a blade of grass and there is Spark in the smallest beetle. All beings have it. The difference is some have brighter Spark than others. The Spark in a cat would be brighter than that in a flower for example. When a human is born with brighter Spark, it changes them. Well, it doesn't change them since they're born that way. The excess manifests in an extra ability. Those people with brighter Spark, with a gift, are called Luman."

"Okay," Jenner said. "You are Luman and I am Human."

"Yes," I nodded. "I met Zemila at Erroin Peritia Academy, a school for Lumankind in India."

"Cool," Jenner said, eyes lighting up. "Hogwarts is real."

"Not quite," I said, smiling. "Nothing so exciting ever happened at Erroin. For the most part, all the subjects were the same as in any Human school."

"So, what can she do? Zemila, I mean?" he asked. But before I could open my mouth to answer, he said, "Dios, that means Nemo is Luman too, right? Is it like a family thing?"

"More often than not it's genetic, but there are outliers. Nemo is Telekinetic and Zemila is an Earth Driver."

"What does that mean? Not the Telekinetic thing, I know what that is, but what is an Earth Driver?"

"Zemila can move earth with her mind. Where Nemo can move anything, he struggles with size, or he did when I knew him. Zemila could, well, I don't know how powerful she is, but I've heard of Earth Drivers who can shake mountains."

"Madre de Dios. This is the girl you have a hard-on for?"

"Jen!"

"No seriously, I don't think you should mess with some chica who could drop a mountain on your face if you upset her."

I laughed, and then yawned. I needed a nap. I needed a tux. I needed Cam.

"Do you think Cam will take me shopping?" I asked Jenner.

"Ha! Are you kidding?" he said, "Of course she will. Go to sleep," he ordered when I yawned again. "I'll call her."

I nodded and headed upstairs.

"You're the best, Jenner," I said over my shoulder.

"I know," he called back.

φ

After a cruelly short time, Jenner shook me awake.

"Cam's here," he said.

"What?" I muttered, still half asleep. I waved my hand over my bedside table. Red lights flashed 1:30 p.m. at me. It had only been an hour.

"Lochlan!" I heard a lightly accented female voice shout up the stairs. "Get your pasty butt down here so I can burn a hole in your wallet!"

I grinned into my pillow. Cam's here.

Perhaps, I thought as I rubbed my face and swung my legs out of bed, perhaps I had two friends. And if things were all right with Nemo, mayhap, I had three.

My lips turned down when I thought I was still lying to them.

"What's wrong?" Jenner asked, seeing my expression.

"You didn't tell Cam anything did you?"

"Dios mio, I had to tell her part of it. I left out all the freaky Magic stuff though. Was that okay?" Jenner asked, worry pulling his thick eyebrows together.

I nodded.

"If you did tell her, she wouldn't care, oh mystical one." He started to bow his way out of the room and I threw my pillow at him. He dodged it easily.

"I'm waiting!" Cam's impatient voice came from downstairs.

"Nemo and Zemila don't know either, Jen, so you have to be careful about what you say to them."

"Qué?" Jenner stopped in the doorway, confused. "But I thought they were Magic Luman Ninja Turtles too?"

"They're Gifters," I said. "Which is a type of Luman. They think I'm a Gifter too, but I'm not, I'm—"

134

"A Druid."

"I am not a Druid," I said a little more defensively than I meant to. "I'm just different." I pulled off my white t-shirt that I had, at some point, gotten a small coffee stain on, and put on a black one.

Cam was now yelling up the stairs in Spanish. Jenner rolled his eyes, left my room and started yelling back in a way only an older brother could.

I pulled on a pair of dark-wash blue jeans and headed to the washroom. Sibling argument drifted up the stairs as I quickly washed my face. A minute later I was bounding down and picking Cam up off the ground in a bear hug.

"Lochlan buddy!" she said as she hugged me tight. "How've you been?"

"Had better days," I told her truthfully.

"Yes, Jenny told me some of it."

I put her down. Cam was of average height and build and she had the same caramel complexion as her brother. Where Jenner was lanky, Camile was soft. Her curves were akin to Greek statues carved at a time where the rounded look of being well-fed was a sign of wealth and, therefore, was the most desirable shape.

"How have you been, stranger, really?" she asked, punching me in the arm. Large brown eyes looked up at me.

She must have just come from the office, I thought. She wore a navy pencil skirt with a pale-pink top and heels that added nearly five inches to her height.

I smiled broadly. I don't know what it was about Camile, but she always made me smile.

"I tried to call. The phone doesn't work both ways for you?" she said.

"Sorry. I've been busy. It's no excuse, I know," I said, leading them both into the kitchen. "I just want to grab an apple and a glass of water."

"No problem," Cam said. She and Jenner both sat down at my kitchen table as I got a glass out of the cupboard.

"Do you want anything?" I offered.

"Just to get a move on," Cam said. "Isn't the event tonight?"

"Yes."

"Go easy on him, Camile," Jenner said. "He's just a sub for the girl's douchebag boyfriend."

"How do you know he's a douchebag?" I asked Jenner after draining my glass.

"Oh right," Cam said. "He isn't going with her to this event tonight because . . ."

"Si," Jenner said with conviction. "Douchebag move."

"Fair enough," I said, downing my second glass of water. "So where are we going?"

"Oh, don't you worry about it," Cam said with a mischievous smile. "Jenner told me you have a little money saved so we don't need to be stingy."

I looked sharply at Jenner who shrugged at me. How did he know I had more money than my lifestyle suggested? Mayhap, it was just an educated guess.

"Ready to go?" she asked.

"Yes," I said, grabbing an apple out of the fridge and following her to the front vestibule, Jenner behind me.

"You coming too, Jen?" I asked.

"Nope, I'm going home to sleep for a few days, thank you very much."

"Right. Thanks, Jenner. For everything." I meant it.

"Yeah, yeah," he said, pushing past me and heading out the front door.

"Don't get all mushy on me. I'll be back for the big reveal. My little sister is treating me to dinner tonight."

"I am not!" Cam yelled out the door at him.

He ignored her. She sighed and turned to me.

"I am," she said.

φ

Shopping with Camile was an interesting experience. It mostly consisted of my following her around a very expensive store, her holding things up, making different faces, and throwing items into my hands.

"So, tell me," Cam said in a hushed whisper as she looked through a rack of black suit jackets in my size. I rearranged the mess of expensive items in my arms. "How crazy is it that your friend has to go to this gala thing the day after her roommate was killed?"

"It is indeed crazy," I said. "She was adamant on the phone, however. She said she had to be there."

"What does she do?" Cam asked, finding a jacket and handing it to me before moving on to a new rack. "She works in media, right?"

"She's a journalist. She has a video blog. I've never watched it but apparently it's pretty popular."

"Because she's gorgeous?" Cam asked.

"Perhaps," I said, with what I'm sure was a dopey grin on my face. Cam shook her head at me. "Wait," I said snapping out of my reverie. "How do you know she's gorgeous?"

"Jenny told me about the sexy brother."

"Naturally."

"He also told me you were crazy in love with this girl before you left

137

university in India. Side note, you went to university in India, so cool."
She handed me another jacket.

"Thanks?" I said, as I tried not to drop everything I had. I looked around for some help.

Wasn't there someone to take these to the—

"Change room!" she instructed.

Never mind, I thought, and walked to the back of the store.

Crazy in love was right. Not like young-love crazy, either. That might have been manageable. Towards the end of my time at Erroin, I started to have strange thoughts about Zemila.

It started as dreams, then daydreams that I would snap out of and wonder where the gruesome, brutal ideas had come from. It was like someone had put my brain on hold and, instead of bad music, it was images of me hurting her.

I hated it. I tried to make it stop. It happened again and again until finally I couldn't take it anymore and hoped distance would make it go away.

I left. It worked. And now she was here.

"I want to see everything," Cam said as I closed the door in the large fitting room. Then I heard a whomp sound as she sat down in one of the armchairs near the mirrors.

I shook my head, trying to bring myself back to the present.

"All right," I called back to her. I decided to try on the navy-blue pinstriped suit first. I hated that one and wanted to get it out of the way. After putting it on, and making sure my shirt laid flat over the fine chain around my neck, I walked out to show her.

"You were right," she said. "I don't like it either. Next!"

The next was a plain navy-blue suit. This one was tolerable. I was not a fan of the black and grey button-up she had picked to go with it. I showed her.

"This one isn't bad," she said. "I like the shirt."

"I hate the shirt," I said with an expressionless stare. "I hate shopping."

"Wahh, wahh," she said, imitating a baby. "Poor you! At least you don't have to wear heels."

"True enough," I said, turning and heading back into the change room. I went through a few more suits and shirts until I got to the one I really wanted. I tried it on and went out to show her.

"Wow," she said, as I turned slowly. "Perfect fit. That's the one."

CHAPTER FOURTEEN

I waited on the vast steps of the National Art Gallery in a black suit, white shirt and bow tie. Cam had been amazed at the perfect fit. Little did she know I had made a couple of minor alterations before showing her the outfit.

Zemila had to be early for the Gala and instructed me to wait outside where she would come to collect me. Huge white pillars, akin to those of the Parthenon, lined the entrance.

To the left of the stairs, a man in a very expensive tuxedo stood pleading with his daughter beneath a sculpture of a huge bronze spider. The sculpture must have been almost ten meters tall, long metal legs reaching out in all directions.

The young girl, perhaps fourteen or fifteen, was in a wheelchair. She wore a flowing pink dress.

Wheeling away from her father, she grabbed hold of one of the legs of the spider and spun herself around. Her arms extended in a perfect and graceful line as her dress billowed out behind her. Before the chair she must have been a dancer.

Giving the wheels another hard push, she headed to the adjacent bronze leg, spinning again and sending herself beneath the belly of the massive spider to the opposite leg. Her movements were fluid and the expression of bliss on her face told everyone watching that she was at peace. Her father smiled, watching his daughter dance.

"Beautiful," I heard from behind me.

Turning, I saw Zemila. She looked stunning in a full-length charcoal-grey dress, so dark it was almost black. The supple material came over her shoulders and fit closely. A thick belt of the same color wrapped around her waist. Below the belt, the fabric dropped loosely to the ground.

Zemila walked towards me, her red lips turned up on one side. She placed two fingers on the bottom on my chin and closed my, apparently open, mouth.

"Thank you," she said and hugged me quickly. "You don't look so bad yourself. No glasses?"

"Yes, I . . ." I paused, thinking back to my decision to not wear them, and what that meant. I wore them to help me be invisible, to blend in.

I guess I didn't want to blend in tonight, I thought, ignoring how unwise that was. I guess I wanted her to see me.

"Thanks for coming tonight," she said, letting me off the hook about my glasses. "I need a friend right now."

"Whatever you need," I said.

I followed her gaze over my shoulder to the young girl in the wheelchair and we stood watching her dance.

"That's my boss's daughter," Zemila said as the girl glided to a stop in front of her father. He knelt down and hugged her.

"Come inside, you can meet her."

Zemila turned to lead me into the gallery and I stifled a wildly inappropriate noise. Her dress was backless but for two strips of fabric running from her shoulders straight down to her waist. She was a goddess in grey and I would follow her anywhere.

"What's this gala actually for?" I asked as I followed Zemila past the Parthenon-like pillars.

"It's the Day Dream Ball. A different charity is featured every year. Last year was for the World Wildlife Fund, specifically for polar bears."

"There aren't many left," I said as we walked down an enormous hallway. Stone statues lined the walls between priceless works of art.

"Right," she said nodding. "I think we're down to two or three families now. Climate change." She shrugged. "This year it's Youth Rights."

"I read your articles," I told her. "I agree the voting age should be lowered, but education reform is important too. A flood of young educated voters could change the—what?" I said, cutting off when she stopped walking.

"I'm just surprised, I guess," she said, staring at me with an expression I couldn't decipher.

"You do good work," I told her with a smile. "I guess the right people noticed it. That's why you had to come, right?"

"Yes. And thank you." She looked pleased and started walking again. "I was invited with a few of the higher-ups from work who attend every year. It's pretty big for my career, but it's going to be a rough night, you know?" she said as she slowed. We had reached a large group of people all milling around the entrance. "Pretending everything is normal will be hard."

I didn't know what to say.

"Whatever," she said, smoothing down her hair unnecessarily. It was in an elegant knot at the base of her neck. "I just have to get through a few hours. It's a great opportunity and there are a lot of people here who can help change things for the better . . . or at least their wallets can."

"I'm sorry," I said lamely. "I don't know how to help you."

"You're here. That helps me," she said, linking her arm through mine. "Let's rub shoulders with some trillionaires, shall we?"

"Let's," I said.

We walked through the large double doors and into the ballroom.

φ

The first hour of the evening passed without incident. For the most part it consisted of me following Zemila from one small gathering of people to another as she promoted the Youth Rights charity and, through the popularity of her work in the field, promoted herself.

"Mr. Talbot is one of the top financial backers of the Right Waters Party," she said to me under her breath.

It was impressive to watch her wiggle her way out of the tight spot with the middle-aged Mr. Talbot, whose watch cost more than most people made in a lifetime.

"I don't even know why he's here. He doesn't want to lower the voting age. All he wants is to get rid of immigrants like me."

"Me too," I said.

"You grew up speaking English. It's different." It sounded like an insult when she said it.

I hadn't grown up speaking English, but she didn't know that.

Zemila made a beeline for a group of NEP members. I silently said a prayer of thanks to Jenner for educating me on the political system. Without him, I wouldn't know NEP stood for New Egalitarian Party or that they were currently the official opposition.

During a lull in conversation, I spotted the girl who had danced around the legs of the bronze spider. Zemila followed my gaze, said goodbye to the group and led me over to the girl.

"My boss," she hissed in my ear as we made our way towards the young girl and her parents.

Their backs were to us and, had Zemila not whispered her boss's name in my ear before tapping the woman on the shoulder, I would have been physically knocked back with the shock of seeing her.

"Zemila, there you are, dear," said the woman with black hair and terracotta skin. She turned to face us. Her dark eyes met my green ones, and recognition flared.

"Oh, Benjamin!" she exclaimed, frantically tapping her husband on the shoulder. "What a coincidence, this is the young man I was telling you about. The one who saved my life."

"Hello again, Ms. Jace," I said, extending my hand.

"Stop that," she said, taking my offered hand and pulling me into a tight hug. "Adrienne is fine, of course." She released me.

"I don't know whether to thank you or hit you," her husband said with a warm and genuine smile as he extended his hand.

I took it.

"She can't stop talking about you. The Irish Prince Charming who pulled her out of traffic." He rolled his eyes playfully at his wife.

"Stop that!" she said again, lightly slapping her husband on the shoulder. "And this is my daughter, Rosamund."

"I knew a Rosamund once," I said, turning to face the girl and shaking her hand. "It's nice to meet you. I'm Lochlan."

"Hello," she said, giving me a shy grin.

"I saw you dancing outside earlier this evening," I told her.

"Oh no!" she squeaked, pulling her hand away, clearly embarrassed. Color flooded her cheeks.

"You move beautifully," I said, kneeling before her. "I'm certain your father would agree?"

I gave him a quick look and he nodded emphatically.

"The Rosamund I knew was similarly gifted with grace and beauty. She was also a little stubborn and extremely passionate," I told her.

"It must be in the name," Adrienne said flatly.

"Don't lose that." I smiled and gave her a quick wink before standing. She beamed at my praise.

"It's nice to finally meet Zemila's boyfriend," Adrienne said, smiling at us. I opened my mouth to correct her, but she cut me off. "So good of you to be here in her time of need." Her expression turned into one of pity as she affectionately patted Zemila on the arm.

"Lochlan is just a friend," Zemila said smoothly. "A good friend."

"Oh," Adrienne said with a small frown.

"Oh," Rosamund echoed with much more enthusiasm. "Oh my God," she said quickly, covering her mouth with her a hand. With a look of horror, she said, "I, punch bowl, thirsty now."

She groaned, her father laughed and together they headed to the hors d'oeuvres table.

"The accident happened about eighteen months ago," Adrienne said, stepping to my side and watching her husband and daughter walk away from us. "It's nice to see a bit of her old self back. It seems I'm in your debt again."

"A debt I will never collect on, Ms. Ja——," I cut off my words as I caught sight of her stern expression. "Adrienne."

An easy smile broke over her face as we both turned back to Zemila, who was looking curiously between the two of us. I gave her a quizzical look, as if to ask what was wrong, but she just shook her head.

"Well, Ms. Jace, I don't want to keep you," Zemila said.

"But I want to keep you," she replied. "I wonder if you both could be moved to my table for dinner. The Thompsons are sitting with me and I never did like them." Adrienne looked around, presumably for someone who could arrange the switch.

"Ahh," she said with a small wave. "There's George now, he owes me a favor and I think he knows who did the seating arrangements. I'll be right back."

With a wave to George, she hurried off.

"Can I get you a drink?" I asked Zemila.

"What the hell was that?" she said, turning to me after watching her boss hurry across the room. "Who knew you were such a damn charmer? I have been working for Ms. Jace for two years! You know her for two minutes and it's 'Adrienne is fine, of course'?" she laughed. She really laughed.

For the first time, the half-sad expression Zemila had been wearing all night melted away. It was replaced with an honest and open smile that made it seem as though, for a moment, she had forgotten about the tragedy of the night before.

I smiled too. I couldn't help it.

"Yes, you can get me a drink," she said, linking her arm through mine and leading me over to the bar. " 'Adrienne is fine, of course,' " she quoted again, laughing.

Leaning against the bar, Zemila looked at me. Her full lips were quirked up in a coy smile. Her posture accentuated her curves. My eyes roved her body before I caught myself.

"I can only remember one other time I've seen you without those enormous glasses on your face," she said after a moment.

"Oh yeah?" I asked, smiling at her.

"Yeah," she echoed. "It was the last New Year's you were at Erroin. I remember we were all at Rossy's, and Nemo was trying to talk Duke into taking a shot of Rossy's Moon with him for the countdown. Duke never touched the stuff again after Dyson drank him under the table, and then there was the countdown, and then . . ." She trailed off and looked up at me.

She took a half step closer. Our eyes locked.

I remembered that night too. The pub was called Roswell's, the All-Luman bar popular with the students of Erroin. Zemila was with her flavor-of-the-month boyfriend, and Dyson came over to me just before midnight.

I should have figured Dyson knew who I really was then. She took my glasses off my face and told me she knew why I wore them, that they weren't real.

I remembered Zemila looking at me the same way she was looking at me now. I think that was the first time she saw me.

"Excuse me?" I heard from what seemed like very far away.

Zemila took another half step towards me. Her hand was resting on my arm and I inhaled a shaky breath.

"Excuse me!" I heard again, and my eyes snapped up to the bartender. "Can I get you two something?" he asked.

"Sorry," I said, stepping away from Zemila, the spell we had both been briefly caught in, now broken.

I felt the absence of her hand on my arm. My heart was racing, and I tried to remember how to talk.

"Canna hame . . ." I trailed off. Those weren't real words.

"Rossy's Moon?" Zemila whispered to me, her lips brushing my ear. I had to grip the bar so my knees wouldn't give out.

She was not playing fair.

She laughed softly before turning to the bartender.

"Two Keil's please," she said.

"You got it," the man said, quickly getting two glasses out onto the bar top and filling them with an amber liquid.

"Thanks," I said to the bartender, grateful my brain was forming real words again. I pressed my thumb to the tip pad labeled $10.

"Adrienne is waving you down. I guess I'm going to have to share you for the rest of the night," she said over her shoulder as she headed in the direction of her boss, hips swaying with every step.

I blew out a breath in a huff as she walked away. I took a moment to pull myself together before following after her.

Conversation flowed easily. Zemila was funny and sexy and, damn, she was smart.

I momentarily forgot how to think when Zemila snaked her arm around my waist and rested her head on my shoulder in the brief calm between the many introductions and conversations.

"I'm happy you're here," she said, big brown eyes looking up at me. "It feels easier than it would've been . . . because you're here."

"You're welcome," I said, and before I knew what I was doing, I kissed her temple.

I froze, midway through the act. Afraid of her reaction, worried I'd crossed a line. But Zemila sighed and leaned into me.

We sat at Adrienne's table. Zemila and Rosamund were next to each other and by the time the meal was over, Zemila had a new fan.

"We are here tonight to raise money for Youth Rights," one of the teenaged MCs said after the last speaker left the stage.

"But it's not just about raising money, we want to have a little fun too, right?" said her co-MC.

"Right!" the girl agreed as she danced through the tables, getting people to their feet.

"Do you know what we're doing this time, Ayba?" the boy asked as he skipped on stage to a familiar beat. He started to clap and we all mimicked his motions.

"I've been looking forward to this all night," Zemila said, taking off her shoes and hiding them under her chair.

"This is an oldie," I said, surprised she knew it.

She smiled, took my hand, and pulled me onto the dance floor.

"I know what we're doing this time, Nodin," Ayba answered him.

The two MCs spoke in time with the male voice in the song.

"This time, we're gonna get funky."

When the music died down there was huge applause for Ayba and Nodin who had freestyle danced on stage as well as performing the best Charlie Brown I'd ever seen. Perhaps a third of the crowd returned to their chairs when the next song came on. I gave Zemila a questioning look, to which she rolled her eyes and started dancing again.

Ayba and Nodin would come out periodically to introduce a singer or DJ. When a young woman of about seventeen, named Felicity Davis, sang the first slow song of the night, I extended a hand to Zemila.

We revolved slowly on the spot. I looked down at her and I saw the corners of her mouth were turned down. Her eyes were sad.

"Are you all right?" I asked.

"Just sad, I guess," she said into my shoulder. "I feel guilty I've been having such a good time when it was just yesterday that—"

"Hey," I said, moving my hand from her waist to her chin, taking it between my index finger and thumb. I tilted her head up to look at me. "I knew Tiffany for all of about ten minutes. She didn't seem like the kind of girl who would have you feeling guilty over something that brought you joy when you needed it."

"You're right," she said slowly, looking right at me, right through me.

My heart started beating hard in my chest, could she hear it? We were pressed so close together. Could she feel it? Bright brown eyes stared into my green ones. I took in an unsteady breath.

Then I blinked and stepped back. Her hand was still held in mine.

"Can I cut in?"

We both turned, and I breathed a sigh of relief when I saw Adrienne and her husband standing beside us. I saw Zemila give a small smile as she took the Benjamin's offered hand. I offered mine to Adrienne.

"Did I ruin a moment?" she asked as we began to dance.

"It was more of a save, to tell you the truth," I said.

"Oh, boy," she laughed. "You got it bad."

"Is it that obvious?" I asked.

"Yes," Adrienne nodded emphatically. "And I'm sure she doesn't really know."

"Well, she's dealing with enough right now, and she's with someone."

"Yes, she is," Adrienne said, looking around the room. "But where is he now?"

"He had a work thing, I don't know. He's kind of a—" I cut off. I didn't need to taint Adrienne's view of a man she had never met.

"Seems like kind of a douchebag, if you ask me," she said with a half shrug.

I laughed.

"Yes, that was precisely the word I was searching for," I said. Adrienne caught the flick of my gaze to where Zemila was dancing. She was smiling in earnest again. It was nice to see.

"Since I have you alone, I wanted to tell you something."

"Aye," I said, a little wary of the change in tone.

"You seem to care about her."

"Yes?" I said it as more of a question than a statement, but Adrienne went on.

"She isn't taking it seriously, even after last night, but . . ."

"But what?"

"But she's been getting some strange letters lately."

"Letters?" I asked. "People still write letters?" I thought of Mrs. Abernathy's full mailbox.

"Some do," she said, a dark expression covering her face. "Some I wish wouldn't."

"What do you mean?"

"I think she is being followed," she said. "She refuses to acknowledge the situation, so there isn't—"

"Someone is following her?"

"Keep dancing gorgeous, you're making a scene," Adrienne said, patting my shoulder.

"Oh, sorry." I hadn't realized I'd stopped.

"Zemila is pretty good about fan mail and I don't know if she's stopped answering this particular fan, or if she ever answered him in the first place. I'm assuming it's a man, but it could be a woman. There is something icky about it. She doesn't think she's being followed."

"What did the police say?" I asked, slowly revolving on the spot. I could feel myself getting pulled into yet another area of Zemila's life where I should be keeping my distance.

"They said to let them know if the guy, or whoever, starts coming around the office," she sighed. "I wanted to tell someone in her life outside of work."

"A friend told me not to get caught up in everything tonight," I said, thinking back to Cam's words to me before I left. "This isn't helping."

"Get caught up in what?" Adrienne asked.

"In being . . ." I hesitated to say it.

"Prince Charming," Adrienne supplied.

I rolled my eyes to try to make it seem like a stupid thing to say.

"Good advice," she said, nodding seriously. "Though she'll need you."

"She's strong," I said. "I don't think she needs anyone."

"We all need someone," Adrienne said seriously. Then changing to a more comical tone she said, "If you need to be someone's Prince Charming, I'm sure Rosamund wouldn't mind."

I'm unsure when it happened, but sometime between the buffet table, saying our goodbyes and leaving the gallery, my hand found Zemila's. Or perhaps hers found mine. We walked that way for a while. She held her shoes in her free hand, walking barefoot.

"Aren't you worried about stepping on a rock, or glass?" I asked her.

"At this point that might be more comfortable than these." She held up her strappy heels. "I felt like after the first song, I should probably wear them for the rest of the night."

"Hopping in heels would have been difficult," I agreed.

"And after the night we were having with Ms. Jace," she said, sighing.

"I wanted to stay on her good side." She bumped into my shoulder.

"What?" I asked. I was happy to see the easy smile on her face and the playful light in her eyes.

"Her Irish Prince Charming?" Zemila said.

I rolled my eyes at her.

"Shut up," I said, bumping her back as she started to laugh.

I joined in too after a moment. It wasn't funny, but Zemila's laugh was one of those infectious ones. It was the kind of laugh you got caught up in, even if you didn't hear the joke.

"Here I am," Zemila said, gesturing to a dark blue VW Golf. I was always a little surprised when I saw her car. It wasn't what I expected. But when I thought about it, it made sense. At her core, Zemila was a practical being.

Pulling open the driver-side door, she stopped. I was already half way into the passenger seat but straightened and looked at her over the car.

"Thanks, Loch," she said. "I really needed the company tonight."

"It was my pleasure," I said. "It was fun."

"Yes. I just—" she paused for a moment and looked to the heavens. I saw tears fill her eyes.

"Mila," I said, walking quickly around the car. She turned into me as I wrapped her in my arms. She hugged me and cried into my shoulder.

My heart ached for her, for the pain she was going through, pain that was likely my fault. I wanted to tell her the truth about me, about my past. I wanted to find a way to ease her pain, but I knew I could do nothing. Nothing except leave, and I didn't think I could do that again.

"I'm sorry," Zemila said as she pulled away from me.

"For what?" I asked, genuinely confused.

"I had a good time tonight, but I think ..." she trailed off, trying to find the words. I waited for her to continue. "I just mean I needed someone tonight, and with Tyler being away, and you. I feel like it's just so easy with you but I don't want to ruin anything. You just disappeared, all those years ago, right when we were, and I just, I just—"

"It's all right," I said, lifting a hand to her cheek. She closed her eyes and leaned in to my touch. "I'm here for whatever you need. I'm not going anywhere."

She sighed and placed her hand over mine before pulling it to her lips and planting a kiss on my palm. Then she released me and turned to get into the car.

I stood, frozen for a moment, trying to piece together the puzzle of mixed messages I just received. Deciding it was better to leave it alone, I hurried around the vehicle and got in.

"Do you still want me to come to the airport with you?" I asked as she started the car and pulled out onto the street.

"It's okay. I appreciate everything you've done tonight. I want to be alone for a little bit before I have to tell Nemo everything."

"I understand," I said. "You must be exhausted."

"You have no idea," she told me.

But somehow, I thought I did.

CHAPTER FIFTEEN

Zemila walked alone down a darkened street, her long loose curls swinging with every hurried step. As she looked over her shoulder, a street lamp illuminated her olive-toned skin and bright brown eyes. Picking up her pace, she fumbled in her bag for her phone.

Before she had a chance to use it, she screamed.

She dropped it.

She tried to run.

Her cries for mercy echoed off the abandoned buildings, accompanied by the clacking of her heels on the pavement and the steady footfalls of a heavy run. My hand reached for her, grabbed her and—

In the brightly lit office building, she sat at a desk, typing furiously on her Intelli-glass tabletop. Sliding and grouping pages into different files, she muttered to herself about her work.

"Hey," said someone from her doorway. "Jace just left for the day, you want anything?"

"No," Zemila answered. "I need to stretch my legs though, I can go." She turned away from the door, pulled an elastic band off her wrist and looped her hair into a ponytail. Moving back from her desk, she left her office for the elevators.

"Lochlan?" she said as she stepped through the elevator doors. "What a nice surprise. What are you doing here?" She looked down at my arm. "Oh my goodness your hand, what's wrong with your—"

Her words were cut off with a grunt.

The doors closed.

Her face twisted in confusion and pain.

Looking down to her stomach, she saw a red stain bloom on her white shirt around the handle of a blade. I savagely twisted it before pulling out of her, and then—

The tall hallways of Erroin Peritia were a sight. Times there had been good. Times there had been simple.

I'm dreaming now, I realized with relief. This one is a memory.

"Hey, Lochlan." Turning, I saw my roommate and best friend. Nemo.

"You're late," I told him. My accent was thick. It felt easy to speak that way. Comfortable. Like I didn't have to hide. Or at least, I didn't have to hide everything.

"Sorry but I was, ahhh . . . well, let's just say I'm back in Nianca's good books." He winked at me.

"You're a dog." I shook my head and grinned.

"Speaking of," he said, nodding to greet a pretty girl with skin the color of dark chocolate who was holding hands with a mountain of a man.

"Duke, Agatha," I said. "How are you?"

"Right as rain," Duke responded in a southern drawl. "Where are the other girls?"

"Dyson said she was coming," Agatha told us. "We're still going to Rossy's right?"

Roswell's. The campus bar.

Good times.

Simple times.

"Oh, there they are," Agatha said. She released Duke's hand and headed towards the two girls walking down the hall. Dyson and—

My breath caught in my throat. It did that every time I saw her. Tall and lean with long wavy dark hair cascading over her shoulders, Zemila smiled at me.

Gods, she was beautiful. We had gone for a long walk around the school grounds the day before. It had started platonically enough but ended with her hand in mine.

A sharp pain shot through my head. A grotesque scene of blood and bodies flashed before my eyes.

"Whoa, are you okay?" I heard from somewhere above me.

My knees collided with the hard marble floor of the hallway. Another image came to me. Hands, my hands covered in hot red blood.

"Lochlan!" said another voice that sounded far away.

I knelt, surrounded by bodies . . . no, just one body, in pieces.

"Aga, what's wrong with him?"

"I don't know!"

Matted long dark hair still attached to a bit of scalp lay inches from me. I reached out my hand, but there was already something in it.

Something soft.

Something red.

Something dripping.

I screamed as the dripping mess in my hand vanished. I clutched at the people around me.

But no one was there.

I was alone.

One hand gripped the coffee table and the other my old mismatched couch. I looked down at myself. My new suit was wrinkled and drenched in sweat. Thin rays of light shone through the gap in my curtains.

I needed to clear my head. I needed to swim.

φ

I ran to the community center. Fast. It helped.

In the change room I tried to find the melody of a song that might calm my mind, but it wasn't until I dove into the pool that my brain focused on something else.

I felt my body panic, then relax slightly as I was submerged. At 5:45 in the morning, I had a lane to myself and, as usual, Tim was doing lengths of front crawl so slowly, I was amazed he moved at all.

I went straight into a butterfly stroke. When my muscles screamed to cease the rapid pace I pushed them to, it became easier to ignore my troublesome thoughts.

Easier, not easy.

Faster, I have to go faster.

My hands were covered in blood again. No, no, that was just water. It was water from the pool.

Hot liquid splattered across my face. I reveled in it. No, I told myself as I turned, pushing off the pool wall.

I reached forward to grab the water, propelling my body through it. I reached forward again to examine a chunk of something on the bloody floor. It was soft . . . brain matter.

It took me two strokes to get to the side of the pool. Pulling myself out and slipping on the damp floor, I hurried to the nearest garbage can as nausea overtook me.

It had been hours since I'd eaten. Only bile came up. I gasped for breath with my head over the garbage can.

As soon as I could, I straightened and looked around for a water fountain. Finding one, I rinsed my mouth before getting back in the pool.

Tim hadn't noticed a thing. His stroke was as steady as ever. If nothing else, this incident proved to me that the teenaged lifeguard fell asleep on the job. He was awake now, I noted as I tried to pick up the intensity of my swim and erase the image of—

Swim, I thought. Just swim.

It wasn't long before Tim and I were forced to share the lanes with other early-morning swimmers. That was usually my cue to leave, but I needed more time.

Slowing to accommodate the other swimmers, I tried to think over everything without seeing images of death. This was not the first time I had had such an intense reaction to a nightmare; they were always about Zemila. The brutal ones were anyways, the ones of her dead, murdered, and by my own hand.

I knew that wasn't the same kind of vision. She wasn't in any imminent danger. It was a warning. It was a subconscious warning of the darkness I knew lived in me. That was why I had left Erroin. That was why I knew I'd have to leave. I would not become a thing of nightmares. Not again.

I had thought the other dreams, the visions, were my redemption, my salvation. I had thought it was my second chance, but somehow, it all came back to her.

My first dream: Melanie Connor. She was the daughter of a friend of

Zemila's. My second dream: Adrienne Jace. She turned out to be Zemila's boss. Third was the douchebag boyfriend. I almost regretted helping him, and then . . . something clicked in my brain.

I felt like an idiot for not putting it together before. Tiffany and the train. I didn't think of it then. She must have been on the train I had disabled.

It was only hours later she was murdered. Murdered the way I had killed the men who had killed Lugh. Perhaps a train crash would have been a better way to go. I shook the thought from my mind. She wasn't the only one on that train. If nothing else, I had saved lives that day.

The thought was of little comfort against the memory that turned into the reality of Tiffany's fate.

If this was truly my redemption, then why was everyone I'd helped connected to Zemila? Perhaps it was not redemption at all. Perhaps it was just further torment.

Further punishment.

Mayhap, I deserved it.

Adrienne's words drifted back to me, "She's been getting some strange letters lately." If all the people in my dreams had died, Zemila would have been pretty isolated. Perhaps this was all an attempt to leave her vulnerable. But then, why was I seeing it?

Confused and frustrated, I swam for another ten minutes before getting out of the pool. I didn't bother stretching or showering before I left. I knew what I had to do, and it had to happen now, before I changed my mind.

Once outside the community center, I hoisted my bag to a more secure spot on my shoulder and started to run. Fewer than fifteen minutes later, I was jogging up to my front gate.

"Why did you go running with that great big bag?" said a raspy voice.

I turned to see Mrs. Abernathy making her way down her side of the front walkway.

"Are you sick?" I asked, slightly out of breath and a little more worried than I expected to be.

"Oh, aren't you sweet," she said, and coughed. "Just a little frog in my throat."

"I'll bring you some chicken soup, shall I?" I said, breathing in deeply. I felt a pang in my chest as I realized too late that I wouldn't be bringing her soup.

"What are you doing with that big bag on your run?" she asked, smiling at me and ignoring my offer. She knew I would bring some over no matter what she said.

I always did. But not this time.

"I was at the pool and I had to rush home," I told her.

"Well, don't let me keep you," she said, shuffling past me and onto the sidewalk. "Oh!" She stopped and, reaching into her bright green handbag, pulled out a small manila envelope.

I walked over to her.

"This was on my doorstep, but they must be for you. Good job, lovey," she said, handing me the envelope. "I'm glad you took my advice. You both look very smart. She's gorgeous."

After patting my cheek rather harder than necessary, and with no further explanation, she waved her hand in an absent sort of goodbye and walked off down the street. Momentarily distracted from my task, I looked down at the envelope and wondered at its contents before remembering it didn't matter.

I had to leave.

CHAPTER SIXTEEN

I jerked awake for the second time that morning.

Upon arriving home, I had showered quickly and had had every intention of grabbing my go-bag and leaving right away. That plan was foiled by a wave of tiredness so strong I felt dizzy.

I had intended to just rest for a moment. I didn't want to sleep. I didn't want to dream. Both happened anyways.

9:45 a.m. I thought of calling Dyson. We had left Erroin together. I could stay with her before moving on. That was the easy part, where to go, where to stay. It was the leaving that was hard.

Jenner would try to find me if I left without explaining. He could do it too. In this digital age, I don't know if I could hide from a man of his talents.

Should I explain? Would he understand?

As though my thoughts had brought him forth, the automated system announced Jenner's presence at my home.

"*Jencilvadonner Hernandez,*" the androgynous voice said a moment before there was a hurried pounding on the door.

I jogged down the stairs and pulled open the door. He gave me a dark and tired look.

"Coffee, now," he said.

"Jenner," I said, trying to think fast. I needed to get rid of him.

"Now!" he said, pushing past me.

I followed after him, head bowed in defeat. If I told him I was leaving, he would try to stop me. I would just make him some coffee, figure out why he was here and send him on his way.

Jenner flopped down at the kitchen table and rested his head in his hands. "Enough for three," he said.

"What?" I said dismayed, almost dropping the French press.

"Cam is on her way."

I groaned.

"I feel the same, but she wouldn't stop calling me. She wants to hear about last night."

I groaned again. Jenner looked up.

"To tell you the truth, so do I, but I could have waited."

"Oatmeal?" I asked.

I knew when I was beat. Or was I was making excuses to stay?

"I make it better than you do," he said, standing.

"You know where everything is," I said, scooping grounds into the French press and looking over at the kettle. It was heating on the stovetop.

"*Camile Hernandez,*" my security system announced. I left the kitchen to let her in.

"You look like the bottom of my shoe," she said.

"Good morning to you as well."

"Yeah, hi. Coffee?"

"Not ready yet."

"What?" she said, outraged, pushing past me.

"Neither of you told me you were coming!"

The three of us sat around my kitchen table with a mug of coffee and bowl of oatmeal each. Jenner took a sip from his mug before letting out a contented sigh. "You make better coffee, I make better oatmeal."

I nodded my agreement.

"So how was last night?" Cam asked me.

"Let the man eat, Cam!" Jenner said.

"¡Qué! Soy curioso ¿Por qué no preguntar ahora?" she said back to him.

"Porque tal vez era horrible y su pobre corazón está roto y él no quiere hablar de eso! Es por eso! Madre de Dios Camile!" Jenner said, leaning forward and staring daggers at Cam.

"Mi corazón no se rompió," I said. Cam was about to say something in response to her brother's reprimand but froze at my words. "Te diré," I continued. "Si quieres saber."

"Yes, I want to know," Cam said at the same time Jenner said, "Dude, you speak Spanish?"

"Sí . . . Obviamente."

"Yes, obviously," Cam said, echoing my words. "Don't care, moving on. How was last night? Was it horrible? Is your poor little heart broken like Jenner thinks it is?"

I looked at Jenner who shrank back in his seat.

"Sorry, man. I didn't know you could understand me."

"Está bien," I assured him.

"So," Cam said impatiently. "How was it?"

"It was," I paused. How was last night? What a loaded question. "Interesting."

"Do tell," Jenner said, earning himself a look from Cam. "What? I'm not allowed to want to know too?"

"Interesting how? Did you two . . ." Cam said, letting the phrase hang in the air.

"We're just friends," I said, trying to keep the disappointment from my voice. "But at the end of the night she apologized to me."

"For what?" Cam asked, right as I put a spoonful of oatmeal in my mouth.

"For flirting with me, I guess," I said after swallowing. "And she was, I mean, we both were. It was just so easy. She said that too, that it was easy. But . . ."

"But she's with someone," said Cam.

"Who cares?" said Jenner.

"Yes, she's with someone. And Jen, you will never believe who I met—" I stopped. I couldn't tell him now. Not with Cam here.

"Who?" Jenner asked.

I looked meaningfully at Cam. Trying to speak without words.

Jenner shrugged.

I squinted my eyes at him.

He gave me an exasperated look.

"What's going on?" Cam asked.

I ignored her question as Jenner nodded at me, his crooked smile growing.

I rolled my eyes. But I trusted Jenner, and he trusted her. I nodded.

"Lochlan is the grandson of an ancient Demon King and has Magical powers!"

Cam froze with her spoon halfway to her mouth.

"Phew! I have wanted to tell someone so bad!" Jenner said.

"Umm," she said.

"Really?" My tone was flat. "Like that?"

"Well how else was I supposed to do it?" he asked, excitement lighting his face. "Now do some Magic!"

"Mayhap, with a little more tact is all," I scolded.

"Wait, you're serious?" Cam said, drawing our attention back to her.

I turned to meet her eyes, afraid of what I would see there.

"Yes," I said, ready for the backlash of disbelief or fear.

"Huh. Okay," she said, before going back to her oatmeal.

"That's it! Dios mio!" Jenner said, almost standing before remembering his legs were still tucked under a table.

"I am inclined to agree with Jenner's reaction," I said. "You seem to be taking this pretty well."

"Lochlan," she said, after a few painful seconds of silence. "There has always been something a little, I don't want to say off, but different about you."

"¿Qué?" Jenner asked.

"For starters, you're really good at blending into the background. It's a little creepy. You just kind of melt away sometimes."

I shifted uncomfortably at her words.

"Si," Jenner said, looking at me thoughtfully. "You do that."

"You also don't need your glasses," she continued. "But they help you be more invisible."

I scoffed and rolled my eyes. I took my glasses off and tossed them on the table. "Apparently they don't help . . . anything else?"

"Well since you mention it, your accent comes and goes, like you're working to suppress it all the time. And sometimes you say weird words...like, really old words."

"Mayhap," Jenner said. "What does that even mean?"

"Right," Cam agreed with a chuckle.

"But how does that make 'demon spawn' not a shock? Sorry, man," Jenner added as an afterthought.

"No," I said. " 'Demon spawn' is pretty close."

"It doesn't, but," Cam said, after a sip of coffee, "I met this guy a few months ago when I was traveling in Asia. We, ahhh," her eyes shifted to Jenner before focusing on her coffee. "We had a good time."

"Ew!" Jenner said.

I punched him in the arm.

"Thank you," Cam said to me.

I nodded, and she continued.

"I actually spent a lot of my trip with him after we met. A couple of weird things happened, first at a casino, then bowling. I mentioned it and he said it was him." She looked at me and said, "He called himself a Gifter. Is that what you are?"

"No, I'm something else. Something older," I said.

"He told me he had . . . a gift," she stumbled over the word. "I didn't believe him."

"And then what happened?" Jenner asked.

"Nothing. Maybe he thought it freaked me out, but the weird stuff stopped happening and a week later I flew to Dubai."

There was a wistful look in her eyes.

"Did you see him again?" I asked.

"I did, but you know how these things go."

"No," I said. "Enlighten me."

"I saw him again about two weeks later in South Korea."

"And?" Jenner and I asked at the same time.

"And he had his face attached to some local," she said, her expression going blank.

"Oh Camile," Jenner murmured compassionately.

"Did you talk to him?" I asked.

"Nah, I just left," she said shrugging it off. "Enough about me. You are a hellion come to reign terror on us all and you were talking about the love of your life who has a boyfriend but was flirting with you shamelessly. Let's talk about that some more."

That made me smile.

"I'd be lying if I didn't say it went both ways," I told her.

"Yes, well, be that as it may—"

"You were going to say something about your visions," Jenner cut in.

"You get visions?"

"No, I mean yes, but not like you think." I explained to Cam as best as I could about each of the nightmares, about telling Jenner the truth and about how I was afraid somehow it was I who'd killed Tiffany.

"Then Zemila's boyfriend came to get her and it was the guy from the coffee shop."

"Hell of a coincidence," Cam said.

"The girl in Fort Totten Park was her friend's daughter, the woman I pulled out of traffic is her boss, and the roommate—"

"She was going to get on the train you stopped," Jenner said.

"We stopped," I corrected. "Aye, she was." I fell back into my chair.

I thought of telling them about my other dreams, the ones that started a long time ago, when I first met Zemila. Would they understand that I didn't want to hurt her? That it wasn't me? Could they? Could anyone? Even I worried I would lose control.

Then a thought resurfaced in my mind. It was the same thought that solved all my problems, the same thought I had been struggling with since I had woken up.

Run. Run and don't look back.

"Where'd you go?" Jenner asked as he finished his oatmeal and stood to put his bowl in the sink.

"Huh?" I said.

"Where did you go just now?" he asked again. He sat back down on the other side of the table and blew on his refilled mug of coffee.

"Just trying to think it all through, why this is happening."

"It's not a magic-man thing or a Druid thing or a sparkly-vampire-werewolf-duck thing is it?" Cam asked.

I grinned in spite of my current thoughts. "No," I said. "I just have to leave."

"Do you need a ride? Where are you headed?" Cam asked. "I have to run a few errands today."

"No," I said. "I have to *leave* leave."

They both stilled, then looked up at me.

"What?" Jenner said, understanding my meaning. "Why?"

"This has happened before," I stood. "Not exactly like this but when I'm around Zemila I just . . . It's not safe for her to be around me. I have to leave."

Fear and anger rose in me as I left the kitchen, headed to the front hall and the stairs to the second floor.

"Oh, come on," I heard from behind me as both Cam and Jenner pushed away from the table and hurried after me.

"That's ridiculous," Cam said. "How could all of this be happening because of you?"

"I don't know!" I called from halfway up the stairs. "I just know it is!"

I heard Jenner follow me into my room.

"Come on, man," he said. "We can figure something out, you don't have to run away."

"Jenner, I appreciate your concern, your help," I said as I pushed my bed to the side, revealing a charcoal black circle drawn on the floor. "Nochtann féin," I said to the ground. Two bags appeared in the center of the circle.

"Whoa," Jenner said.

"And I couldn't have done it without you," I continued. I swung the backpack over my shoulders and picked up the small duffel.

"Don't ask me why, but I know if I stay here, Zemila will be next. She'll die. By my hand or by another, and I can't let that happen. It can't be me," I said, pushing past him and down the stairs.

"What does that even mean?" Jenner protested.

"Lochlan?" Cam's voice drifted up to me from the living room.

"It means I have to go, Jen," I said.

"Lochlan," Cam said more urgently.

"I just know I have to." I slid on my shoes and reached for the front door.

"Lochlan!" Cam shouted.

I froze with my hand almost on the door handle.

"You can't leave," she said.

I spun around to argue but stiffened when I saw what she was holding.

"I don't think your leaving will help," Cam told me. "I think she's already in danger."

The manila envelope Mrs. Abernathy had given me. I hadn't given it a second thought. My mind had been so preoccupied.

"Good job, lovey." Mrs. Abernathy's words drifted back to me. "I'm glad you're taking my advice. You both look very smart. She's gorgeous."

I should have paid more attention.

I should have listened.

"Oh, Gods," I breathed as Cam handed me several photographs.

One was of Zemila on the front steps of the National Gallery. I was standing a few stairs below her. It must have been taken when we were watching Rosamund dance.

Another was of us sitting together at dinner. She was laughing; I was looking at her. I flipped to the next picture, not needing to examine my own expression to know what I would find there.

Next was us dancing. I could see she wasn't wearing her shoes. The last one was by her car, her cheek resting in my hand as we stood close together.

"Turn that one over," Cam instructed. I looked up at her, then obliged.

My breath caught in my chest as I saw the words written in a harsh red scrawl:

She's mine. Not yours.

Mine.

CHAPTER SEVENTEEN

Though I hoped my connection to Zemila was to help her, to save her, the bloody dreams I kept having made me believe otherwise. I never thought I'd miss seeing strangers in deadly accidents. But once I decided to say, and the dreams stopped, I did.

I missed waking up with a purpose. With a mission. With someone to save. Now I woke up trying to rid my mind of the blood and torment.

I had a purpose though. I would save her. I would save her from whoever had sent me those pictures.

And if fortune favored me, mayhap, I'd also save myself.

Though I'd swam yesterday, nearly vomiting in the pool hadn't been the release I was going for. My body itched to get back in the water.

I hummed an old favorite while I went through my morning routine before heading to the Community Centre for a swim. This particular song had been stuck in my head recently. Perhaps it was because I was "praying for the end of time" a little more than I normally did.

As usual, Tim beat me into the water. Less usual, he left the pool just after I did.

"Tim!" I said, surprised when I felt the cold draft of air waft into the sauna where I was stretching. "Short swim today?"

"Oh hello, Lochlan," he said in a raspy baritone. His slight accent reminded me he'd grown up in Jamaica. He moved slowly over to the bench across from me and sat down.

"Yes, just a short swim," he told me. "I have been scolded by my husband and my doctor."

"Oh, have you?" I said with curiosity. I continued my stretching routine and asked, "Too much swimming?"

Tim scoffed. "The doctor says I need to stretch more and the husband says I need to slow down."

Slow down? I thought. Any slower and he wouldn't be moving at all.

"I'd be going backward if I was going any slower," Tim said, annoyed. He extended his left leg and unenthusiastically reached for it with his right hand. "He's not even going to believe I was stretching. If you get a call from an angry man named Usman, you better back me up, kid," he said and pointed at me.

I laughed. "No problem." I had never met Tim's husband; in fact, this was probably the longest conversation we'd ever had.

We stretched in silence for a while, the only sound his exasperated sighs when he switched positions.

"You know what?" Tim asked, as we both left the sauna.

"What?" I replied.

"You're the weirdest young person I've ever met." He gave a sharp nod as if to emphasize his point.

"Oh really?" I said, turning to look at him over my shoulder. "Why's that?"

"What young man in his right mind spends so much time stretching?" he asked in earnest. "You don't have to worry about that stuff until you're old, like me, and have someone nagging you."

"I'm certain the nagging comes from a place of love," I said, smiling and opening my locker.

"Yes, well when Usman calls, you can tell him that's where sarcasm comes from too."

φ

"Loch." Jenner jogged up behind me, entering the door of Tjart Tech and Security seconds after I did. "I see you've decided to stay with us a while longer. I have to admit, I thought you might run off after Cam and I left on Saturday."

"No," I said, walking towards the elevators as Jenner fell into step beside me. "I think I'm past running. I think it's too late for that now."

"Okay, well. I'm happy you're staying," he said soberly. "I'm happy I'm not losing my friend."

"Thanks, Jenner," I said.

"Cam was worried too," he told me.

"Worry not, I'm here to stay. Hey," I said, pointing at his coffee cup and glad of an excuse to change the topic. "Did you see your blond this morning? Does he work at the café or is he a customer? You never did tell me."

"He works there," Jenner said with a devilish smile. He had been going there nearly every day and mentioned the guy almost as often. Turning his cup around I saw a smiley face under his name on the cup. We stopped in front of the elevator and in turn, pressed our hands to the sensor.

"Does that mean you've spoken to him?" I asked, stepping back and waiting for the doors to slide open. The crooked smile dropped from his face and his shoulders slumped a little.

"I wish. I'm pretty sure he does this to all the cups."

"Sorry about your luck," I chuckled and stepped through the doors that slid open in front of me. "Mayhap, you should speak to him?"

"He makes the drinks, he doesn't work cash. I think it would be weird."

We waited while a few other people scanned their palms and filed into the elevator.

"What's the number today?" Jenner asked, as we started moving.

"Monday morning, I'm thinking I'll get fifteen before lunch."

The elevator stopped, and two people got off. An impatient man in a navy-blue suit jabbed the close button.

"Wow, fifteen," Jenner said. "I don't think you'll get it. I'll say twelve." Our floor was next and as we stepped off, I could hear the close button being jabbed hard again.

"Are we betting today?" I asked.

"Está bien—Hey wait!" Jenner said, stopping dead in front of me. I almost collided with him. Spinning around, he pointed an accusing finger at me.

"Do you ahhh, use your ahhh . . . you know!" He waved his hands in the air and finished in a whisper, "Diablo Magic stuff?"

I smirked as I walked passed him into my cubicle. He hurried into his own, and immediately dropped the window panel. Leaning through it, he said, "That's cheating!"

"You are so much better than me that if I didn't cheat, I would always lose," I told him.

"That's fine," he said, a broad smile on his face. "We can bet something today if there is no cheating."

"Not a chance," I said.

"Ahh well," he shrugged. "I'll beat you anyways."

φ

Seven hours and fifty minutes later, I picked up a call I hoped would be my last. "Good Afternoon, Tjart Tech and Security, Tech Division. My name is Lochlan. How may I help you?"

"Oh hello," said the man on my screen. "It's you."

I squinted at him.

"I'm sorry, do we—" and then it came to me. "Oh, we take the same bus."

It was Tired Guy.

He looked more rested than the last time I saw him. His eyes, I thought. I don't remember them being different colors. They were both blue, but one was much darker, almost grey. I mentally shrugged and tuned back into what he was saying.

"Small world," he chuckled. "Anyways, I just installed a home system and I need it activated."

"No problem," I said, opening the activation program. "I just need a bit of information from you."

"Yes, of course."

I rattled off the list of questions and he, in turn, gave me all the information I needed. His name was Greg Simmons and he lived only a few streets away from me. It was a brief call and when I hung up, I opened the window to see if Jenner was still working.

An annoying, high-pitched, electronic song met my ears as the window opened between us. Looking through it to his screen, I could see the old-school graphic of a frog dodging traffic.

"So, I guess you're done?" I asked.

"Just waiting for you. I shut down my call line when I hit thirty-seven."

"Whoa! Good day!"

"Si, gracias," he said, pausing his game. "And you?"

"Twenty-eight, five hang-ups," I told him. "People were cranky this morning."

"I only had three. Ready to go?" he asked, grabbing the navy hoodie that was crumpled at his feet.

"Yes," I said.

Reaching for my coat, I thought of my suit jacket that Zemila still had. Should I ask for it back? I hadn't spoken to her since Friday night at the Gala.

That had only been a few days ago, but it felt like much longer.

Shaking off the thought, I swung my messenger bag over my shoulder and headed for the door. I looked down at my watch as Jenner and I headed towards the elevators. There was a message from Zemila.

"What?" Jenner asked. I hadn't realized I had stopped dead in my tracks as I read it.

"Zemila asked me to help her move into her boyfriend's apartment on Friday," I said flatly.

"What?" he nearly shouted.

"That's weird, right?" I asked, starting to walk again.

"Si, super weird."

"It would be good to see Nemo though," I thought aloud. "Try and mend fences with him a bit."

"Uh huh," Jenner said with a dreamy look on his face. "I'd mend a fence with him any day. Can I come?"

"Gods, Jenner," I said, and punched him in the arm.

"What?" he said with a smile. "Jealous? Sorry, you're not my type."

I shook my head and laughed. The elevator doors slid open and we scanned our palms in turn before entering.

"I'll tell her we're both coming then?"

"This is a terrible idea and you shouldn't go," Jenner said flatly.

"I'll make you pizza," I said in a sing-song voice.

"Done."

CHAPTER EIGHTEEN

"Madre de Dios!" Jenner said in an exasperated tone from the back seat. "What are we even doing here? I didn't think you were serious."

My eyes drifted from his reflection in the rear-view mirror to the mid-sized moving van we were parked behind. I had gone back and forth all week. The truth was helping Zemila move was an excuse to see her.

"She asked for help," I said. "And her brother used to be my best friend. I haven't seen him since he got here."

"You mean he won't see you?" Jenner asked.

"Or he's been busy? Or something," I said hopefully.

Yesterday, Zemila had called to see if I could still help her move everything from her apartment with Tiffany to her new place with Tyler. I told her I could come by after work to unload the truck.

"Just to sum up," Jenner said. "You're here to help the love of your disgustingly long life move into her boyfriend's apartment. I'm here to make sure you don't make a fool of yourself." He took a breath. "Why is she here?"

We both turned to look at Camile, who had been quietly sitting in the driver's seat.

"Who else was going to drive you?" she said, rounding on her brother.

"I'm here to make sure Loch doesn't make a fool of himself. You're here to watch, don't lie," she added quickly before Jenner had time to speak.

He gave a half-nod, half-shrug gesture.

"The real question is, Lochlan, why are you here?" she said.

I sighed and opened the passenger door.

Cam and Jenner followed me up to the second-floor apartment where a door was propped open by a few small boxes. The apartment was incredible.

High ceilings and large windows with long, dark curtains neatly drawn to either side were the first things to catch my eye. The navy-blue material framing the windows matched perfectly with the rug that lay between the black leather couches.

"Wow," I heard Cam say from behind me. I turned to see what she was looking at. A perfectly-polished glass dining-room table surrounded by slate grey chairs. An ornate white and navy centrepiece finished the look.

"So he's a loaded Doucheb—," Jenner started to whisper, but was cut off by something large, black and furry that came streaking out of a back room towards us.

His words turned into a high-pitched screech. He jumped back and collided with the door frame before regaining his balance.

"Are you okay?" Cam asked, stunned at her brother's reaction to the mixed breed now sitting in front of him.

"Si," he said. "Yes, it just startled me."

Cam's shocked face turned to one of amusement as she looked at Jenner and the dog.

"You guys made it!" Zemila said, walking through the same door as the dog had.

"Hi," I said, and waved awkwardly at her. She walked towards me and engulfed me in a warm embrace.

"Thank you so much," she said into my ear.

"How are you?" I asked.

She pulled away before answering.

"I'm okay. Tiffany's parents left today. The funeral was two days ago. It was tough."

"I'm sorry," I said, not knowing what else to say.

"Hi," Zemila said, turning to Jenner and Cam.

"Oh right." I'd forgotten they were there. "I brought some help. This is my best friend, Jenner."

"Hola," he said still looking worriedly at the dog.

"Oh, sorry," Zemila said. "Oriole, do'ci."

The dog stood immediately before trotting over to her right side and sitting at her heel. Zemila extended her hand to Jenner.

"You helped my brother with his flight. Thank you."

"And this is his sister, Camile," I finished.

"Hi," Cam said, shaking Zemila's hand too.

"You guys have met Oriole," she said looking down at the dog. "She is friendly enough."

"Belgium Sheepdog?" I asked squatting down and offering the back of my hand to Oriole. "And maybe Akita?"

The dog growled at me, showing teeth, and I quickly pulled my hand back.

"Friendly?" Jenner asked.

"Oriole," Zemila scolded. "Sorry, that's so strange."

"That's okay," I said as the dog stared at me, teeth still bared.

"You're right about the breeds though," she said with a shrug. "I'll get the boys. They're around here somewhere." She turned and headed for the closed door behind her.

"Your timing couldn't be better," she said over her shoulder to us. I don't think she noticed Oriole was still in a guard position between her and me. "The truck just got here. Nemo is probably still asleep."

Cam's head snapped up quickly.

"Tyler!" Zemila called. "Nemo!"

"What, babe?" I heard from the other room. The dog seemed to relax at the sound of Tyler's voice.

Or got tired of growling, I thought.

"Lochlan and his friends are here to help us. Come say hi," Zemila said.

"Yeah, in a minute," he called back.

I saw Jenner roll his eyes and I stifled a laugh before catching a glimpse of Cam.

"What's up, Cam?" I inquired.

She looked like a deer in the headlights.

"Sorry," Zemila said, with a slightly embarrassed look. "Nemo!" she called again and went over to another door opposite us and banged on it twice. "Spavaš skoro dva sata, lenjčugo!"

"Evo, evo, I'm up, jebote!" came at her through the door. "It has not been two hours."

"Bogdan?" Tyler said, pointing at me as he walked into the room. I turned to see Oriole winding herself happily around Tyler's legs as he walked.

"Hi," I said dryly.

He ignored me, dropped to one knee and rubbed the belly of the dog who melted at his touch.

"Lyle, is it?" Jenner said, intentionally getting his name wrong. He stepped forward and offered his hand.

"Tyler," he said, looking at Jenner's hand for an unnecessarily long period of time as he stood before shaking it. Jenner was several inches shorter than Tyler and looked up at him when he spoke again.

"Isn't that what I said?" Jenner gave Tyler what appeared to be a sincere smile. "Sorry, anyway, Lyle, this is my sister—"

"Cam?"

Everyone, even the dog, turned.

Nemo stood in the doorway of the room he'd occupied, shock plain on his face.

"Hey, Nemo," Cam said, nervously tucking a few strands of wavy black hair behind her ear. "How was the rest of your trip?"

"Yeah," he said, stepping out of the doorway and coming towards us. "I mean, I'm good, it was good," he corrected.

"You know my brother, right?" Cam asked, stepping back as he joined the now awkward meeting circle.

"Yeah," Nemo repeated. "Thanks again, Jenner. Hi, Lochlan," he said, finally turning his attention to me.

"So how do you two know each other?" Tyler asked, looking between Nemo and Cam.

"We met traveling," Nemo answered, his eyes going back to Cam.

"Oh," Zemila said in a quiet, knowing voice.

"Ooooooh," Jenner said, much louder than was necessary.

I looked at him. How was it possible he was so tactless?

"Okay, well," Zemila said, clapping her hands together. "Let's start moving me in? Tyler, can you put Ori in her cage, please?" And without another word she left the apartment. I immediately followed her.

"Nice job," I said, as we went down the stairs. "I didn't know how to get us out of that one."

"Thanks," she said, over her shoulder. Once outside, we waited for a few seconds for the others to catch up.

"So he told you about her?" I asked.

"Yep," she said.

"Details later?" I said, with a devious grin.

"Nope," she said, smiling.

"It was worth a shot," I said, and we set to work.

The next couple hours passed uncomfortably but without serious incident. Oriole growled at me every time I came within five feet of her cage, and though I tried to talk to Nemo, he avoided me. Eventually, Zemila told me she had no idea what was wrong with Oriole, and to just give it time with Nemo.

"You were his best friend," she said. "Then you and Dyson disappeared. It was hard for all of us, but hardest for him. He's not good with loss."

I assumed "all of us" included the two other people from our social circle at Erroin, Agatha and Duncan. I didn't consider anyone else when I left. I just knew I had to go. I didn't think about who I left behind.

I noticed Nemo trying to talk to Cam. He had about as much success with her as I was having with him. Every time he approached her, she found something else to carry or something to unwrap. Once she just grabbed my hand and pulled me out of the apartment.

"What the hell was that?" I asked when we were out of earshot.

"Can you just . . . not? Okay?" she demanded.

"Okay," I said. We hid in the stairwell for about five minutes, sitting in an awkward silence. When I tried to leave, she shot me such a look that I sat unmoving until she told me it was acceptable to return.

The only two people who seemed to be unaffected by the palpable tension were Tyler and Jenner. Jenner was enjoying watching the various conflicts and Tyler seemed to be totally oblivious.

It wasn't until we were almost done that anything notable took place.

"Oh my God!" I heard Zemila shriek from the kitchen. Oriole barked loudly in response, scaring Jenner, who was placing a glass vase on the mantle beside her cage. He let out a high-pitched shriek of surprise. I turned just in time to see him fumble and save the vase.

Putting down the tiny hex key, I cursed the small table that should never have been taken apart in the first place, before going to see what was going on.

"Oh my God, oh my God, oh my God!" The mantra got higher pitched every time it was chanted, each time accompanied by the dog.

There was the sound of a box falling over and rapid footsteps. Tyler laughed.

"So you like it?" he asked.

"Like it? I'm so happy! I really need to get away. Thanks, baby."

I walked into the kitchen to see Zemila and Tyler embracing, watched by Cam, Jenner and Nemo.

"What's going on?" I asked Nemo.

"He's taking her to Paris, four-day trip. How cliché." Nemo rolled his eyes and looked over at me. He was a couple inches taller than my 6'2". I looked up at him a bit.

"Did you really expect any higher-level thinking from someone she picked?" I asked.

Nemo snorted. It was a bit of a running joke at Erroin that Zemila tended to pick duds.

"Remember that one guy?" Nemo whispered to me.

"Oh yes, I know exactly who you're thinking of."

"Yeah?" he asked.

"No!" I said through a quiet laugh. "There were so many, how could I remember?" I made quotes in the air with my fingers. " 'That one guy'?"

Silent laughter shook his body. He was always an easy mark.

"Let's just the four of us go get something to eat," I suggested. "Leave these two to their . . ."

"Unpacking?" Nemo barely got the word out.

"Cam, Jenner," I said as Nemo gave up trying to hide it and burst into hysterical laughter. Zemila and Tyler broke apart. "Let's go get something to eat."

"Oh, let me just—" Zemila started.

"No, no," I insisted. "You two still have so much—"

"Unpacking!" Nemo nearly shouted. "Sorry, sorry," he said before hurrying from the apartment.

I rolled my eyes and gestured for Cam and Jenner to follow him out.

"Thanks for all your help," Zemila called after us. I waved before shutting the door.

By the time I got to the front of the apartment building, Nemo had somewhat recovered from his outburst.

"Oh, man," he said as he swung his arm over my shoulders and led me down the street. "It's been too long."

CHAPTER NINETEEN

Jenner tried to convince us to go to his favorite karaoke bar, but Cam strongly objected. "Come on, Cam," Jenner said to her, exasperated. "You sing every single time we go there."

Nemo suggested a small pub nearby that had good wings and his favorite beer. We agreed. Not ten minutes later, Nemo headed down a short flight of stairs to a semi-basement with a blank, faded-red sign over the entrance.

"I'm not sure what the real name of this place is," Nemo told us over his shoulder. "But Zemila said most people call it Red Space."

We walked through the door and into a dingy bar that had a distinctly prohibition feel to it. I liked it immediately.

"Is this your kind of place, Gramps?" Jenner said to me as we walked in.

I gave him a sharp look. He looked back at me confused.

"Jenner," I mouthed, shaking my head and throwing a look towards Nemo's back. Luckily, he was walking ahead of us and was not aware of our silent conversation.

Jenner's mouth opened in a silent O, and he nodded.

"Is here fine?" Nemo asked, pointing to a booth.

I sat next to Cam and Jenner sat opposite me. Nemo went up to the bar to order.

"He doesn't know about your . . ." Jenner waved his hand in the air like he was a witch casting a spell over a cauldron.

Cam gave a nervous look towards Nemo who was flirting with the woman behind the bar. She scowled.

"He thinks I'm a Gifter. Half witch, half demon," I said, drawing Cam's attention back to Jenner's question.

"Isn't that kind of what you are?" she asked.

"Yes," I said. "I didn't want to lie to everyone at Erroin, but something just didn't feel right about telling them the whole truth."

"Why?" Jenner asked.

I opened my mouth to answer, when Nemo returned with a pitcher of Cracked Antler and four glasses.

Good, I thought. I didn't have an answer anyway.

"The wings are going to be about ten minutes," he said as he sat down opposite Cam and started to pour the beer. "I got a few different sauces since I didn't know what you all liked."

"Thanks," I said, accepting the glass he handed to me. The sentiment was echoed around the table.

"New beginnings?" I said, raising my glass to his.

Nemo looked at me for a moment, as if considering. Then he nodded and raised his glass to tap mine. "New beginnings."

Jenner and Cam raised their glasses too. Cam avoided Nemo's eyes. There was silence as we all drank.

"Nice," said Jenner, turning the glass to read the name. "Cracked Antler."

"Do you get along with Tyler?" I asked Nemo.

Though Zemila had only just packed up her apartment, both she and Nemo had been staying with Tyler.

Nemo snorted.

"It hasn't been so bad," he told me. "He's at his office a lot and he's good to Mila."

"How's she doing?" Jenner asked.

"Mila?" Nemo said. "She's kind of thrown herself into work. I think she's trying to avoid thinking about what happened."

"Any news on Tiffany's case?" Cam asked.

Nemo's eyes locked onto hers. It was the first time she'd spoken directly to him.

"Umm," he said self-consciously, seeming to realize what he'd done. "No, not really. Not that we've heard anyway."

"What was that thing you were talking about, Cam?" Jenner said, snapping his fingers at his sister. "Pájaro del cielo. ¿O algo así?"

"Sky View," Cam said.

"Yeah, why don't they use that?"

"That's not real, is it?" asked Nemo.

"What's Sky View?" I asked.

"It's a government surveillance project used mostly overseas in war-torn cities," Cam said.

"But it's not over here?" Nemo said. "I heard it's not even over there, it's just a rumour."

Cam opened her mouth to reply but Jenner cut her off.

"I have tried to find any tangible evidence of it, but there's nothing." He smirked at his sister.

"Then why did you even bring it up?" Cam asked, annoyed.

"I still don't understand how this could help with Tiffany's case, even if it was real. Does it watch everything all the time?" I asked.

"Essentially, yes," Cam said.

"In theory," Nemo said. "Sorry," he added after a sharp look from her.

Jenner started to laugh but turned it into a cough and became absorbed in his drink.

"In theory," Cam echoed with an irritated look at Nemo, who also became absorbed in his beer. "It's unmanned aircrafts taking pictures of a given area every second."

"That's creepy," I said, thinking of the implications. "How big is the given area?"

"There are varying reports," Cam informed us. "But most say around fifty square kilometers."

There was a moment of silence interrupted by the arrival of the wings. They smelled amazing and came with five small silver cups of sauce. "Hot, Medium, Honey Garlic, Chipotle, and Maple Syrup," the waitress told us.

The next several minutes were filled with taste-testing the different flavours and meaningless conversation. Jenner, who was never good with spicy foods, accepted Cam's bet that he couldn't eat a whole wing dipped in the hot sauce, then spent the next six minutes with a mouth full of sour cream.

"You owe me dinner," Jenner said to Cam when he could speak again.

When the pitchers were empty, and the wings were nothing but bones, Nemo brought the conversation around to a more serious topic.

"A weird thing happened this morning at Tyler's," he told us. "Zemila had a big bag of fan mail to go through."

"I can't believe people still handwrite fan mail," Jenner said.

"I know right?" Nemo agreed. "I was looking through and one caught my eye. I didn't open it but when Mila saw it, she snatched it away and threw it in the garbage."

"Love letter?" Cam offered, not making eye contact with Nemo.

"I doubt it," he said. "I heard her and her boss arguing on the phone later about something. She said going to the police was unnecessary and that it was no big deal."

"What do you think they were talking about?" said Jenner, leaning forwards with interest.

"Sounded like a fan writing her or something," Nemo answered.

"What did the envelope look like?" Cam asked.

"It was a small manila one," Nemo said, and Cam threw me a meaningful look.

I shook my head ever so slightly to try and tell her "not now," but Nemo saw.

"What," he said. "What was that?"

"It's… ahhh," I said, trying to think of how to say it.

"Lochlan got an envelope like that too," Jenner said with his usual level of tact—that level being zero.

"It was creepy," Cam added.

"What was in it?" Nemo asked.

"Guys," I said. "We have no idea what was in the envelope Zemila got. Perhaps they have nothing to do with each other. Mayhap, it was someone . . ." but I trailed off, seeing the expressions on Jenner's and Cam's faces.

I was trying to convince myself they weren't connected, but I didn't even know why.

"There were some pictures of me and Zemila," I told Nemo. "From when I went to that gala with her."

"Okay," Nemo said, not understanding. "Like from the photographer?"

"No," Jenner said. "Like from someone hiding in the bushes and taking pictures to threaten Lochlan to stay away from her."

"What?" Nemo said loudly. A few tables looked over at us.

"Shhh," Cam said.

"Nice, Jenner," I shot him a reproachful look.

"Yeah," Cam said. "Real delicate." Then she swore at him in Spanish.

Nemo was still looking confused as he followed the back and forth.

"There were some pictures of us outside the gala. She was crying, and I hugged her." I stared at the table as I spoke. "On the back of the picture the guy wrote—"

"Mine. She's mine," Nemo said.

"Yes," I looked up at him. "How did you know?"

"She mentioned something on the phone," he said. "She flat-out refused to go to the police, but does she know about the pictures you got?"

"No," I said quickly.

"Maybe she would go to the police if she knew?" Cam thought aloud.

"No," Nemo and I said at the same time.

"She's going away," Nemo continued. "She's had a lot on her plate and I want her trip to be a good one. She'll be fine with Tyler. He's all right. He'll keep her safe." He said the last part like he was trying to convince himself as much as us. "But maybe we could try to find out a little more. Talk to her boss?"

"Yes," I said, nodding in agreement. "I can call Adrienne and set up a meeting. I met her at the gala."

"You also—" Jenner started, but I cut him off with a look.

If Nemo had been paying attention, he might have noticed. Lucky for me, he was trying to catch the eye of the server.

"Can we get the bill?" he asked when she came over.

I would tell Nemo everything when it became necessary. I had told him about some of my early nightmares at Erroin, before I knew who or what they were about. The last thing I wanted was him finding out the real reason I left. Or worse, that everything happening to his sister could be my fault.

CHAPTER TWENTY

"Lochlan Ellyll here to see Adrienne Jace," I said to the round-faced woman with rich brown skin sitting behind a huge white reception desk. On the wall at her back, written in silver letters with blue backlighting, were the words Journalism And Communication Enterprises.

Nemo had decided if Zemila wasn't going to take the threat of a stalker seriously, then we would. It was an admirable notion, but there were a couple of problems. Luckily for him, I was the solution.

First, Nemo wanted to read Zemila's fan mail to try and find out who was stalking her but had no way of actually getting it. Second, he was staying with Zemila and Tyler so even if he did have the mail, he couldn't very well read it at the dining room table.

That's how I got talked into going to Ms. Jace and asking for the fan mail, then keeping it at my house... because that wasn't creepy at all.

"I'm sorry but Ms. Jace has cancelled all her appointments for this afternoon," said the receptionist, looking me up and down.

I could tell, in her mind, that my blue jeans and black t-shirt had been found wanting.

"I just spoke to her this morning," I said, certain there had been some kind of mistake.

"I'm sorry," she said again. I opened my mouth to speak but she held up a finger to stop my words, and said, "JACE Media, how may I direct your call?"

I stood and waited as she finished. Looking down at my watch, I saw I only had about twenty minutes before Zemila would be back in the building. The likelihood of her running into me up here was small, but Nemo took her out to lunch all the same.

"Yes," the receptionist said into the silence, her finger still in the air in front of me. "Yes… no… I'm sorry? Yes, I understand but Mr. Irving said she is not to be… yes…"

Ah, I thought. Adrienne didn't cancel her appointments. Someone else did.

"Yes, that would work… If he called, yes… thank you!" she said brightly before turning to me and lowering her finger. "As I was saying before—"

"Have you been working here long?" I cut her off.

"About seven months, but I don't see what—"

"And do you work five days a week?"

"Yes, but—"

"So, you were here the day someone pulled Ms. Jace out of traffic on her way to work?"

There was a sharp intake of breath. I grinned.

"Irish Prince Charming," she said in a rush, with a look of horror on her face. "You're Irish Prince Charming."

"In the flesh," I said, still not entirely comfortable with this particular nickname. But as it was getting me what I wanted, I didn't complain.

"Ohmigod, I am so sorry!" she said, standing immediately. "Ohmigod-ohmigod-ohmigod. This way."

I nodded and followed her past a stone fountain in the corner of the huge waiting room and down a bright, white hallway.

"I'll take you right in, please don't—" she stopped herself and moaned. "I'm so sorry, I'll—"

"Not to worry, Ms.?"

"Birch," she said. She slowed to look back at me. "Wendy Birch."

"Ms. Birch," I continued, placing my hand on the small of her back and guiding her forward. Floor-to-ceiling white double doors ended the hallway. "My waiting will be our secret."

She seemed to sag in relief and hurried forwards. She pulled opened the doors before I could get there and popped her head in. "Ms. Jace, a Lochlan Ellyll for you." Then she turned to me. "Go right in."

"Lochlan!" Adrienne said, as she stepped out from behind a massive, glass-topped desk. She touched the corner as she walked past, and the scattered images and articles strewn across the intelli-glass tabletop disappeared. "I hope you weren't waiting?"

"Not at all," I said as I heard the door click shut behind me.

Adrienne embraced me before holding me at arm's length, saying, "Please tell me you came here in search of an agent. I have had six calls about you since the gala." I looked at her, surprised. "Okay, four. Two were from Rosamund but she doesn't count."

"How is she?" I asked.

"Good, good! Can I get you a drink?" Adrienne asked, gesturing for me to sit in one of the two straight-backed armchairs in front of her desk. Instead of sitting, I walked to the window and looked out over the city.

"Water would be great," I said. "Thank you."

As Adrienne walked back around her desk, I surveyed the office. It was on the top floor of her building, so naturally the view of the city was amazing. I could tell she had selected this office carefully as its windows lined up with the only gap in the skyscrapers that crowded the blocks around her.

"I own the airspace there," she told me as she pulled a couple of glasses from a waist-high stainless-steel cabinet under the window behind her desk.

"Really?" I asked. She handed me the glass full of water. Hers had a darker liquid.

"Yes, it was expensive but worth every penny," she told me.

I slowly turned away from the view, my eyes scanning the wall to my right. It was covered by a large bookcase filled with what looked like a little of everything. I saw books on law, science, history, popular culture and even a small vinyl collection at the bottom.

The wall opposite was full of frames: pictures, articles and awards were arranged in a scattered, yet organized, fashion. A comfortable couch and a black coffee table looked out of place beneath the frames.

"Great space," I said, finding a seat.

"Yes," she said. "It'll do. How has Zemila been, really? She puts on a brave face here but…"

"She's all right. Her brother is in town and I think that helps," I said.

She nodded knowingly. "Yes, I thought he would be. She told me he cut his trip short to be with her. And what do you know, she's going away."

"Yes, off to Paris with her boyfriend," I said.

"Hmm." Adrienne sounded disapproving. "Well, the way Zemila looks, maybe I should be talking to her brother instead of you."

"That may be," I agreed. "He's looking for work. He's also quite concerned about some of the fan mail she's been getting. He's been staying with her and I guess something turned up there. He read it and—"

"You want her written fan mail."

"I do. I'm assuming it's where the troubling letters have come from."

"It is," she said. "It's no problem to get that for you." She tapped the desk twice with two fingers. "Whitney, get in here." Then she said to me, "I'm assuming you only want what has been deemed threatening?"

"I think her name is Wendy," I said as she lifted her fingers from the desk. "And, yes."

"I know it is," Adrienne said, winking at me. "But it makes her work harder when I get it wrong."

"Tough," I said.

"Yes, Ms. Jace," came an out-of-breath voice from behind me. She must have sprinted down the hallway.

"Collect Zemila's written fan mail, the ones in the blue bags, and have it waiting by your desk in four minutes."

"Yes, Ms. Jace," she said, and hurried from the room.

"I'm so sorry to rush you out," Adrienne said, turning back to me. "I have this meeting tonight. I'd tell you about it, but I can hardly stand to think of it." She finished her drink.

"It's not a problem. This will be a huge help," I said, standing. "For her brother's peace of mind, if nothing else."

I was positive it would be more help than that, but she didn't need to be involved any more than she already was.

"Well, I'm happy someone is looking out for her," Adrienne said, slowly walking with me to the door. "Just make sure if you find anything, you talk to the authorities."

"If Zemila will let us."

She nodded. "Right."

I looked at a picture on the wall of a girl on stage leaping through the air. "Is this——?"

"Yes, isn't she beautiful?" Adrienne said, looking fondly at the image of her daughter, arms outstretched, graceful and strong.

"Yes," I agreed, looking at the photo more carefully.

"That was three weeks before the accident."

"It must be so hard for her," I said, not being able to imagine what it would be like to not only lose the ability to walk, but also to lose my craft.

"Yes, but she's strong," she said.

"Like her mother."

"Oh," Adrienne scoffed. "Now you're just sweet-talking me. Let's go."

She led me to the door and down the hall.

"Thanks for this, Adrienne," I said, as I picked up the two enormous mailbags, full to bursting with many colored envelopes.

"Let me know if you need anything else." She walked me to the elevator and said, "Down, lobby. This will take you right down, no stops."

"Thanks," I said again. She smiled and turned back in the direction of her office.

"Get me the usual from RidgeBean would you?" Adrienne barked at her receptionist as I stepped into the elevator.

"Right away, Ms. Jace," she said as she hopped out of her seat.

Adrienne caught my eye and, as the door was closing, said, "Thank you, Wendy."

I saw Wendy's elated expression and got another wink from Adrienne before the doors slid shut.

CHAPTER TWENTY-ONE

I walked past Arlington and Metcalfe on the way to the train station. It seemed like so long ago I had first met Adrienne, so long ago I had first woken up with images of a lost girl in my mind. I had more questions now than I did when this first started. Hopefully the bags of mail I carried would help answer some of those questions, although I wasn't optimistic.

Thankful it wasn't rush hour, I lugged my bags onto the half-full train. The meeting with Ms. Jace had been short, which was good. I wanted to take the mail home before heading back to work.

Twelve stops after getting on the subway, I got off and caught a bus that would take me almost to my doorstep. I found a seat, putting the mail on it and standing to take up as little room as possible. Even though it wasn't rush hour, almost every seat on the bus was taken.

I yawned, feeling tired as a strange dizziness came over me. My vision slid out of focus at the same time as the bus lurched into motion. My hand scrabbled to find purchase on the overhead rail. Just as I grabbed hold, the bus driver let out a strangled cry of protest before there was a screeching banging sound and the bus stopped abruptly.

"What the . . ." the driver said as he leaned forward to open the bus doors.

Everyone who wasn't staring at their watch or phone leaned forward to see what was going on.

The dizziness was gone as soon as it had come. I shook my head and yawned again.

That was strange, I thought, before mob mentality took over and I also leaned forward to see who was getting on the bus.

A man climbed slowly up the few steps, gripping the railing for support. Though there was no sun and the day was warm, the man wore long pants, a heavy coat, gloves and sunglasses. It wasn't until he walked right past me that I recognized him.

"Greg?" I said, before I had considered if I wanted to speak to him. He turned slowly and grabbed my arm as the bus started forwards again. I winced at the strength of his grip. I steadied him, and he released me.

"Sorry," he muttered.

"Are you all right?" I asked. "Do you want to sit?" I started to move the bags of mail.

"Oh no," he said in a gruff and raspy voice that didn't sound like him. "Thank you, Lochlan, I'll be just fine."

I was surprised he remembered my name.

"Are you certain?"

"Yes, yes," he said. "What's all this?"

He pointed at the large bags and reached for the opening of one, pulling out a letter.

"Fan mail," I said.

"Yours?" he smiled. It was more of a leer. It didn't suit him. "I didn't know you had a pseudonym."

I chuckled, feeling uncomfortable and wishing I hadn't spoken to him in the first place.

"No," I said. "It's for a friend." He replaced the letter, grunted, then swayed on the spot again, almost falling when the bus stopped.

"Are you certain you're all right?" I asked again.

Greg moved away, towards the open door, nodding as he went. He just made it to the steps as the doors started to close. They sprang open again as he stepped down and out of the bus.

It was strange he'd only stayed on for one stop. I was sure he lived by me. But the thought took a back seat to the mail I carried.

Would I find the untidy red scrawl on pictures taken from behind trees and over park benches? Or was this a wild goose chase? Would I find the answers I sought? Or was all of this just paranoia?

The paranoia of an old man who had been young for too long.

φ

"This is all from a video blog?" Jenner asked after work, when we were back at my place. We stood in the kitchen, staring at the bags of mail I had left beside my kitchen table.

Cam grabbed a handful of letters and started to look through them.

"Nope," she said.

"Cam's right," I confirmed. "This is just a fraction. Just the ones that are—"

"Threatening," Cam finished, reading the single word written across each envelope.

"And," I added, "this is just the snail mail. Two months ago, they had to disable the comment section on all her videos and articles."

"This can't all be from one guy?" Cam asked, pulling one of the letters out of its envelope.

"I don't think so," I told her. "Apparently most of them are more xenophobic than stalker."

"I can see that," Jenner said in a flat voice. He turned the page he was reading to face me. Letters were cut out of a magazine like in old movies and read: "You're not fooling anyone, go back to your country you three-holed—"

"What!" Cam cried, snatching the paper out of her brother's hand before I had finished reading it.

"Where did you get that?" Jenner asked me as I pulled off the thin navy long-sleeved shirt I was wearing.

"What?" I asked.

He pointed at my arm.

"Whoa," Cam said as she reached up, crude letter forgotten. She touched my arm. I winced where she held me and looked down.

Peeking out from under my black t-shirt, a dark bruise was forming.

"It's almost like a hand," Cam said as she wrapped her fingers around my forearm just as Greg had done.

"Someone on the bus grabbed hold of me pretty hard," I explained. "He was going to fall."

"That's a hell of a grip to leave a mark like that," Jenner said. Cam nodded.

"I guess," I said. "Where's Nemo?"

"On his way," Jenner said.

Cam scoffed.

"What is with you two?" I asked, sitting down and pulling a few letters towards me. Cam threw me a look that stung. "Whoa, sorry I asked."

"One thing you need to know about mi pobre hermanacita," Jenner said, smiling with sickening sweetness at his sister. "Is that she doesn't fall often, but when she does . . ." He left the sentence hanging in the air. Cam showed him a rude hand gesture.

"Aye, you fell hard." I said.

"I don't want to talk about it," she said as she sorted the letters in front of her. "It's done now."

"I'll take that as a yes." I smirked at Jenner who was grinning ear to ear.

"Camila," Jenner crooned. "Come on chica, get over it. He's here, isn't he? He's trying to make it up to you, isn't he?"

"That's not the point!" Camile said, slamming her open palm down onto the table. The crooked smile left Jenner's face. I felt the grin slide off mine.

"Do you want to talk about it?" I asked with caution. Jenner shot me a warning look.

"Not particularly," she said.

"Hey, I told you about Zemila."

"Dude," Jenner said. "Who cares? She's loco."

"I'm curious," I shrugged, grabbed a handful of mail and turned my attention back to Cam.

"There isn't much to tell," she said, giving in. "We met when I was traveling and got along well, like we had known each other forever, like we were instant best friends." She paused for a moment. Seemingly transported back to their first meeting. "I felt like myself around him, my full self. Like finally I was comfortable in my skin. It was . . ."

"Then what happened?" Jenner asked, now interested.

He was such a romantic.

"We traveled together for a while, a few weeks maybe. I would play his wingman sometimes, and he would play mine. It was fun. The weekend before we were going our separate ways, things became . . . less platonic."

"I don't know if I want to hear this," Jenner said, opening another letter.

"We went out on the Friday night, and I saw this girl, the type he'd be into. But on our last weekend together, he said he'd rather spend it with me. I remember feeling," she tapped a spot on her chest. "Light, like there was a balloon inside me filled with helium."

"And—" I prompted when she drifted into silence.

"They did the nasty," Jenner said, now fully enjoying his sister's discomfort.

"No," she said. "But we danced and did," for a moment she looked embarrassed, and with a half glance at Jenner, said, "other stuff."

"Straight people are weird," Jenner said to me. "So uptight."

"Oh, shut up," Cam said, punching him in the arm. It looked like it hurt.

"Can we skip to the part where you can't stand to be in the same room as him?" I asked, wanting to get to the meat of the issue.

"We had a great day together on Saturday, went out again that night and then—"

"Got nasty," Jenner said in a lurid voice, still rubbing the spot on his arm where Cam had hit him.

"Why do you have to say it like that?" Cam asked.

"Moving on," I said.

"Anyways, Sunday, I was flying out to Dubai and he was going to Hong Kong a few days later. I didn't expect anything, I knew how he was, but then he said he wanted to meet in Korea a few weeks later and fly back together. He said he was going to let me know his plans."

"You got your hopes up," I said.

She nodded.

"And he bailed," I guessed.

"Yes . . . No . . ." She groaned and threw her head into her hands. Her voice became muffled. "If he had just told me he wasn't into me that way it would have been fine, we could have gone back to the way it was, or we could have tried . . ."

She looked up. Her eyes went back and forth between my face and her brother's.

"It's not fair to be mad at him," she admitted. "I'm upset with myself. I felt so terrible after all that happened, and I felt terrible that I was feeling terrible."

"I don't get it," Jenner said.

"Neither do I," I said.

"Like, what's so wrong with me that I need a guy to feel good about myself? It just brought up other issues, you know?"

"No," Jenner said. "I still don't get it."

"Neither do I."

"I need more female friends," she said.

The ID system announced, "*Nemanja Alkevic.*"

"Seriously!" Cam shouted to the heavens. Jenner laughed and volunteered to get the door.

Cam got up moments after Jenner. She muttered something under her breath about needing a minute. I gave her a few seconds' head start before following her.

"Hey, Nemo," I said as Jenner opened the front door. I took the stairs two at a time, following Cam.

I heard Nemo and Jenner move into the kitchen at about the same time as I knocked lightly on the bathroom door. The tap was running and

Cam spoke quietly over it.

"Go away Lochlan, I'm an idiot; let me be an idiot for two minutes."

"You're not an idiot," I whispered through the door. "Can you just let me in?"

For a few heartbeats, there was only the sound of water hitting the sink. Then the tap turned off and the door opened a crack. I went in.

Cam was sitting on the edge of the tub.

"Your place is weirdly clean for a guy," she said with a sniff. "Have I ever told you that?"

"Thank you?" I asked before closing the lid of the toilet and sitting across from her. "What's really going on?"

"You're a guy," she said, rubbing her face. "You wouldn't understand."

"I don't think you're giving guys," I put the word in air quotes, "enough credit."

She looked up at me cynically.

"All right, perhaps I wouldn't understand, but here's the thing," I explained. "It's going to be as weird or uncomfortable or normal or amazing as you make it. He wants to reconnect with you. He wants to be around you. Do you want to be around him?"

She nodded.

"Then stop stressing about it. It may be that you'll get hurt again. It may be that it will be great. The only thing that's for certain is you'll never know if you don't try."

I got up and left the bathroom. By the time I got halfway to the kitchen, I heard her following me.

"Lochlan," Nemo said when I walked into the kitchen, "Where'd you go?"

"I had to grab something from upstairs," I said. "Beer?"

"Sure," he answered.

"Me too, amigo," said Jenner. "And I think we should move into the living room. Your kitchen isn't big enough for all of us."

"No problem," I said, taking four bottles of Cracked Antler out of the fridge.

"Is one of those for me?" I heard Cam ask.

"Hey Cam," Nemo said. "How are you?"

"I'm all right," she answered without making eye-contact. "Did I hear we're moving to the living room?"

"Si," Jenner said. "Grab a bag."

Once we were set up on the couch with Nemo sitting on the floor, and envelopes were scattered in front of us, we set to work.

Categories were made. All xenophobic letters went in one pile, solely misogynistic was another, and a third pile was made for letters that suggested the writer might be following Zemila. Those were the important ones.

"In this one, the guy says he saw her, but then calls her a wet-back Mexican," Nemo said. "Does that go under stalker or xenophobe?"

"I'd say xenophobe," Cam answered, reading the letter over Nemo's shoulder. "It seems like he just saw her out somewhere, not like he was following her. See here," she reached over and pointed at something on the page. "Here he talks about how she ruined his grocery shopping experience with her Latin accent. That doesn't even make sense, she's Serbian."

"Right," Nemo said, no longer looking at the letter but staring up at Cam. She didn't notice.

"Nemo," I said, bringing him back to earth.

"Yes?" He didn't look away from her, but then seemed to snap out of it. "Yes," he said again.

Coughing awkwardly and tossing the letter into the xenophobe pile, he changed the topic.

"Lucky Mila's boss likes you," he said. "You must have made a real impression at the gala."

"Gala?" Jenner said. Then before I could stop him, he said, "Or maybe when he saved her life."

There was a beat of silence before Jenner looked up at me, realizing his mistake.

"What?" asked Nemo.

"It was nothing," I said. "She was just walking ahead of me one day. When she went to cross the street, a car came speeding out of nowhere and I pulled her out of the way."

"Good thing you were there," Nemo said, giving me a strange look.

"What's that look for?"

"You met Tyler before you knew he was with Zemila too, right? I overheard them talking about it. You spilled coffee on his suit."

"Yes," I said, trying to sound casual and reaching for another envelope. "Weird coincidence."

"And you saw Tiffany at the train station the day she was killed," he continued.

"What are you getting at?" I asked, getting defensive.

"Well, we're all looking through this mail for someone following Zemila around and you seem to have 'bumped into' a few people in her life."

He put air quotes around the words "bumped into." I took a deep breath.

"I don't know what to tell you, Nemo. I was happy I was there to help Adrienne. I was less happy about the incident with Tyler. Most of the coffee ended up on me."

"And then you showed up at her place right after she found Tiffany's body," Nemo said, his voice growing louder. The coffee table between us shook. "How did you get there so fast? How did you know?"

"Oh, so now I killed her?" I said, my voice getting louder too. The letter I held was crushed in my hand.

"Well this wouldn't be the first time you were obsessed with my sister," he accused, standing up. Now it wasn't just the coffee table; everything in the room seemed to be shaking.

"And did I take pictures of myself with her at the gala too?" I said through gritted teeth. I rose to my feet, suppressing the surge of power I felt building in my core. The letter in my hand began to smoke.

"Hey," Cam said, standing quickly and placing one hand on Nemo's chest and the other on mine, separating us. "Sit."

Neither of us moved, but at her touch, everything in the room stilled. "Now!" she said.

Nemo flopped into a cross-legged position on the floor, glaring at me.

"Lochlan, ahora!" she said in a warning tone.

I did as I was told and sat down. The singed letter in my hand was barely legible. Luckily, I had already deemed it irrelevant and so I had no qualms about throwing it away.

"We are all here because we want to help," Cam said, taking her seat. "Right?" she said with a hopeful look at Jenner.

"Si," Jenner agreed. "We want to help."

"Okay," Nemo said. He took a calming breath before asking, "Why?"

"What?"

"¿Qué?"

"Huh?"

We all spoke at once.

"Well," Nemo said. "I know why you're here," he pointed at me. "But you two don't even know Zemila. And you," he said looking at Cam. "You can barely stand to look at me, let alone be in the same room."

"We, ah—" Jenner started, with a nervous look at me. Camile's gaze slid my way as well.

Finally, all three pairs of eyes were on me.

"What's really going on here?" Nemo asked.

"Camile and Jenner are here because of me," I said.

"Yeah," said Nemo. "I got that part, but why?"

"If Lochlan is going to tell the whole story from the beginning," Jenner said. "I'm going to need another beer."

I did start at the beginning, the very beginning. At first, he was hurt I'd lied about what I truly was when we were at school, but he understood the instinct to protect myself. The way he and Zemila grew up had taught them self-preservation. In his own way, he hid from his past too.

Then I told him about my dreams of Melanie Connor, then of Adrienne, Tyler, the train and, finally, Tiffany.

"So, you had multiple dreams of the first girl, but only one of all the others?" Nemo asked.

"Yes," I said. I had never thought about that before. "Perhaps because I acted right away with the others."

"But you were too late for Tiffany?"

"Yes," I said again. "It was only after that I started putting the pieces together. Zemila mentioned a friend who had lost her daughter, then Tyler showed up, then the gala where I met Adrienne again."

"And no visions since then. Tiffany's death was the last one."

"Si," said Jenner. "That's weird, right? Why would they just stop?"

"Someone is giving them to you," Cam suggested.

"But why?" Nemo asked.

"Maybe," she continued. "Maybe they wanted you to be around Zemila and they wanted her vulnerable."

"Even if that was true," Nemo said. "Who would want that and to what end?"

"To help Lochlan get a date?" Jenner suggested.

"Ha-ha," I said over Nemo's snort of laughter. "Very funny."

"He's got a point," said Cam.

"What?" I turned to look at her.

"Well, the dreams stopped after you were firmly reinstated as her friend. They stopped only after you were truly back in her life. Do you know anyone who has that kind of power? To put images in your mind?"

"Any of the Old Gods could do it, but most of them are dormant and the only one who would do me harm is dead."

"Balor," Nemo said. "Your grandfather."

I nodded.

"The dreams didn't stop," I said, thinking. "They just changed."

"What do you mean they changed?" asked Cam.

"If I'm thinking of them as you suggested, as someone or something putting images into my mind, they haven't stopped, but they aren't about helping people."

"What are they about?" Jenner said before draining the last of his beer.

"Me," I said. "They are about me becoming Famorian."

"Is that possible?" Nemo asked.

"Yes," I explained. "Famorians are made, not born. And it almost happened once, a long time ago."

"But it didn't happen, right? You didn't turn into one of them." Nemo looked thoughtful, like he was working through something.

"No, it didn't happen," I said.

"Why not?" he asked.

"I left. I ran away," I admitted.

"And you've been running ever since," Nemo said. "That's why you left Erroin. Something happened, and you were afraid of becoming one of them."

"Yes." I looked up at him, willing him to understand, to forgive. Willing him not to ask for the particulars.

"What happened the first time?" Cam asked. "What started the change?"

"Anger, loss," I said, losing myself in memory. "No, that wasn't the real reason."

They all waited. I didn't speak. Shame was heavy on my tongue.

I had never intended to go this far, to tell them so much. But mayhap, if I did, if I trusted them, they could help me stop it from happening again.

"Lochlan," Nemo said, and waited for me to make eye contact with him. "It's okay. We aren't going anywhere. Nothing you say will make us want to leave."

Of that, I was unsure.

"Killing," I said. "Killing for unjust reasons, killing for killing's sake, and enjoying it. That's what starts the process. Once you start to turn, you crave the destruction. It infests your mind and it makes you want more. So you kill more, and you love it more. The more you destroy, the faster you turn, until there is nothing left but a shadow of the person who was. And the bloodlust."

"The three brothers," said Jenner.

"What?" asked Nemo.

I had left that part out of my initial telling. I didn't want him to know the worst of me.

"The way Tiffany died," I explained. "It was the same way I killed the men who murdered my brother."

I told him how that dream had really happened. Cam hadn't heard this part either. Jenner had. He looked thoughtfully at me as I spoke.

"That's horrible," Nemo said. "Thinking you had done those things to her. I'm sorry I suspected you."

"That's all right," I said. "I can't blame you. I had the same thought."

"Someone wants you to turn," Cam said.

"But what does that have to do with Zemila?" Jenner asked.

Cam gave me an apologetic look before she spoke.

"Correct me if you think I'm getting this really wrong, but the first time you started to turn, it was after you killed three men. They had murdered your brother to avenge their father."

"It's like a Celtic soap opera," Jenner said.

"Then you brutally killed them and took pleasure in it," Cam finished and looked at me.

I nodded. Heat flooded my face. I remembered that righteous anger. I remembered getting lost in it.

"No judgement here, man," Nemo said. "If someone hurt Mila, I would—"

"Exactly," Cam interrupted. "Why bring Lochlan and Zemila back together? Why draw him to her? Why make him seem the hero in her eyes?" She looked around at all of us, waiting for us to catch up to where she was.

"Oh my God," Nemo said, eyes widening.

"What?" Jenner said.

"But who would do this?" I said.

"Do what?" Jenner asked.

"Someone wants Lochlan close to Zemila," Cam explained to her brother.

I nodded as she spoke. Slowly, things seemed to fall into place.

"Because if they're close," Cam said. "If they are close and something happens to her—"

"I would take pleasure in killing whoever did it," I finished flatly.

"This is . . ." Nemo started.

"It's a lot," Cam finished.

She was right. It was a lot. I felt the weight of the world drop on my shoulders. I felt shame press in on me as I got up and walked over to the corner of the room. I leaned on the wall and sunk into myself.

After killing the three brothers, my bloodlust was uncontrollable. I had taken over my grandfather's remaining Famorians before Llowellyn brought me back from the edge. Before he told me we both had to leave.

Did Llowellyn just postpone the inevitable? I wondered. Could I ever be redeemed?

"Ahhh!" Jenner yelled, pointing at me.

My head snapped up.

"What the hell, Jenner?" Cam said.

"Look he's doing it!" Jenner told her.

"Doing what?" I asked.

"Oh my God, he is," she said.

"What!" I demanded. I looked from Jenner to Nemo to Cam, confused.

"You're melting away," Nemo said. "You're trying to hide from us."

"It is freakin' creepy, man!" Jenner exclaimed.

I pushed off from the wall behind me. "Oh, I—I didn't realize."

Jenner turned to Cam and started speaking in rapid Spanish. She looked at him as though he was crazy.

So did I.

Nemo, who didn't speak Spanish, looked back and forth, confused.

"You need a night out," Jenner said, breaking the silence that had stretched through the room.

I looked up at him quizzically.

"Yes, you," he said to me. "You who looks like someone just told you there was no Santa Claus. Like someone who thinks so little of his friends, that they would abandon him because of something he did thousands of years ago. Dios mio, you're old as time!"

I smiled weakly.

"You don't need to hide from us," Cam said.

"I don't think this is the time for an outing," I said.

"Then when is?" Nemo, the eternal party boy, asked. "When is a good time to let go and have some fun?"

"And," Jenner added. "It's my birthday."

Cam looked at him sharply.

"Is it?" Nemo asked.

"No!" Jenner yelled. "But I want to go to Once More and I want to do it now!"

"But—" I started.

"NOW!" Jenner yelled. "Okay . . . maybe not right now. But in the very near future."

"It seems like you've been dealing with this for a while," said Nemo.

"Very, very near," Jenner repeated.

"I've been dealing with it for an hour," Nemo continued as if Jenner hadn't spoken. "And I feel like I need to let loose."

I took a breath to start speaking but he cut me off again.

"Honestly, this stuff is scary. Someone is going to try to hurt my sister. And they are doing it by trying to hurt my friend, to turn him into some kind of monster. That terrifies me. But being scared and panicking are two different things."

"You can't dwell on this 24/7, amigo." Jenner said. "You need a break or you won't need to be a Famorian to go loco."

It's not like we could go to the police with this, I thought.

"What's Once More?" Nemo asked.

"Jenner's favorite bar," Cam said, looking at Jenner.

"Don't pretend you don't love it. I know you want to go."

"It's pretty cool," Cam said to Nemo.

"And I bet you're going to make him do that thing with you." Jenner said to his sister.

"Tell me it wouldn't help," she said.

"What are you two talking about?" I asked.

"Friday night is mixed night and they have live music," Jenner told me with a sly grin.

Nemo's phone rang and he tapped his watch to answer it.

"Hello," Nemo said.

"Come on Lochlan," Cam said. "Friday night. What's the harm?"

"All right," I agreed. An infectious smile broke over Cam's face.

"Oh hey, Mila, why is your number blocked?" Nemo asked the image of Zemila on his watch face.

"It's a work phone and Ms. Jace is over-protective," she answered. "Did I just hear we're going out on Friday? Are you at Lochlan's?"

I groaned and Nemo shot me an apologetic look. He knew as well as I did, the night would be easier without Zemila.

"Yeah, I am, and yes, we are," he said.

"Are you working out your plan to win Cam back?" Zemila asked.

Nemo flushed.

"Hi, Zemila," Cam called out as Jenner roared with laughter.

"Oops," Zemila laughed awkwardly. "Sorry. Hi, Cam."

"Right," Nemo said through gritted teeth.

"I was just calling to check in. Going out on Friday would be great, right, Tyler?" she called over her shoulder.

I groaned again. Cam patted my arm sympathetically.

Nothing could ever be easy, I thought.

CHAPTER TWENTY-TWO

"Finally!" Jenner proclaimed loudly as he walked through the doors of Once More With Feeling. A large sandwich board outside told us Friday night was live karaoke.

Cam and I followed Jenner into the bar at a distance as he'd started a happy dance and we didn't want to get injured.

The bar was in an old opera house without the original stage. Red velvet hung from the walls, from the high ceilings down through several small balconies and lower levels.

"Cool place," I shouted to Cam over an amazing rendition of Billy Joel's "Piano Man." She nodded.

"Is that guy actually playing?" I heard Nemo ask behind me. "That's amazing."

Where the original stage would have been, a smaller one rose about a foot off the ground. It was covered with instruments. Several stands to the left of the stage held two guitars, a bass and a cello. There was also a small brass and woodwind section.

My eyes shifted to the drum set and then to the small upright piano, played by a scrawny man with long fingers that danced over the keys. The improvisation on the solo was incredible and he had a deep, raspy voice that lent itself to the melancholy song.

"Yep!" Jenner said excitedly. "This is the greatest bar in the world."

He led us over to a table off to the side but still in view of the stage. Before sitting, I turned to look up at the many levels and rows of seats. Capacity must have been 500 when this was an opera house. I wish I could have seen it then.

The walls were covered with old and older posters of shows and performers, one of which read, "Grand Opening of the Imperial Theatre, July 27th, 1914."

"Gramps," Jenner said. He had caught me looking at the poster. "Where were you in 1914?"

"Do you know what started the next day?" I asked him, as I slid into the booth next to Nemo. Jenner and Cam sat beside each other, across the table from me.

"Oh, come on," I said to the blank expressions that met my question. "Think, 1914. What happened in 1914? That led to something else happening in 1939?"

"I know this one!" Jenner said, snapping his fingers and cursing in Spanish under his breath.

"I actually know this one," Cam said, taunting her brother. "Would you like me to tell you?"

"A war! It was a war!" Jenner announced proudly.

"Yea," Nemo said. "The War of all Wars, or something like that."

"The War to End All Wars," Camile corrected.

"And then there was a bigger war, like twenty years later." I opened my mouth to speak but Jenner cut me off.

"Madre de Dios, were you in those wars?"

"Yes and no," I said. I was saved the trouble of answering further when Cam waved to someone over my shoulder. I turned to see Zemila and Tyler heading towards us.

Cam stood to hug Zemila before sliding back into the booth. Tyler and Zemila moved in beside Jenner, opposite Nemo, Cam and me.

"Are you settling into the new place well?" I heard Cam ask Zemila.

I gave Tyler a sort of nod-wave. He completely ignored it. Zemila's answer to Cam was covered by a question from Nemo.

"Have you gone through any more mail?" he asked, turning away from Cam as much as he could in the small booth.

"No," I told him, a worried expression clouding my face. Jenner leaned in. Tyler, who was chewing a large piece of gum, gave us a strange look before Cam distracted him with small talk.

"I told him to take a break from it," Jenner said.

"Yeah, okay," Nemo looked at me. "Maybe we could go through some more tomorrow?"

"Yes," I said.

"This place is amazing, Jenner," Zemila said, effectively bringing the table back to one topic. "I can't believe I've never heard of it."

"It's gone a little underground, I guess," Jenner said. "Maybe because it's a mixed club."

Nemo looked at Jenner quizzically. At the same time as Tyler muttered, "maybe because it's for losers," under his breath.

"Mixed," Jenner said, in answer to Nemo's unasked questions. "Any creed, color, gender, orientation, and everything in between."

"Isn't that everywhere?" Nemo asked.

"Oh, you sweet beautiful naïve straight boy," Jenner said as he patted Nemo on the hand.

"How have you not heard about all this 'rights to refuse' garbage?"

Zemila asked.

"I've been traveling?" he shrugged and looked apologetic.

"Well this place doesn't have any of that," Jenner said. "What it does have, right now anyway, is Cam." He looked at his sister. "Just wait until you hear her sing."

"You can sing?" Zemila asked Cam.

My eyes drifted to Tyler possessively holding Zemila around the shoulders as he eyed the other patrons. He had practically pulled her onto his lap.

Cam rolled her eyes at her brother before answering.

"A little," she said.

"A little!" Jenner almost left his seat. "She was the lead in every musical at our high school!"

Cam couldn't contain her smile.

"Really?" Nemo said, interested. I was surprised too. I had no idea.

"Go sign up for your song," Jenner said. "They're over there. I can see Misha. But the stage manager is there."

He pointed to a group of people sitting not far from the stage, then to a man with a clipboard leaning against one of the pianos and singing along. Cam's small smile grew wider as she gave me an odd look before hopping off the booth bench and walking towards the stage.

"What was that about?" I asked Jenner.

"I'll tell you in a few minutes," he said as his sister made a beeline towards the stage manager. I saw them speak briefly before he pointed at the same group of people Jenner had indicated.

"Do you sing?" Zemila asked Jenner.

"Oh no," he told her. "I just love the atmosphere here."

He looked over his shoulder at Cam. She was smiling and clapping as the group of people she was talking to got to their feet and went to set up for their set.

"I don't tell her often," Jenner said. "But I love it when Cam sings. Her voice is amazing."

"Well I can't wait," Zemila said, "Right, Tyler?" She nudged him in the ribs.

"What, babe?" he asked, clearly not having heard any of the conversation.

"Nemo," Jenner said. "Switch spots with Lochlan."

"Why?" Nemo protested.

"So I can stare into your dark and mysterious eyes," Jenner answered sarcastically. "Can you just do it?"

He threw a look at Cam who was now on stage. A band was setting up behind her and she gave Jenner the thumbs up.

"Okay," Nemo said, confused.

"Jenner," I slid out of the booth and waited for Nemo to go in before me. "What are you up to?"

"I think Cam heard you singing the other day," he told me with a mischievous smile. "I had to look up that old song, but she knew it by heart."

My eyes widened in horror as I sat down, now on the edge of the booth, ready to run. "Oh no," I groaned, and as if on cue, the twanging guitar riff drifted over the crowd. "This isn't happening."

"Oh, it's happening," Jenner said, nodding excitedly.

"Kill me now," I requested as Cam started to sing.

"Well I remember every little thing as if it happened only yesterday," she sang. And she was good. "Parking by the lake and there was not another car in sight. And I never had a girl, looking any better than you did," she pointed at me as she brought the mic away from her face and back again.

"No!" I yelled, but I was smiling uncontrollably.

"And all the kids at school, they were wishing they were me that night."

The crowd roared.

Seventy years later, and Meatloaf still had it.

She sang on to much whistling and applauding. A few tables emptied onto the dance floor, singing with her.

"I don't know this song," I heard Zemila say, but I had eyes only for Cam. She had taken the mic off the stand and was making her way over to where we sat.

She stopped a few meters away from me, the crowd parting for her, before starting again in a slow march, in time to the music.

"I'm not getting up," I said as Cam sang.

"I betchya you are," I heard Jenner yell.

Cam, now right in front of me, grabbed my shirt and pulled me to my feet, much to the approval of the crowd. She shoved the mic under my nose.

Everyone seemed to take a breath at the same time.

The band stopped and the bar went silent in anticipation.

I stared at Cam. She stared back, raising an eyebrow in challenge. I shook my head, giving in.

"Ain't no doubt about it we were doubly blessed," I sang and the band started in perfect time. "Cause we were barely seventeen and we were barely dressed."

We sang together for another couple of lines. A moment later, a server appeared at my side with a second mic, tapped the top once and handed it to me, before hurrying away. I turned with a look of half-hearted exasperation, to see Nemo and Jenner in stiches, Tyler looking confused, and Zemila wearing a smile that didn't quite reach her eyes.

"Go!" yelled Nemo between gales of laughter.

All right then... Let's go.

I raised the mic to my lips and sang my way to the stage.

I used to sing as a boy, every day with my brothers, then later on my own. It makes me sad sometimes. It makes me think of better times. Times long past. Times lost forever.

But here, with the crowd pushing me forwards and Cam dancing and singing to me on the stage, here I found pure joy.

"Okay, here we go," said an elderly man with a cane in one hand and a mic in the other. "We got a real pressure cooker going here."

Cam pulled me off stage and for almost a full sixty seconds she threw me around behind the curtain, occasionally poking out a leg or an arm and getting a big laugh when she yelled, "Am I hurting you?" into her mic.

By this point I knew my role and how to play it. I took the mic from Cam and she pushed me back to the middle of the stage.

"Stop right there!" I threw my head side to side in time with the music. "I gotta know right now!"

Cam walked seductively onto the stage.

"Before we go any further do you love me, will you love me forever?"

Totally absorbed in the moment, and almost taking out the old man as he tossed his mic to Cam, I put everything into the song.

Cam sang the "Let me sleep on it" bit with as much gusto as I sang my parts. Though I thought the crowd could get no louder, it did.

We went back and forth, playing our respective roles, the Cautious Lover and the Cautious Committer, until finally, the Cautious Committer gave in.

"I couldn't take it any longer, Lord I was crazed," Cam sang, and threw herself to her knees. The crowd hollered their approval.

She looked over at me with a devious smile and I couldn't resist singing the last verse with her.

"So now I'm praying for the end of time, to hurry up and arrive."

Singing together, we turned to the crowd in front of us. Cam danced over to share her mic with the drummer for the last few lines.

When the song was done the crowd exploded.

Cam and I hugged tightly.

"Thank you," I said so only she could hear. "More than you can ever know."

At some point through all that, the weight I had been carrying around with me since the very first dream had lifted. If only for those few minutes, it was paradise.

We took a quick bow before stepping back to recognize the band. All of us took a final bow together. Next, we made a beeline for the bar where I insisted on buying the musicians a drink.

"That was fun!" the drummer, Misha, said. She was younger than I had expected her to be. "My band has that in our repertoire, but we keep losing our lead singer."

"Have you guys been together a while?" I asked, as the next act was warming up.

"Yes, we have," Misha said. "I know Cam from law school. I'm the reason she knows that song." She smiled brightly and looked over at Cam, who was talking animatedly to the bass player.

"Really?" I said, interested.

"Yes," she nodded. "My parents are big Meatloaf fans and our band is called The Dashboard Light."

I laughed. "Great name."

"Thanks,"

"Drink?" I asked.

"Yes, please!"

After a few drinks, and as The Dashboard Light was trying to convince Cam to join their band, I made my way back to our table. Flopping down across from Zemila, I asked her, "Where is everyone?"

Her eyes were closed, and she took in a deep breath before opening them. She stared at me for a moment, bright brown eyes locking onto my green ones. My breath caught. Then she cleared her throat and answered me.

"Tyler had to take a business call. Nemo is playing Jenner's wingman." She nodded in a direction over my shoulder.

I followed her eyes and saw the pair of them talking to a couple of guys, one of whom was in the process of playfully shoving Jenner when I looked over.

"And you know where Cam is," Zemila finished sourly.

"Sorry?" I asked, turning away from Jenner, who was now whispering in the ear of the man who had shoved him.

"Nothing, Lochlan." She said it the way people say someone's name when they're upset. Attached to the end of a sentence, a name changes its meaning, and Zemila's meaning was plain.

"Forgive me," I said, squinting at her through my thick black frames. "Have I done something to upset you?"

Her fingertips drummed hard on the top of the table. My eyes moved from her quick fingers up to her stony expression as she searched the crowd.

"Why would you think you could upset me?" she said.

I heard a rattling sound. My eyes flicked down quickly to see the glass salt shaker vibrating against the table, hitting the pepper shaker with its jerky movement.

"Sorry?" I asked again, my gaze back to her. "What exactly does that mean?"

As if answering my question, both the salt and pepper shakers flew across the table and smashed into the wall.

"Damnit," she swore, looking angrily at the mix of broken glass, salt and pepper now littering the table.

"Gods, Zemila. How did you do that?" I asked, staring at the pepper shaker, trying to figure out how she had moved it. "You're an Earth Driver."

"What's it to you?" she spat.

"Okay, what is your problem?"

She looked at me sharply, bright brown eyes turned cold. The glass and salt scattered across the table shook.

The glass, I thought. Her powers were growing.

"I don't have a problem," she lied, and for the briefest of moments her eyes moved to the bar and back to me.

I followed her gaze again.

"Cam?" I asked, totally baffled. "Are you jealous?"

"Excuse me?" she said. "Jealous of what? I'm in a relationship, I'm happy. I'm going to find Tyler."

She stood and stormed off without another word.

The salt and glass slowed their eerie dance and returned to their natural state of stillness. I stared at it, perplexed. Not only at Zemila's strange outburst, but also at how she could control glass.

I scanned the crowd to see if I could find anyone.

Maybe I should go after her, I thought. I was worried her growth in power could somehow be connected to me. I wondered how long it had been going on.

I stood up and weaved my way through the crowd to the front door. Taking the stairs two at a time, I tried to catch up to her.

My eyes did a quick scan of the group of people standing just outside the door. Walking away from them, and looking up and down the street, I tapped my watched with the intention of calling her.

"Call Zemila," I said as I walked further away from the noisy street. I started to turn down a side street, but quickly changed directions when I saw two people pressed up against the side of the building.

"Whoa," I said, turning away. A woman with pink hair had pinned her partner in a shadowy alcove. "Sorry."

Zemila didn't pick up.

I made my way back past the crowd, through the front door and over to our booth. Cam was still chatting with Misha, Nemo was hovering awkwardly behind them, and Jenner was laughing at him. I smiled a little but was plagued with worry about Zemila.

I flopped down in the booth. Someone had come by and cleaned the glass off the table. Salt and pepper were still stuck in the grooves of the dark wood.

Someone sat down across from me. Tyler.

"Have you seen Zemila?" I asked. "She was looking for you."

He ignored me. He was staring at something across the room. Someone across the room. A woman with pink hair.

She smiled seductively at him and winked.

"That was you?" I said. He stood and grabbed his coat, eyes on his phone.

"Tyler!" I shouted over an average rendition of "Lies of Love," a recent and widely overplayed pop hit. "Tyler!" I repeated. I stood and grabbed his shoulder, turning him to face me.

"Get off me," he spun around, shaking off my hand.

"What the hell was that?" I said, gesturing towards the pink-haired woman. "With that girl?"

"Oh, Mary?" he said with a smug expression. "Why do you care?"

"I care about Zemila," I told him. "And I think she'd care about you and Mary outside in the alleyway."

His expression went stony and he stepped towards me.

"Yeah, you do care about Zemila, don't you?" I stepped back, and he closed the distance. "I see how you look at her," he said, shoving me in the chest.

I wasn't prepared for it and stumbled. He advanced on me.

"But you're nothing to her," he went on. "You're like a pet puppy. You're there when she needs a pick-me-up, but she comes to me when she needs a man."

He shoved me again. This time I was ready. This time I didn't move. My blood boiled, and I felt the tingle of fury crackling between my fingertips. I made fists with my hands to try and stop the Magic that pooled at my core and sparked at my fingertips. Then I spoke in a voice of forced calm.

"She's my friend." I breathed slowly. "You shouldn't—"

"I shouldn't what?" he hissed, cutting me off. "Mary was just congratulating me on my new promotion. Seems the head office likes what I do and wants me to work there."

"Your head office is in California," I said, remembering a snippet of conversation.

"How the hell do you know where I'm moving to?" he asked, forgetting that he had told me, told everyone. His company was all Tyler had talked about when we were moving Zemila in.

"You're moving? Does Zemila know?"

"Hey, guys," Nemo appeared beside us with a nervous expression. "What's going on?"

"What's going on is your little buddy here has the hots for my girlfriend and has decided to keep tabs on me."

"What? Lochlan, what's he—" but before Nemo could finish the question, Tyler leaned close to me and whispered.

"It doesn't matter who else I fuck while I'm with her. She'll never choose you."

Before I decided to move, I pushed Tyler away from me and swung. Fist connected with flesh as a crackle of power radiated off my body.

Somehow, in some corner of my brain, I must have been thinking. Had I not been, I would have killed him.

"Lochlan!" I heard several voices cry.

I felt something hard at my back and looked down to see two hands pressed into my rising and falling chest.

I was breathing hard.

Trying to stay calm.

Nemo had pushed me away from Tyler and into a nearby wall.

"What the hell is wrong with you?" Zemila screamed as she helped Tyler to his feet. I hadn't even noticed he'd fallen. "I tell you I'm happy and you punch my boyfriend in the face? God!"

"I…" I tried to explain but something was happening. I tried to calm down, but rage kept building. "Zemila, I…"

"You what?" she said angrily, half holding Tyler up. "What could have possibly happened to make this okay?"

"I… I…"

My heart was racing, and my breath came short and ragged. A crazed bloodlust came over me and every time I blinked the scene before me changed.

Blood everywhere and three men dead by my hands.

Broken glass and Tiffany dying the same way.

Long dark hair attached to skin attach to bone lying next to—

I squeezed my eyes shut, pressing my palms hard into them, trying to scrub the awful images away and trying not to scream. It didn't work. Another image replaced them. One I had seen before.

It was an image of me, looking into a mirror. Two green eyes stared back at me. I blinked and one of the eyes turned to stone.

I raised a hand to remove my glasses. A hand of stone pulled them roughly off my face and crushed them into powder.

"No," I said, pushing away from Nemo. I was back in the bar. Back to what was real.

"No!" I shouted, before sprinting out of the bar and into the night.

I ran, and kept running, not knowing where and not caring. I ran until the pain in my legs forced my brain to focus on the ache instead of on the images of blood, death and destruction.

And then I ran some more.

CHAPTER TWENTY-THREE

Rays of sun woke me. For a moment, I couldn't remember where I was or how I'd gotten there. I looked up at the many branches of the large oak tree I sometimes sat beneath when I wanted to escape reality. It was in a park some fifteen minutes away from my house. It reminded me of home, and of my brothers.

At least I ran in the right direction, I thought as I stood up.

My whole body ached. Every step seemed to be painful and I took a few moments to stretch. When I felt like I could move in a semi-normal fashion, I looked down at my watch. 6:25 a.m.

At my slow and stiff pace, the trip home took an extra ten minutes. By the time I got there, Mrs. Abernathy was leaving for her morning walk.

"Lochlan, dear," she said, a look of horror on her face. "What in the world happened to you?"

"Oh," I said, looking down at my sweat and dirt-stained clothes. "I ran home. Well, a little further than home, and slept under a tree." I was too tired to lie. And in this instance, I didn't see the point.

"Why on earth did you do that?" she asked.

"You know what, Mrs. Abernathy? I'm not quite sure."

"Well, I'm happy I caught you," she said. "I wanted to thank you for the soup you gave me. I felt so much better after eating it. It was just like magic."

"You're very welcome," I said.

It was an old recipe but not a family one like I had said after I'd given it to her the first time.

Though I haven't aged past twenty-three, my body is completely human. Over the years, I have learned how to beat the common cold with no more than chicken, vegetables and a few spices. No Magic required.

"You could sell that recipe and be a wealthy man," she said, not knowing I already was.

"I'll think about it and get back to you," I chuckled.

"Tell me," she said. "How is that nice young girl you've been seeing? Those pictures were beautiful. Strange angles but nice pictures."

"She's just a friend," I said.

"It didn't look like that to me."

"She's headed off to Paris with her boyfriend today. I'm a little late to the game."

"If you say so," Mrs. Abernathy said as she started to make her way down her front path. "You are obviously in love with the girl. Your face lights up whenever you talk about her. But what do I know? I'm just an old lady." She smiled at me, then pushed open her front gate and started down the block.

"Real love goes both ways," I said softly, before turning to go inside.

I managed to shower before falling into bed for a couple hours. When I woke up again, it was almost nine. After my usual oatmeal and coffee, I packed my gym bag and headed to the pool.

Since it was Saturday morning and almost 9:30 when I arrived, the community center was packed. I weaved my way through the many screaming children and cursing parents, heading for the change rooms. There would only be one lane open for swimming today, but the real reason I had come was the hot tub.

To my surprise, the lane for lengths was empty but for a lost pair of water wings and a few pool noodles. I blissfully welcomed the panic and release when I dove into the water. After swimming long enough to get beaned in the head by two flutter boards, and nearly taking out a nine-year-old on one of my turns, I decided to call it quits.

"Tim," I said to the man sitting in the hot tub. My aching muscles welcomed the heat of the bubbling water. "How are you?"

"Oh hello, Lochlan," he said in his deep baritone. "I don't normally see you here on a Saturday. I always thought it was because you didn't like people."

"Well," I said, looking over at the crowded pool. My vacated lane had been taken by a group of girls playing the roughest game of water polo I'd ever seen. "I had some stuff to get off my mind. The water helps."

Tim nodded slowly. "We all have our sanctuaries."

"And I see Usman is allowing you to keep yours?" I asked.

"At a steep price," he said, a look of annoyance on his face.

"Really? What's that?"

"Volunteering." He shuddered.

"Now who's the one who doesn't like people?" I laughed.

"Oh, I don't mind people," he said, shifting so the jet of water behind him hit a different spot on his back. "Especially young people. They are so optimistic; they see the world as a beautiful place. Not you, though," he said, looking at me sideways. "You've seen darkness. You've seen more than your years show."

I looked at him, not responding. Not knowing how to respond. He was right.

"Anyway," he continued. "People I like. It's politicians I can't stand."

"He's making you volunteer with a political group?" I asked, my stunned expression making way for a rueful grin.

"In a way," he said. "He's got his panties in a knot about this new immigration thing the Right Waters party is going on about. You heard about it?"

"Yes," I said. Jenner kept me well-informed.

"I don't think anything will come of it, but he's sure we're headed for war." Tim sighed. "Maybe I shouldn't be so hard on him. We're both immigrants and have faced our fair share of xenophobia and homophobia. I guess I'd rather not think about it, but Usman . . ." he trailed off.

"He's a fighter," I supplied.

"I guess it takes one to know one," he said, tipping an imaginary hat to me in agreement.

φ

I got home just before noon and found Nemo sitting on my front porch.

"Hey," I said, making him jump. "Sorry to scare you."

"Just now? Or last night when you ran off after decking Tyler?" he said.

"Ummm."

"I called," he explained. "Before I came over, I mean. But with everything that's going on, I was worried. After I dropped Zemila and Tyler off at the airport, I came here."

"I left my phone here," I said, looking down at my wrist where my watch usually was. "I went for a swim."

Nemo nodded.

"I brought lunch," he said, holding up a brown paper bag. "Let's talk inside."

I walked up the few steps to my front door. After I scanned my palm and punched in the door code, he followed me in.

"Couches or table?" he asked me.

"Up to you. I'll get us some water."

"Okay," he said flopping down in my living room and pulling a small coffee table between the two couches.

Minutes later, I was setting two water glasses down and sitting across from Nemo. He handed me a sandwich.

"Thanks," I said, reaching for it. He pulled it back before my fingers touched the wax paper it was wrapped in.

"It comes with a price," he told me.

"What doesn't?" I asked. And though I thought I already knew the answer, I said, "What's your price?"

"An explanation."

"Did you think I wouldn't give you one if you just asked?"

"Let me check my records . . ." He dropped the sandwich on the table in front of me and opened an imaginary filing cabinet.

I picked up the sandwich.

"Would you look at that!" he said, reading a pretend file. "It says here the last time you ran off without a word, you fell of the face of the earth for five years."

"Never going to live that down, am I?"

"It's been like three weeks," he said. "I get to hold this over you for at least a year."

"Fair enough," I said.

"Start talking," he told me. So I did.

It didn't take long.

"And when I saw the girl inside, she was winking at him," I said between bites of the pastrami sandwich Nemo had brought. "I asked him about her, and he basically told me he was going to mess around with whoever he wanted."

"Douchebag," he said.

"Right," I agreed. "Then he said he was moving away, and I asked if Mila knew."

"She doesn't," Nemo said. "Not as far as I know."

"He started shoving me and . . ." I took a large bite of my sandwich.

"Okay," Nemo said, filling in the rest for himself. "Well, I don't think I would have done any different. Tyler has a black eye by the way."

"Whoops," I said.

"But throwing a punch isn't really in your wheelhouse."

I nodded.

It used to be. But he didn't know that.

"I think it was because of Zemila and whoever has made me see these visions," I said, deciding to be honest and hoping he could help. "It's like she's a trigger for my darker side."

"Darker side?" he asked.

"My Magic isn't like your gifts," I explained. "You own your power; you don't have to ask for it. I do."

"You have to ask for Magic?"

"Yes," I said. "I have to ask Magic, Magic with a capital M. It's kind of alive. It's hard to explain."

"Is it like the Force?" Nemo asked.

"Wow. No wonder you and Jenner get along so well."

Nemo smiled. "Jenner's a good guy."

"Yes, he is," I agreed before continuing to explain the complexities of Magic. "Casters gravitate to one side of Magic or the other. Dark or Light."

"What's the difference?" Nemo asked.

"Dark Magic is more powerful, but it comes at a greater cost."

"Like Blood Magic."

"How do you know about Blood Magic?" I asked surprised.

"Since you told me who you really are, I've been doing some research. This whole 'Magic is alive' thing connects a few dots for me."

"A spell powered by blood is one of the strongest kinds of Magic," I explained. "The cost is a life. The life of the Caster, or the life of another."

"I'm guessing there isn't a lot of self-sacrifice when it comes to Dark Magic," Nemo said.

"No," I answered. "There is not."

"Have you cast blood spells before?"

I paused.

"It is a black mark on my soul I can never be rid of," I said. "And my greatest fear is I will do it again."

"And that's what you think someone is trying to make you do. Somehow, through Zemila?"

"It's possible."

"But who?" Nemo said, standing. He balled up the paper sandwich wrapper before beginning to pace slowly back and forth across my living room floor.

"That's the sixty-four-million-dollar question, isn't it?" I said.

"It has to be one of the Old Gods," Nemo said. "One of them must need you for something. Cethlenn, or one of the other Gods who supported Balor? Or maybe something about your mother Ethinn?"

The depth of his research impressed me. Cethlenn was the one who foretold the death of Balor by his grandson Lugh. She was Balor's wife.

"It's possible," I said again, finishing my own sandwich and crumpling the wrapper as Nemo had done.

"How would you kill one of them?" Nemo asked. "If you had to. How would you kill a God?"

"The Tools of Lugh," I said immediately. "You could kill a God with the Tools of Lugh."

It had once been my mission to track down those tools. Lugh himself had hidden them and taken the secret of their locations to his grave.

"I've never heard of those," Nemo said.

"Three tools. Lugh of the Long Arm, Lugh of the Long Hand, Lugh Master of Skills, imbued them with his power," I said. I could hear my accent grow thick.

"What are they?" Nemo asked.

"If you know enough about Balor and Lugh to know who Cethlenn is, you would have heard of the Tools. The Long Arm," I said, and waited to see if Nemo could put the pieces together.

"The Spear," he said, realization lighting his face.

"The Long Hand," I offered next.

"The Sword," he said nodding. "Fragarach, The Answerer."

"And what has already been wielded by Lugh to kill a God?"

"The Stone," Nemo whispered.

"So, you have heard of them," I said, fingering the chain at my neck. "It's important you know these three objects are more than just weapons. Lugh hid them for good reason. Since he is dead, if someone possesses all three of his tools, they also gain his power."

"You've tried to find them." It was a statement. Perhaps he could see the answer in my eyes. "But you didn't."

"No, and thank all that is holy I did not. If I had, in the state I was in…" I shook my head.

"Could the Tools kill you?" he asked.

"No, there is only one way I can die," I told him. "Nemo, If I go over—"

"You won't," he said, staring at me.

"If I do," I said. "You have to drown me."

CHAPTER TWENTY-FOUR

Nemo came over Sunday and Monday night to go through the mail with me. On Tuesday night, Jenner and Cam joined us. It was only on Wednesday, the fourth night of continued company and the night Zemila was supposed to come back from Paris, that I realized their true intention. They wanted to make certain I was all right.

It was good, knowing I had friends who cared about me. It was good to have people I could speak openly with. This was a new experience. It was something I could get used to.

"Uh, guys," Nemo said from his cross-legged position on my living room floor. Jenner and Cam were each stretched out on my couches and I was sitting in a chair I'd brought in from the kitchen. "I think you should take a look at this."

He held up an image of Zemila standing outside the JACE building doing an interview with some local politician.

"It looks like a professional photo," said Jenner, taking the photo out of Nemo's hand.

"Not from that angle," Cam said. She was right. The angle was odd.

"Turn it over," Nemo told Jenner, and he did. My brows pulled together as I saw the spiky red writing.

"What?" Cam asked. Jenner laid the photo down on the coffee table.

"I love seeing you in my favorite color," she read aloud. "I love that you wear it for me. You wore red three times last week. I want you to wear it again tomorrow."

There was a beat of silence.

"Well that's creepy," Jenner said. There was a murmur of agreement. I stood abruptly and headed to my office.

"Locher?" Jenner called after me.

"Just a minute!" I yelled back.

I opened the bottom drawer of my desk and took a small manila envelope from it, then headed back to the living room. I pulled out a photo, flipped it over on the table, pushing aside fan mail as I went.

"Whoa," Cam said, seeing the sharp red writing on the back of the photo saying "she's mine." She placed the two pictures side by side. The words on the back of the photo of Zemila and me were identical in color and style to the back of the one Nemo had found.

"There must be more," Jenner said. "It can't just be these two."

"What was the envelope like?" Cam asked Nemo. He handed her a small manila envelope.

"Same as mine," I said, holding up a duplicate.

"Well that makes things easier," Jenner said as he started to sweep piles of white envelopes back into the bag.

On Monday, Adrienne had called and asked how things were going. She also told me there had been a third and fourth bag of threatening mail if I was interested in looking through them as well.

"I don't know how they were missed," she had said. "They were all together, but we do have other writers who are popular. They were mixed in with theirs."

It took only about five minutes to separate all the small manila envelopes and another thirty to look through them for the distinctive red writing.

These bags of mail weren't like the first two. Most were legitimate fan mail. There had been a very elaborate birthday card from a young girl named Hazetta who said she wanted to be just like Zemila when she grew up. I set it aside to give back to Adrienne. Zemila should see that one.

Eventually we had a row of eighteen photos, mine included, all having the same spiky red writing on the back. There were no dates on them, and they all appeared to have been hand-delivered because there was no postage either. Still, we placed them in what we thought was chronological order.

The first few were fairly harmless. I guessed that was why they weren't marked as threatening. "You looked beautiful today," or "I loved your show this week." Slowly, it escalated to things like, "I told you to wear my favorite color today," and "you will be mine."

The last one was nearly illegible. The back of the photo was covered with red writing in all directions. Only some words were distinguishable. "Soon… Together… Whore… Beauty… Love me… Slut."

On their own, the words made no sense, but the combined message was clear.

"What now?" Nemo asked. He had grown quiet as more and more envelopes and photos were found. "We have to go to the police, right?"

"I don't think we can," Jenner said.

"What do you mean you don't think we can?" Nemo asked, his voice rising. "Look at all this! Obviously, this insane guy is stalking her!"

"Yes, but she won't acknowledge it," I said.

"She hasn't seen this!"

"And even if she did," Jenner continued, "I think something would have to happen before the police got involved."

"Something would have to happen?" Nemo shouted. "What the hell does that mean? Like they wouldn't do anything unless she was attacked?!"

"I don't know," Jenner said. "The law doesn't always make sense."

Nemo stood up with an angry grunt.

"We can try and find him though, right?" I looked to Jenner. I was scared too, and thankful Zemila had been out of the country for a few days.

"Yeah," Jenner said as his eyes flashed between Nemo and me. He looked like he was doing some quick thinking. "Yes, yes we could."

He pulled out a small white rectangle from his pocket and placed it on the table. Then he looked at the wall to his right, the one we usually played video games on. Nemo was currently pacing back and forth in front of it.

"Cam, trade places with me. Nemo, sit," Jenner ordered before he traced a pattern into the top of the white rectangle. It lit up, projecting a screen onto the wall and a keyboard in front of Jenner's fingers.

"So," Jenner said as he tapped furiously on the holographic keyboard. "We know he is dropping off the letters by hand." The screen split in two, both showing the front of the JACE building. "And we know he was there on the day Zemila interviewed that guy who lost the run for mayor."

"Redford Justal," I said. The man in the picture Nemo had found.

"Yes," Jenner said, shooting me an impressed look.

"I guess you're rubbing off on me." I gave him a bleak smile.

"I guess so." Jenner did something and the screens split from two into four. "There," he said, as all four screens showed different angles of the day Zemila had interviewed Mr. Justal.

Jenner started to fast-forward through the interview.

"Now the angle of the photo." Jenner looked over at it and then back at the four camera angles projected onto my wall. "Means he would have been standing . . ." He clicked a few times. "Right . . . here."

When all four screens showed a small grouping of people staring in the same direction, Jenner returned the speed to normal before freezing it.

"This is a frame from the JACE front-door camera. Unfortunately, the resolution isn't great, but I think we have enough to do a basic facial recognition."

"You should do this for a living," Nemo said, amazed, as Jenner's hands flew across the blue holographic keys.

"Thanks," Jenner said. "Instead, I'm stuck inside all day with this fool." He pointed his thumb in my direction.

"Sorry, friend," I said. "Do you want some help with this part?"

"Already done, amigo," he said.

Nine faces popped up on the screen. They all looked like photos off driver's licenses.

"These are the people standing there," he said, pointing to the small cluster of people, all looking in the same direction. "Because of what was written on the second-last one, I think it's safe to assume it's a man sending these."

"Yes," I said, mentally cringing at the memory of those crude words. Nemo's face turned stony.

"So, we can rule out these." Three of the nine faces were female and disappeared. "This guy is too old, this kid is too young," he muttered and two more disappeared. "Okay, there we go."

We all looked at the four men staring back at us from the screen.

"What now?" Nemo said.

"Now," Jenner turned to us. "We all are going to be bored stupid watching surveillance feeds. The facial recognition can do a lot, but if someone is wearing a hat, glasses, is partially turned away, has different facial hair than the image given to the recognition software, it can mess with results. We'll just have to watch it."

"That could take weeks!" Nemo said.

"Months," Jenner corrected. "But I think if we got a little help from our friendly neighborhood wizard—"

"I'm not a wizard," I said, studying the pictures on the wall.

"— then we might be able to do it a little faster."

"Yes," Nemo said, turning to me. "Remember the time you cast that memory spell and helped me remember that twenty-page paper I lost?"

"You can do that?" Cam said.

"Could you do that again? But different, to help?" he asked.

"Can you control time?" Cam asked.

"No," I said, which wasn't entirely true. "But I don't think we need Magical assistance."

I walked towards the screen and pointed at the man on the far left.

"What?" asked Nemo. He turned to see who I was pointing at.

"It's him," I said, putting the pieces together in my mind.

"How the hell do you know that?" Jenner asked, surprised.

"I know him," I said.

He looked healthier in this photo. His cheeks were fuller than they had been on any occasion I'd seen him. His complexion was rosy, his eyes were a sharp blue and he didn't look tired at all.

"Greg Simmons," Jenner said as he pulled up the man's information. "I'm going to ask again: how the hell do you know it's him?"

"He rides the same bus as me and . . . and . . ." My knees almost gave out and I backed up to sink down onto the couch.

"Lochlan, are you all right?"

I was unaware of who spoke. It didn't matter.

"No," I whispered. "Impossible."

I thought again of the last time I had seen him. I remembered the lurch of the bus, the surprise of the driver, the dizzy spell preceding his appearance.

"He wore sunglasses to hide his eyes." I wasn't certain I was speaking out loud or if anyone could understand my meaning. "The gloves were to cover his hand, and he . . . the way he walked."

I thought again of my head spinning, but it wasn't a spinning, it was more of a pressure. It was more of a—

"How could I have been so stupid?" I exclaimed, jumping off the couch.

"Lochlan, what are you talking about?" Cam asked.

"Yeah, fill us in, would you?" Nemo demanded.

"I didn't put it together. Not until just now. This guy, Simmons, I first met him the morning after Melanie Connor was found. Then I kept seeing him. He called me at work once," I said, looking at Jenner. "And the last time I saw him, I had this feeling."

"What kind of feeling?" Jenner asked.

"Power," I said. "I didn't recognize it then. It hit me so hard I just felt tired. I didn't know it was possible. He's supposed to be dead."

"You didn't think what was possible? Who's supposed to be dead?" Jenner asked.

"Balor," I said. "Balor is alive."

"No," Nemo said after a second of silence that seemed to last on for minutes. "He can't be. No, he can't be. You said Lugh killed him."

"He must be. He is. I'm certain," I said, pacing in the small space not taken up by furniture and scattered letters. "That's what I felt."

"Greg Simmons is Balor?" Jenner asked.

"No," I said. "He's a follower. Balor turned him."

"What does this mean?" Camile asked.

I thought back to the stone-grey undertone of his skin.

"He is Famorian now," I said.

"Zemila should be calling me any minute to come get her from the airport," Nemo said, panic running through his words. "She told me she would let me know when she landed. I think we need to tell her everything."

"Yes," I agreed. "Is Tyler with her?" I didn't think he would be of much help if Simmons tried anything but the thought of her not being alone calmed me.

"No," Nemo said, and my heart skipped a beat.

"Why the hell not?" Jenner nearly shouted.

"His business trip was extended and Zemila found out he'd accepted an offer from his California office," Nemo said, nodding at me. "She didn't want to stay with him. I think she ended things."

"I'd rather she not be alone," I said.

"Me too," he agreed. "We could just go over now?"

"I'll drive," Cam said.

"I'm coming too," Jenner said.

"Jenny, the car only seats five. We're just picking her up from the airport," Cam protested.

"I'm not going to be the only one left behind!"

"Don't be ridiculous. Lochlan isn't coming either," she said.

"Yes, he is," Nemo corrected.

"I don't need to come," I said, though I wanted to.

"You're coming," Nemo demanded.

"So am I," Jenner said.

Just as Cam opened her mouth to continue arguing with her brother, Nemo's phone rang and we all went silent.

He looked at his watch to pick up the call.

"That's weird," he said. "She usually video calls. Hey, Mila, have you landed?"

For a moment, no one answered.

"Is the third son of Ethinn listening?" hissed a raspy voice.

CHAPTER TWENTY-FIVE

Panic gripped my body. I couldn't move. I couldn't speak.

"Who is this? Where is Zemila?" Nemo's words were sharp.

I already knew who it was.

"Because if the third son of Ethinn is listening," the voice continued, ignoring Nemo's questions. "I have a message for him."

My eyes flicked to Jenner, then to Nemo's watch and back. Jenner nodded once and traced the call.

"Greg," I said.

"There he is," he hissed.

"Greg, where is Zemila?"

"Oh, right here, right here," he said quickly.

There was a thud and a cry of pain. Cam gasped, Nemo sucked in his breath, and everything in the room started to shake.

"She can't talk right now," Simmons continued. "She's a little . . . tied up."

Two of the beer bottles were shaken off the coffee table and crashed to the floor. I looked at Nemo. He needed to calm down.

"You won't hurt her again, Greg," I said as evenly as I could.

"Won't I?" he hissed.

"No, you won't. I've seen your letters. You love her."

There was a deep gravelly sound that I barely recognized as laughter.

"Oh, there you and I share something in common, Ethinnson. Our love goes unrequited. But that is beside the point."

I stepped over to Nemo and laid my hand on his shoulder, casting a minor spell of tranquility. In a moment, everything in the room stilled. He took a deep breath and nodded to me.

"What is the point, Greg?" I asked. Jenner gave me the thumbs up to tell me he had Simmons' location.

"My Master wants you," Simmons said. "He will take you as you are or turn you to his cause. Turn you, like he turned me."

We all knew what that meant. If I went voluntarily, Zemila would be fine. If not, she would be murdered in the hopes I would kill her killer.

"Your Master wishes you to take her life," I said. "Then for me to take yours."

"But I don't think it will come to that, do you?" he asked. "Better not chance it. Your grandfather has waited a long time for you. Tick-tock, tick-tock."

And the line went dead.

For a moment, no one moved. No one spoke. Finally, Cam broke the silence.

"Jenner, you have the address?" He nodded at her. "Okay," she continued. "Obviously he wanted us to have it, but we have to go anyway. What choice do we have?"

"You're not going," Nemo told her. "It's too dangerous."

"It's me he wants," I said, stopping Cam's protest. "I'm going alone."

Perhaps I should have expected the backlash. Perhaps I should have been prepared, but the explosion of protest caught me off guard.

Nemo was insisting he and I would go together, and Cam and Jenner would stay behind. Jenner was saying he was the only reason we had a location, and he was able to make his own decisions. Cam started to demand she be brought along, but was the first to stop speaking.

"What are you doing?" Nemo asked her as she walked towards the door and then stopped, waiting with her arms folded.

"Unless you're flying there, you need a car. I'm the only one with a car," she said simply. "The sooner you stop arguing, the sooner we can leave. I'm driving."

"I can get there on my own," I said. It would take more energy than I could spare, but if it would keep all of them safe, it was worth the risk.

"You'd need the address," Jenner said.

"And she's my sister so don't even think about leaving me behind," Nemo added.

"Jenner," I held out my hand. I had seen him write down the address and close the screen before anyone could see it. Sneaky bastard. "Give it to me."

"You're not going without me," Nemo said again.

"I'm going alone and that's final!" I said through my teeth, trying and failing to remain composed.

"Why!" Cam shouted. "Why? Because we aren't thousands of years old? Because we don't have your power? Because we aren't strong enough? We've helped you! You couldn't have done all this by yourself. Is it because we're Human?"

"Speak for yourself," Nemo said. Cam shot him a look.

"Why do you have to do this on your own?" she said softly. Stepping towards me, she reached up and cupped my face in her hands. "You are not alone."

But I was.

I had been since Lugh died.

That was the punishment for my actions, for my vengeance. I was alone because I wasn't safe. There was darkness in me that tainted everything I touched.

"You are not alone," Cam said again, bringing me back to the present.

I looked down at her. She wasn't tainted. She was good and kind and she was my friend. I looked to Jenner, then Nemo. Both faces held expressions of steely determination.

Slowly, I took in a deep breath and nodded. I turned to look at Jenner, silently pleading for him to keep himself safe and stay behind.

"Not a chance, amigo," he said, handing over the address. "Besides, if I don't come, how are you going to get green lights all the way?"

The sun was ducking behind the horizon as we left. My hand found the chain at my neck. The small pendant at the end of it sat heavier than usual on my chest. Nemo was behind the driver's seat, nervously levitating a few loose coins. The soft clinking the coins made in the air above his hands accompanied Jenner's directions. Jenner had been right. We needed him.

What would have normally taken us forty minutes was halved. Not only did we have all green lights, but he also diverted traffic out of our way and, when he couldn't, diverted us away from the traffic.

"No way I could get you two to stay in the car?" I said from the passenger seat, looking at the decrepit warehouse Jenner had directed us to. Light spilled out of a carport at the end of a long laneway.

A clear invitation from Simmons.

"Not in your lifetime," Cam said.

"Which is like, forever, right?" Jenner said, putting his tablet in the back pocket of the seat in front of him. "So... no. What's the plan?"

"Go in and get the lay of the land," I said.

Nemo looked at me, worried. "What if—"

"If Balor is there?" I asked, cutting him off. "If Balor is there, I bargain for your lives, you take Zemila, and you leave."

"The plan can't be to leave you there," Jenner said, indignant.

"It's not," I said, pulling my chain out from under my shirt. The small stone hanging on it was entwined in gold wiring. I handed it to Nemo.

"What's this?" he said.

"Balor can never have this," I told him. "If he's there, you have to take it to my brother Llowellyn. I don't know where he is. Jenner can help you find him."

"But what is it?" Jenner said, repeating Nemo's question.

"Don't take it out of the gold wire. That conceals its power. Balor might be able to sense it if you do."

"What's so special about a bit of rock?" Cam asked, parking the car outside the circle of light flooding from the open door.

"This stone—" I said, putting extra emphasis on the second word as I looked at Nemo. "—is a fragment. There are three pieces. Dyson has one of them and my brother has the other. From there, you're on your own. That's all I know."

I saw his eyes light up and look at the necklace with a new understanding.

"But you said it would—"

"I know," I said, nodding. "But when all three Tools of Lugh are brought together, the bearer carries his powers. I trust no one else with this. You will be strong enough to do what needs to be done if I turn."

"Guys," Cam said, pointing.

Instead of telling me I wouldn't turn, Nemo followed Cam's gaze.

The long silhouette of a man stretched out the open door. I felt a wave of power wash over me before an icy voice whispered in my ear.

"Tick-tock, tick-tock," he said in a sing-song voice.

Everyone in the car jumped.

"Lochlan," Cam said with a shuddering breath.

"I hear it too," I told her.

It sounded like his lips were a hair's breadth from my ear. Like he was only talking to me. We'd all heard it that way.

"How long do I have to watch the clock?" he continued to sing as his figure vanished from the doorway.

We got out of the car and started to walk slowly towards the open door.

I saw Nemo put my chain around his neck and tuck the stone under his knit long-sleeve. The chain itself held heavy protection spells. As long as he wore it, and Cam and Jenner were close by, no permanent harm could come to them.

"Tick-tock, tick-tock," Famorian Simmons continued. "Towards him all of us will flock."

"He sounds crazy," Jenner said. "Like clinically crazy."

"Turning someone can do that," I said as we approached the door. "It makes them more aggressive... more violent. The process shifts things around upstairs." I tapped my temple with a finger.

"Tick-tock, tick-tock," he said again. "My Master uses me to talk."

I held my hand out to stop the others before we entered the warehouse.

"I can only feel two people in there and the second one is definitely

Zemila." Nemo nodded at my words, his brows creased together in concentration. "I don't think Balor is here, but even so, you two stay close to Nemo."

Cam and Jenner both nodded in agreement.

"How can you be sure?" Nemo asked.

"Tick-tock, tick-tock," hissed Simmons. "My Master also seeks a rock."

I froze. The fact Balor was after the Tools wasn't exactly hard to believe, but it did complicate things. He wasn't here. If I survived tonight it would be a race to the finish. It would be a race either way. I just hoped I'd be on the right side.

"How can you be sure?" Nemo asked again.

"I remember what he felt like," I said. "His power, his chaos. I am certain."

That kind of darkness wasn't here tonight. There was only a fraction of it in the warehouse.

Slowly, I walked into the huge open space. It took a moment for my eyes to adjust to the bright light. Zemila was blindfolded and tied to a chair, at the other end of the warehouse. Old crates lined the walls and water-stained floor.

"Stick-rock, stick-rock," hissed the Famorian.

Now the voice came from all around us, booming off the walls.

"Come inside so the door can—"

There was a clattering bang behind us as the garage door slammed, locking us in. I resisted the urge to turn, grab my friends and bolt for an exit.

"Zemila," Nemo whispered and rushed forwards.

"Wait!" I cried, but it was too late.

He hadn't noticed the light haze hanging in the air just feet in front of us. As soon as his body came into contact with it, it threw him backwards. I was caught in the spell too, and before I knew it, we were both hanging upside-down in the air.

"Hide," I managed to say to Jenner and Cam. I pointed my chin at the crate by the door and they ran over and crouched behind it.

"Lochlan," said the Famorian, but his voice sounded normal this time. Or as normal as Greg Simmons would ever sound again. I saw him for the briefest of moments as I rotated in the air. He was walking towards us, dragging one leg limply behind him.

"You came, how nice. And you brought friends."

We drifted through the air towards him. Nemo's fingertips could just touch the ground. His hands scrabbled to find purchase but to no avail.

"Nice trick," I said, gesturing to my ankles, held up by nothing. "A Spark catcher."

"Good boy," he said, reaching forwards and patting me on the cheek with his stone hand. The pat was more of a slap and I felt hot liquid run up my face from my now bleeding lip. "Just a little something for those of us who shine a little brighter."

"I can't use my power," Nemo said to me, panic building in his voice. "Why can't I use my power?"

"Well that's kind of the point!" Simmons shouted.

Limping towards Nemo, Simmons raised a stone fist.

"I bet you had to use a crystal, didn't you," I taunted. Simmons' hand stopped mid-swing and he turned to me. "I bet Balor didn't brighten your Spark at all. I bet he just gave you a few trinkets and sent you on your way."

"You'd like to think that, wouldn't you?" he said, turning to me. That was my intention. "You'd like to think he didn't trust me, but he trusts me! He trusts!"

"Trusts you?" I laughed. "He gave you a green crystal and told you how to work a spell! It's powerful. I can't break it. The crystal would have to be destroyed to end the spell. But you . . . you are not powerful."

Simmons cried out as he raised his fist, his grey face contorted with rage. I braced for impact, hoping he wouldn't puncture a lung if he broke my ribs. But the hit never came.

I laughed.

"You aren't allowed to kill me," I said.

He knelt in front of me and I spat blood on his face.

Simmons closed his mismatched eyes and wiped at my blood with his human hand, smearing it, rather than removing it.

"No," he whispered. "I'm not. But I can kill him." He nodded at Nemo.

"Bring it, asshole," Nemo spat.

Simmons looked over at him with a smile.

"Nemo, shut up!" I said, thinking fast. I needed to keep Simmons' attention on me. "Would killing him make Balor trust you? You don't even know. You don't know your Master, not the real him. Not the true King of Demons."

"I know!" Simmons yelled, shaking slightly. His face was inches from mine. Spittle sprayed me as he shouted. "I know him!"

"You don't know what I do," I said. "You can't know what I know. That's why he wants me."

Simmons laughed. He stood up, threw his head back and laughed.

"You think that's why he wants you? You were only ever valuable to him because you were the easiest of the three brothers to corrupt. Already tainted and easiest turned."

My heart sank. I knew that to be true.

"Easier to find than your brother. Easier to manipulate." He pointed at Zemila. "You have value to him as a soldier. He knows you will serve him in the end."

"Don't listen to him, Lochlan," Nemo said.

"The prophecy," I whispered.

"The prophecy!" Simmons laughed again. "The prophecy was never that Balor would die at the hands of Lugh. Ethinn bore three sons!" He turned and walked towards Zemila. Nemo and I drifted helplessly behind him as he continued. "You think you know him as I do? You think you know him, and you really thought one death would stop him!"

We stopped moving abruptly.

"Zemila?" Nemo said softly.

She tried to speak but the duct tape over her mouth prevented her.

"Silence!" Simmons cried, raising his human hand and slapping Zemila across the face.

"Don't touch her!" Nemo said, struggling against his invisible bonds.

"That's not up to me," Simmons hissed, raising his hand again. This time he looked at me before he swung.

"Stop!" Nemo screamed.

"That's up to Lochlan." Simmons raised his hand again.

"If you touch her one more time—"

But I never learned what Nemo would do if Simmons did touch her one more time. At that moment there was a resounding bang, followed by an explosion of light. Nemo and I crashed to the ground.

Half the bulbs in the warehouse shattered, releasing a shower of sparks before they died.

"What?" Simmons said, turning in the semi-darkness. Cam and Jenner were standing over the remnants of a green crystal. "Oh, how cute. Your Humans are trying to help."

The spell he had trapped us with was broken.

Simmons raised his human hand. Cam and Jenner were lifted off their feet and, with a throwing motion, Simmons hurled them sideways into the nearest cluster of crates. My eyes widened in fear at the display of power.

He shouldn't be able to do that.

"Camile!" Nemo cried, scrambling to his feet and trying to run towards her.

A shelf carrying cardboard boxes soared through the air and exploded at our feet. It threw Nemo backwards, but I had seen it coming and had had time to shield myself. For a moment, my fear for his life immobilized me.

"Cam!" I heard him groan from behind me and I breathed again.

If he was talking, I thought, he couldn't be too badly injured. Lugh's Stone would keep him alive.

Stumbling to my feet, I threw aside the fragments of splintered picture frames and broken glass from the boxes. I saw Simmons reach into his pocket and pull out a red crystal. He tossed it in front of him and a wall of flame shot up between us before disappearing.

Nemo was limping forwards, one hand directed at the ground. I could see the shimmer of his gift. He used his telekinesis like a cane, pushing the ground away, keeping him standing. His leg was broken.

"Lochlan, what's he doing to them?" Nemo asked, pointing towards Simmons.

"Oh, Gods," I said as my gaze followed his hand.

Cam and Jenner were on the ground behind Zemila, shrouded in shadows and twitching. Every few moments one of them let out an agonizing cry of pain, then gasped for breath they couldn't find.

"What's he doing to them?" Nemo frantically asked again.

Simmons was standing over them, eyes closed and muttering.

"Beginning the ritual," I said. I could see the bone protruding from Nemo's lower leg. It was a wonder he was still conscious, let alone standing.

"What ritual?"

"Turning them into Famorians. Like him," I said.

"But they haven't killed anyone!" Nemo said, lurching forwards to help them.

In his haste to get to his sister, Cam, and Jenner he forgot about his leg. Without the use of his gift, it crumpled under his weight. He cried out. It was a cry of anger as much as pain.

"Cam! Zemila!"

"Lie still," I ordered, stepping quickly to him and moving my hands over his leg.

"Cam! Zemila! Cam!" he cried over and over again, struggling to get up.

"I don't have time for this," I said under my breath, and slapped Nemo in the face.

It was shock, not pain, which stopped his shouting and made him look at me, fury in his eyes.

"I need you to stop moving so I can heal your leg. Shouting will do nothing." He opened his mouth to protest but I cut him off. "There is a protection cast between us and them."

I reached for a hunk of splintered wood and threw it in the direction of the Famorian and his captives. It disintegrated upon meeting an invisible wall that rippled with red flame before becoming translucent again.

"I can take it down, but you need to be at full strength when I do, if we're going to have any chance of getting out of here."

"Okay," he whispered with a nod. He stopped moving.

"This is going to hurt," I said. He nodded for a second time. I picked up another piece of broken wood from the splintered crate and shoved it between his teeth. "Bite down," I said, and began to cast.

I chanted as I pressed the bone back under the skin. Nemo screamed, biting into the wood between his teeth. But he held still. That made it easier, and in a few moments, it was done.

My head spun a little, but I shook it off quickly.

"Are you okay?" he asked.

"I'm fine," I said, taking a moment to sit on the ground. "I haven't done this much casting in a long time. How does the leg feel?"

He stood on his own and tested it.

"Good," he said, looking down at me. "You could give Aga a run for her money."

I laughed with little humor. Our school friend Agatha Roberts could heal broken bones without the pain and without needing any time to recover.

"What's the plan?" Nemo asked, offering me his hand. I took it and he pulled me to my feet.

"And how can he turn them if they haven't—" he cut off when Cam let out a high-pitched scream.

"We don't have much time," I said. "He can force a change, but it is painful. I guess Balor gave him a little something extra after all."

"How do we stop him?" Nemo asked.

"I'll distract Simmons, get him to stop the ritual. You get Zemila, Cam and Jenner to safety," I said simply.

"He'll kill you," Nemo said.

"He might," I told him.

"Zemila will be harder to get away," he vocalized my thoughts. She was still tied and blindfolded.

"I agree this isn't ideal," I said, trying to find a way to get everyone out alive. "The alternative is—"

"No," Nemo said. "No self-sacrifice today. We can do this. You are not alone, Lochlan."

"All right," I agreed, knowing if it came down to it, I would do whatever it took to keep my friends safe.

"You see that circle around them?" I pointed to Cam and Jenner laying in the middle of a dark symbol drawn into the ground.

"Yes," Nemo said.

"When I take down the protection spell, break the circle. That will stop the ritual."

Nemo turned, and I knew he was looking at the large drawing of twisted knots under the now limp bodies of our friends.

"I'm ready," he said, bringing his hands together, drawing power to him.

"Go when I tell you to and not a moment sooner."

"You're sure breaking the circle is enough to stop the ritual?" he asked.

"I'm sure," I said as I drew a small blade out of thin air.

"How do you know?"

Before I answered, I sliced open a gash in my left palm.

"Because I wrote the spell he used to put it there."

CHAPTER TWENTY-SIX

Blood Magic. It was hard to work at the best of times. This was not the best of times.

"Ag mo caitheamh," I said, touching my right fingers to the fresh blood before beginning to paint glowing symbols in the air. They glowed the same color as the fiery ripples of protective wall that stood between Simmons and us.

"Nasgadh ag mo nwyfre ag mo gà tothaim," I continued to chant under my breath.

Simmons, still casting, noticed nothing. He thought his wall protected him. He thought he was safe.

He was wrong.

I had cast that protection spell without a crystal long before his ancestors had left Europe, and now a tangled knot of fire and blood hung in the air before me.

"Ready?" I asked Nemo.

"Just say the word."

"Gada," I said as I threw my spell at the invisible wall.

My symbol shot forwards, smashing the protection spell when it made contact. The symbol did not disintegrate as the wood had. Instead, it turned the invisible wall to glass and shattered it.

Nemo sprinted from my side towards a row of boxes. Simmons whipped around, his mismatched eyes finding my green ones.

"Neat trick," I said. "Too bad it's one of mine."

The symbol that had broken the protection spell still hung in the air. I reached out with an open hand, closed my fingers and pulled it towards me. At the same time, Simmons spotted Nemo sprinting around behind him, attempting to get to Cam and Jenner.

Simmons reached into a pocket, no doubt for another spell, but before he could, I threw a white-hot ball of energy towards him. It knocked him off his feet, and the symbol spread like a net, trapping Simmons on the ground.

Nemo threw the telekinetic energy he'd drawn to him onto the edge of the symbol trapping Cam and Jenner.

The concrete cracked. The ritual died.

Before I had time to react, Simmons broke through my containment spell and, faster than I thought was possible, he was at Zemila's throat with a knife.

"No!" I yelled to him, taking a few hurried steps forward.

Nemo, who was trying to revive Cam and Jenner, looked up. He started to stand, but Simmons pulled her chair closer to him, the silver blade pressed to Zemila's skin.

"Don't move," Simmons cried. "I'll kill her! I'll do it!"

"I don't think you want to do that," I told him, taking a slow step forward. "I don't think you want to hurt her."

"My Master commands it," he ground out, in a voice sounding like stone against stone.

"I read your letters," I said, cautiously taking another step towards them. Trying to keep my voice calm. "I know you loved her once. Do you not still?"

"Mine mine mine," he muttered. "Tick-tock, stick-rock... stick... mine... tick-rock."

He sounded like he was glitching. Whatever was left of his human self was warring against the Famorian taking over his mind.

He might have been a good man once, I thought. He might have just been a fan before Balor had corrupted him.

"You don't have to hurt her," I said.

The Famorian looked up at me, and for a moment, just a moment, the man Greg Simmons looked back. He lowered the blade and ran his human hand down the side of Zemila's cheek. His shoulders seemed to relax when his skin touched hers.

His hand brushed against the duct tape over her mouth and a look of surprise crossed his face, as if he hadn't realized it was there.

Slowly, he removed it.

There was a long silence. No one moved. No one breathed. Nemo held Cam's head in his lap, but his eyes were fixed on his sister. I stood meters away, waiting to see what would happen next.

"Lochlan?" Zemila whispered, as though testing her voice.

"It's all right, Mila," I said.

I stepped forward. Simmons roared. He put the blade back to her throat, this time breaking skin. A thin line of blood snaked down her skin.

"Whoa! whoa!" I shouted, holding up my hand. "Wait!"

"Mine mine," he cried out. "Mine mine stick-tock!"

"I'm sorry," I said, understanding.

It had angered him that she'd said my name.

"Yours," I reassured him.

Behind him, I saw Cam and Jenner slowly wake up. I had to keep Simmons focused on me.

"All right, she's yours. She won't say my name again," I said as much to Zemila as I did to him.

"My Master wishes her dead tick-tock," he said, tears falling from his blue eye. "Lugh the false God killed no Demon King stick-rock. Mine mine."

Fear ripped through me and I fought to keep it from turning into panic.

"A false prophecy and a false God carried a false death sentence to my Master. And he has returned. Returned for you," he finished in a whisper.

My heart pounded in my chest.

"And here I am," I said.

"After the first brother destroyed the Eye of Balor, you stood in your grandfather's place," Simmons growled. "You led his armies, you carried his legacy. Now he calls on you to stand by his side. His right hand. His spear. Stick-rock, tick-tock." He twitched violently on the last few words, cutting Zemila deeper.

She let out a small whimper.

He didn't notice.

Nemo, Cam and Jenner moved towards the door at the opposite end of the warehouse. Silently, I thanked Nemo for his strength and courage, for getting two to safety while his sister was in mortal danger.

"Blood Magic is dark. You have used it again this night. They all know. They know tick-tock you crave it."

I took a chance and stepped forward. He stepped back, pulling Zemila with him.

"He knows you crave her blood on your hands," he said.

"I don't," I told him.

"He knows you dream of her death."

"That's not true," I said, knowing it was.

"He knows you yearn to be the one who ends her light, who eats her Spark."

"No!" I fought for composure as the images that plagued my dreams flashed before my eyes.

Zemila dead by my hands, her blood splattered across the floor.

The Fomorian laughed.

"He has seen it in your mind—he has put it there, to guide you!"

"Guide me?" I murmured, forcing the images away. Willing my mental barriers to be stronger.

"Just as he guided you here," he said. I looked sharply into the mismatched eyes. "To her!" My gaze flicked from Simmons to Zemila. "To him."

Balor. It all came back to Balor.

The dreams. The visions. The bloodlust.

He had forced me to see those things. First, at school, trying to delude me into killing the woman I loved. I was stronger than the images he'd made me see. I left school. I left her. He lost his hold.

But he had found me again. He poisoned the mind of an innocent man. He forced that man to commit horrific acts, and then showed them to me. He isolated Zemila while pushing me back into her life.

Then he poisoned my mind again. He tried to delude me again. Tried to force me to kill, if not her, then her murderer.

But it would not work. I would not allow it to work. I would not be his puppet again.

"No," I said, looking up at the Famorian. "You have failed."

He smiled maliciously.

"But I have her now," he said, removing the blade from her throat.

He stroked Zemila's face with his stone fingertips. She flinched away from him. He growled and hit her. The chair rocked from side to side with the force of the blow, almost toppling her sideways.

"You have nothing," I said.

"I have your friends—" the words died in his throat as he turned to look at the spot where he had left his two captives, two captives that Nemo had taken to safety without his notice.

"You have nothing," I spat out the last word.

He would not win this day. I was sure of it.

With a roar of fury, he stomped his feet and waved his arms like a child. I saw a flash of silver narrowly miss Zemila.

"Mine!" he roared. Lifting the chair Zemila sat in, he smashed it to pieces. His human hand knotted in her hair and pulled. She screamed. Simmons dragged her against him and started walking backwards, away from me.

I advanced, Magic sparking across my skin, determination and fury pushing me forward. I would not be what the Old Gods destined. I only made it a few steps before Simmons put the knife back to her throat.

"One more step," he warned me.

I froze for a moment, weighing my options. If I could get a little closer, I could cast a protection spell around myself and extend it to her. She would be safe. I was sure of it. But I had to get a little closer.

I took one more step forward.

He slashed the dagger across her neck.

Time seemed to stretch as I reached forward, trying to stop it, trying to act faster, trying to undo what had already been done. Zemila's hands clutched at her throat, trying to stem the flow of blood pouring from her, trying not to die.

I was wrong . . . And I'd failed her.

There were spells that could bring back the truly dead, but I would never cast one.

For a moment before death, the body and soul hang in balance. After that moment they separate. If brought back together, if brought back to life, that person is brought back as something else.

Something grotesque.

But in that moment one spell may be cast. One spell may work.

In my long life, I had heard tell of this spell being used three times. Only one was successful.

The first time was an apprentice of my brother's. So wrought with pain after his wife's passing that he tried to work the spell after her body and soul had parted. His soul was ripped from his body as he tried to reunite hers.

The second time was a woman in the mid-twelfth century. Her partner had been beaten to within an inch of her life for the love they shared. She cast the spell and it worked, the two fled and were never heard from again.

The third time was by a man who had been spurned by the woman he was courting. In a blood rage, he killed her. The moment she died, he realized what he'd done. He attempted to undo it. He began to cast, but Dark Magic consumed him. It ate his soul and commanded his body. He took the lives of thousands before he was finally killed.

That's the choice I weighed in my mind as I watched Zemila fall. Would I be consumed by the Magic? Would it kill me? Or maybe, just maybe, would the spell work?

Only Zemila had that answer. I knew why two of the three spells had failed. But as I saw her limp form crashing to the ground at the feet of the Famorian, I knew I had to try.

Zemila's skull smacked the concrete as time returned to its normal pace. The ground beneath her was stained with the blood spurting out between her shaking fingers.

Simmons roared again. Again, he reached down, grabbed a fistful of Zemila's hair, and dragged her behind him. Then he moved towards the open door Nemo, Cam and Jenner had escaped through.

Quickly, I stepped forwards and dropped to one knee in the pool of blood left by Zemila's mortal wound. I slid the fingers of my still-bleeding left hand into the dark liquid and began to cast.

"Ag mo breatha, ag grà mas grà, nasgadh corp a anam, nasgadh breatha a breatha."

The words fell from my lips as if I had known them all my life, whereas, in truth, I had only heard them uttered once in a hushed tone at the end of a forbidden story.

My hand burned as the red blood turned black and snaked its way up my arm. The liquid twisted and turned, knotting itself as it scorched my skin and I chanted.

"Ag mo breatha, ag grà mas grà," I repeated over and over willing the spell to work.

The pain was agony as it traveled up my arm and spread across my chest. When it reached my heart it seemed to magnify, and in that moment, I knew it had worked.

Light flew down the marks that Magic had left on my arm and into the pool of blood in which I knelt. From there it seemed to come alive. The dark blood turned to molten gold as the spell moved through it. The Magic followed the blood trail leading to Zemila's body.

It encircled her, throwing the Famorian off, and lifting her into the air. Simmons shrieked with anger as he flew backwards from the force of the spell. Scrambling to his feet, he tried to reach her. The spell kept him back.

I watched, still chanting, fighting the desire to pass out from the pain, fighting the blackness slowly narrowing my field of vision.

The skin of Zemila's neck knit together. I gazed in wonder as her cuts and bruises disappeared and she was slowly lowered to the ground. She lay there for a moment, still bathed in bright gold light.

In a matter of seconds, she regained consciousness. Her hands moved from her healed throat to the blindfold still covering her eyes.

She removed it.

Slowly, she pushed herself up from the floor, gazing around the warehouse. Her eyes fell on Simmons.

Zemila was fierce and beautiful as the spell released her. It had done its work. The light surrounding her, connecting us, vanished, and I collapsed.

There would be a price for this Magic. I knew that. There was always a price for blood. But on this day, I would happily pay it.

I struggled to my hands and knees, trying to stay conscious. Trying to find the strength to finish Simmons. But I didn't have it. The spell had taken everything from me.

I looked up to see Simmons and Zemila staring at each other. Her hands were at her sides, fingers outstretched.

I staggered to my feet and swayed on the spot before dropping back down to one knee.

"But you're mine," I heard Simmons scream. "Mine!"

Unable to stay kneeling, I collapsed, fighting to keep my eyes open.

"You're made of stone," I heard Zemila say from far far away.

She clenched the fingers of her right hand into a fist. There was a blast of swirling dust. Simmons screamed in agony, clutching for the stone arm that was no longer there.

"You're mine," she said.

And I saw no more.

CHAPTER TWENTY-SEVEN

Mist clouded the horizon as a dark shadow fell over high stone walls. A boy followed the sound of chanting down a corridor. He moved quietly; he knew he shouldn't be there.

Light and sound came through the crack between floor and door. The rhythmic words called to him. He pushed open the door and the chanting grew louder. Vapor rose through the air, swirling but never touching the hooded men calling it to this world.

The chant faltered. The men looked up. The vapor went for the boy. He collapsed, clutching his eye, and the course of his life was set.

Two young boys ran ahead of a third who was far behind. They called to him, taunting him for his slowness. The third boy tripped in his haste and started to cry. The second boy stopped to aid him. The first turned as well.

All three had dark hair and green eyes.

"Let him cry," said the tallest of the three. "He needs to be strong, like me."

"It hurts him so much, Lugh," said the second boy, a mirror image of Lugh but for the kindness in his eyes. "It hurts me too."

"Stop crying," said Lugh, throwing his kind-faced brother off and grabbing hold of the smallest of the three. He pulled him to his feet, dusted him off, and said, "You will get faster. That is why I run ahead of you."

The smallest boy nodded and wiped his tear-stained face.

"We are stronger together," Lugh said, and kissed his brother's cheek. "You are not alone."

Still the smallest, but no longer a boy, he stood back to back with his brother. They were outnumbered. They were surrounded. The foul breath of the Famorian hoard misted the early morning air.

"Where is Llowellyn?" he asked.

"All right there, Little Lochlan?" Lugh said with a smile. "Llow will be along any moment now."

Several Famorians advanced and the two fought as though they shared one mind, protecting each other and slicing down any foes in their path. Suddenly they were joined by a third.

"Have you got it?" Lugh asked of the newcomer.

"I have," said Llowellyn. "Let's get you to him."

"Stronger together." Lochlan said it more like a prayer than anything else.

"Not alone," Lugh agreed, and they advanced.

The triplets stood at the bank of a small lake, so deep even at its edge it was black.

"Hard to believe it's been eight years," said the first born and tallest of the three. His wide chest and broad shoulders were covered in a dark cloak. His hand rested on the hilt of a sword that was seldom drawn.

Strength and leadership made Lugh a good King who was rarely questioned.

"Hard to believe," said the man to his right.

Perhaps an inch separated the height of the King from his brother, the second-born. Their build and dress were identical but for the presence of the blade. Llowellyn solved his problems in other ways. Compassion and reason were the weapons he wielded.

"I think that day was hardest on you, Llow," said the smallest of the three, standing on the King's left side. He was the third-born grandson of the Demon King they had slain eight years ago on this very ground. His brothers dwarfed his height and lean build. He wore no cloak, and though no weapons were visible, Lochlan kept himself well protected. His defiance often got him into interesting situations that his wit got him out of.

"Sometimes when I sleep," said Llowellyn, "I can still hear his scream, I can still feel his agony, his darkness." He looked at Lochlan. The worry was plain on his face.

"Fear not, brother," said Lochlan as he moved between the other two. He threw an arm around each of them before leading them away. "As long as I have the two of you, I am protected."

Lugh nodded and allowed himself to be guided away.

"Stronger together," Lugh said.

Llowllyn and Lochlan answered in unison. "Not alone."

φ

Light and sound seemed to crash into me.

"Llowellyn?" I cried. "Lugh?" Confusion slowed my mind as I looked around. Where were my brothers? Why was I alone?

A hand pressed on my shoulders and a blurred shape appeared over me. I reached for the blade concealed at my hip. It wasn't there. I checked for the blade at my left ankle. Nothing. My right ankle. Nothing. I wasn't wearing the garb I kept them in. Panic flared in me.

Where were my brothers? Why were they not here? I needed them. Pain and dizziness swelled in my mind. I rolled over and retched before the blackness took me again.

φ

"How is he?" I heard.

"Fine now," a second voice said. "I think."

"Has he stopped throwing up?" asked yet another voice.

"Yes," the second voice said.

"And his injuries?"

"Healing normally. Like a human, but . . ."

"What?"

"Look at this."

I felt a hand run up my arm and onto my chest.

"Dios mio," said the first voice and, again, there was nothing.

φ

Bright white light shone in the distance. My eyes were shut, and I squeezed them tight. It seemed like an eternity I stayed that way, the light growing brighter on the other side of my lids. Eventually, I relaxed and took in a deep breath of air.

When the smell of something comforting and familiar reached my nose, I opened my eyes.

Coffee, my brain registered.

I blinked in the bright light of morning. The sun streamed in through my living room window. Turning to the side, I saw a man slumped over and asleep on one side of the couch across from me. Though his arm was thrown up over his eyes to block the sunlight, I knew who he was.

Curled up beside him was a girl. She looked so small with her knees pulled up to her chin and a blanket wrapped tightly around her. Her short dark hair covered most of her face.

Nemo. Camile. My friends. My brothers may be gone, but I was not alone.

That meant it was Jenner making coffee, I realized.

I got up slowly, almost falling back down in the process and nearly hitting a bucket of black liquid. Or was it solid? I didn't waste time thinking about it.

As quietly as I could, I made my way down the short but familiar hallway to the kitchen. Standing over the stove, stirring what was no doubt a pot of oatmeal, was Jenner.

"I guess we won?" I said.

Jenner jumped, taking the pot with him. It clanged back down to the heating element as he turned, wide-eyed, to look at me.

"Madre de Dios, you're awake," he said, rushing forwards and throwing his arms around me. I stumbled back with the force of his hug, steadying us with a hand on the doorframe.

"I'll take that as a yes," I said with a chuckle. "But you'll have to fill me in on a few details."

Jenner released me. His eyes were brimming with tears. He sniffed and turned away quickly.

"Sit, sit," he said.

"Jenner?" I asked, watching him pour a cup of coffee and press it into my hands.

He paused in his movements. "You've been in and out of consciousness for a while now," he said. "We didn't want to take you to the hospital, but we didn't know what to do."

"How long?" I asked.

"Four days." He sniffed again. "It's been pretty rough for all of us."

"Where's—" I started to ask, but Jenner cut me off.

"Zemila's fine. She's physically fine anyway. She calls a couple times a day to check in on you. She'll be happy to know you're awake."

I nodded. I was disappointed she wasn't here, waiting for me to wake up like the others were.

I shook myself mentally. What did I expect? She was stalked, kidnapped and tortured by an ancient demon because of me. Her friend was killed, her life thrown into chaos. I should be happy she was alive. I was happy she was alive.

"Sit," Jenner said again, placing a bowl of oatmeal in front of my usual chair.

I did and was hit with a wave of hunger. The oatmeal and coffee were hot, but I scarfed them down with little regard for that detail. Jenner refilled my mug and bowl twice more before I slowed.

I looked up at him sheepishly.

"Sorry," I said, wiping my mouth.

"It's okay," he said. "All you've done for four days is puke black something and scream about I don't know what."

I looked up at him in confusion. He scooped oats into a fresh pot of water.

"Jenner," I asked, "what happened?"

280

He grated fresh nutmeg into the oatmeal before giving it a stir and sitting down with his own mug of coffee.

"Come on," I urged. An anxious knot had formed in my stomach. "What happened?"

"You'll have to ask Nemo about some of it," he said. "Maybe I should wake him up. I don't even remember it all." I realized he was talking more to himself than to me.

He looked at me. Something on my face must have conveyed what words could not. I just needed to know. Whatever it was he could tell me. That was good enough for now. I needed to know.

"Okay," he said, nodding. "I remember going to the warehouse and seeing Zemila. You and Nemo got caught in this invisible web thing and Cam and I hid." He looked at me and I gestured for him to continue. "We heard you say you couldn't break it and it was attached to a green crystal. So we snuck around looking for it while Simmons was distracted with you."

"You saved us all," I said. "We would have been finished if you hadn't destroyed that crystal."

Jenner smiled blandly and took a sip of his coffee.

"Then something happened. I couldn't move. There . . ." he stumbled over the words. "There was a lot of pain. Nemo said Simmons tried to make us like him." He looked up at me.

"Jenner, I'm so sorry," I said.

"It's over now and we all made it, and like you said, I basically saved the world," he said with a crooked smile. "Though I suppose you guys helped."

I chuckled weakly.

"Anyways, the next thing I remember was Nemo and Cam pulling me to my feet and leaving the warehouse. We hid by the door so we could see what was happening." He paused. "I just hid. Scared. Useless. I'm the one who should be sorry. I would never have forgiven myself if you died because I did nothing."

"You're a good friend," I told him.

"Doesn't feel like it," he said. Disgust colored his next words. "From where I was hiding like a child, we saw Zemila being dragged by Simmons. She looked like she had been knocked out or something."

They didn't know, I thought. They didn't know and Zemila hadn't told them. Mayhap, she didn't remember either, how close she came to death.

"Then this jet of light hit her, and she was lifted off the ground. Something happened and then she woke up. She looked so . . ." he trailed off, thinking of how to put into words what he wanted to say. "She killed him, Lochlan."

I shouldn't have been surprised, but I was. I didn't think she had it in her.

"She turned his limbs to powder and choked him to death with the cloud of dust," Jenner said, eyes wide, as if he was seeing it happen again. "She did it all without moving more than her hand. It was the most amazing and horrible thing I have ever seen. He was just a man once. I don't know if he deserved that."

We sat in silence for a moment.

"I don't think he did," I said, breaking the silence. "But I also think the man he was . . . that man was killed by the monster Balor turned him into. He didn't deserve any of it."

"When she was finished with him, she ran to you," Jenner continued. "We thought you were dead. Pale as anything, drenched in sweat, covered in this black liquid. Then you started convulsing.

"We brought you home; you shook the whole way. It went on like that for a couple hours. When it finally stopped, you were still for a while. Next you started talking, screaming. Eventually that stopped too.

"Then you started vomiting this blackness. Dios mio, we nearly took you to the hospital then. Cam was going crazy. I was too. Nemo was the voice of reason. He said it was the same liquid that was all around you after you did whatever you did. He said it was coming out of you now, and that was a good thing. It was helping you. I guess he was right.

"You got your color back a bit after that. It must have tired you out because you slept for three days, talking in your sleep. Talking about your brothers."

Silence filled the room again. Again, I was the one to break it.

"I should have never involved you in all this. I should have left when I had the chance. None of this would have happened." I breathed a shaky breath, trying to compose myself. "Mayhap, I should go now."

"Where?" he asked me harshly. "Where would you go?"

"I don't know," I said honestly. "I really don't know."

We stared at each other for a moment before a voice drifted in from down the hall.

"Lochlan?"

"He's in here," Jenner called to his sister.

"Nemo, get up," Cam said. I heard what sounded like a pillow making contact with someone who was very much asleep.

"Huh? What?" Nemo's sleepy voice asked.

"Lochlan is awake."

CHAPTER TWENTY-EIGHT

Life has a way of moving on. It's remarkable when you think about it. We learn, or we don't. Things change, or they stay the same. But no matter what, time passes, and life moves on.

The first change I noticed was in the spare bedroom. No, the person who was unpacking in my previously spare bedroom.

"I thought I would move in," Jenner said without a hint of embarrassment.

My house seemed crowded, but it was comforting. Cam was spending a lot of time here and since Nemo was around her every chance he got, he was here too.

Zemila sent a message saying she was happy I was doing better. Nemo told us when Tyler had returned from Paris, they'd officially split up. Zemila had found a nice bachelor apartment on the other side of the city. Currently Nemo was sleeping on her floor.

"It breathes on my face," Nemo said after a particularly bad night.

"It's a she," Cam replied.

"Whatever," Nemo said. "Dog breath waking me up in the middle of the night and hair everywhere. I need out."

My strength returned after a few days, but it took a week to work up the nerve to go see Zemila.

It took me an hour to get to her new place on the public transit. Whenever the bus lurched to a halt, I tensed, waiting for the Famorian that never came.

I knew the anxiousness would pass with time. A memory drifted back to me. "Ah yes," I'd said to Dyson during exam period at Erroin. "Time is a fickle mistress. A witch with a capital B if you're picking up what I'm putting down."

The smile faded from my face as the bus stopped suddenly. I winced. I was happy when I got off and started walking.

A few minutes later, I looked down at my watch to see that the address was correct before knocking on the front door.

Footsteps were accompanied by barking before the door sprang open.

"Oh," Zemila said, looking flustered. "Hi, I umm, wasn't expecting you."

"Hi," I said nervously. "I didn't know if you would agree to see me. Nemo said you were . . ." My eyes flicked down to the black dog growling at me. "Upset with me."

A muscle jumped in Zemila's jaw as she clenched her teeth. "Oriole, quiet," she snapped. The dog growled softly as silence stretched between us.

"Can we talk?" I asked.

"Is that not what we're doing now?" she said coldly.

All right, I thought. This wasn't going well.

"Right," I said, and cleared my throat. "How have you been?"

"Fine," she said, her hand moving over her throat.

The image of her throat being sliced open flooded my mind and I squeezed my eyes shut for a moment. She dropped her hand and shifted self-consciously.

"I'm fine," she repeated.

I nodded. We stood in silence.

I reached out a hand to her, but a loud bark made me jump. I rolled my eyes. "Gods," I said. "You want to do it this way, fine."

I dropped to one knee, took in a deep, calming breath, and locked eyes with the dog.

It only took a second. Oriole whimpered, dropped her nose, and ran up the red-brown carpeted stairs.

"What did you just do to my dog?" Zemila asked.

"Can I come in?" I asked, ignoring her question.

Zemila looked at me.

"You lied to me," she said. I nodded. "About everything."

I thought about contradicting her. I thought about telling her not everything was a lie, about how often I'd wanted to tell her the truth. I thought about explaining how I always tried to tell as much of the truth as possible. But I didn't.

I nodded again.

"If I let you in," she said. "You will answer all of my questions honestly." I hesitated, then nodded a third time. "A lie by omission is still a lie."

I sighed heavily, wondering if I would live to regret this. "I'll tell you whatever you want to know," I promised. "I won't hold anything back."

"Okay," she said. "Come in and close the door behind you."

She turned and followed her dog up the stairs.

A white banister bordered the stairwell. As I reached the top, I saw it opened into a large and sunny space with slanted ceilings on one side and floor-to-ceiling windows on the other.

"Wow," I said. "How did you find this place?"

The windows opened onto a small balcony. A sofa and two chairs were in a semi-circle around a coffee table at the window. A curtain hung from the ceiling to create a half-wall for a bedroom.

Zemila ignored my question as she crossed to the kitchen and switched the oven off. She must have been cooking. Turning, she faced me and placed her hands on the island that stood between us.

"What was the spell you cast?" she asked me.

"It wasn't a spell," I said looking at the dog. My attention moved from the white couches, over a chair with a blanket covered in dog hair, to her dark eyes. "She's protective of you because she knows I'm dangerous." I looked over at the black dog staring at me from her bed in the corner.

"We just understand each other now." My eyes met Oriole's and she immediately dropped her gaze.

"No, the spell. The one that saved my life," Zemila said. "I know I should have died. What happened?"

"Of all the questions." I shook my head, not looking at her. "You test my word of honesty right away. I don't think you want to know the whole truth of this answer."

"I do," she said. "I know I should have died, and then what happened to you after . . ." she trailed off. "Explain it to me," she demanded.

"All right," I said. "I don't know the original name for the spell, but I know it's old and dangerous."

"Why?" she asked, still standing, unmoving, both hands flat on the island's white top.

"Because, well…" I had to tread lightly here. But I couldn't lie, I wouldn't lie. Not anymore.

"When a caster works a spell, it's not the same as you using your gift,"

I told her. "Your gift is reliable. It's always there. If you practice, hone your skills, you always know what you are going to get.

"For most beings like me, we favor a certain type of Magic, Light or Dark. When we cast, we ask for the spell to work. We ask for the Magic. You command your power. I request mine. Do you follow?" I asked.

She nodded.

"For most beings like me, our request will be answered. But because of my gifts, I am different. I am not partial to Light or Dark Magic. Both come when I call, and then I choose."

"That doesn't sound so bad," she said.

"Dark Casting is an evil thing. Powerful, but evil," I told her. I was leaning against the white banister now.

"Why don't you just choose Light Magic every time?"

"I do," and in the interest of total honesty I added, "I do now."

"But you didn't used to." It was a statement, not a question.

"No," I confirmed. "There was a time where I chose Dark Magic."

"Why?" she said, leaning down onto her forearms.

"It's stronger. It feels... better, more powerful. But it changes you. It eats at your soul."

"What does this have to do with the spell?" she asked.

"The spell in question needed both kinds of Magic, and some Casters can't control it."

Zemila nodded. "When we found you, you had blood and black stuff all over you. That was part of it?"

"Yes," I said. "It's Blood Magic. That's why it's Dark. But..." I hesitated.

This was the part I knew she didn't want to hear.

"But what?" she asked impatiently.

I looked away from her.

"But it's also Love Magic. That's why you need the Light."

"Love Magic," she repeated and pressed herself away from the island. Standing back to lean against the counter, it seemed like she was trying to get as far away from me as she could.

"Most powerful thing in the world," I said, refusing to meet her eyes.

"Okay," her tone was flat.

If she didn't press any further, I swore to myself this would be my only omission. This would be my only lie. She didn't need to know that for the spell to work properly, she had to love me too.

"I want to know your story— the real one. The one you've already told Cam and Jenner and Nemo. I want to know it too."

I told her everything. About Balor and my brothers, about the Tools of Lugh and the powers they held. I told her about the blood rage taking me after my brother was murdered and that I had almost become Famorian myself.

I told her about my years of loneliness and the few who helped me through. Finally, I told her about how I came to be at Erroin, about the dreams I had there. I told her I was certain I had been thinking those horrible things, but it was Balor all along.

"That's the real reason you left?" she asked, making eye contact with me for the first time since I'd started to recount my life to her.

At some point in my telling, we'd drifted over to the couch. Even so, this felt like the first time she'd really looked at me since letting me into her apartment.

No, since before she was kidnapped.

Since the gala.

Yes. That was the last time she'd looked at me this way. Like she was really seeing me. Like she knew my soul.

A shiver ran down my spine as I looked back at her. I wanted to touch her, to feel the heat of her body against mine. I wanted to truly know her and for her to truly know me.

Instead, I kept speaking.

"Good timing, I guess, that Dyson needed some help," I said, feeling uncomfortable and looking away. "That's why we left together with David."

"Who is—" she stopped. "Never mind. I can wait for that story. What happened next?"

I told her I had stayed with Dyson for a while before moving here and getting a job. For a few years everything seemed normal, then I started to dream again. I confessed I thought it was a gift, my redemption.

But I was wrong.

It was another curse in a cursed life.

"And now I know he's out there somewhere," I said.

"So what's the real prophecy?" she asked.

She tucked her feet up under her and turned to face me fully. My arm was extended along the back of the couch behind her. She let her head fall to the side and looked at me, resting it against my arm.

"I'll have to look into it some more but what I got from Simmons' ramblings was Balor must be killed three times, once by each of his grandsons."

"But your brothers are dead," she said. "Aren't they?"

"Llowellyn is alive," I said.

"Where?"

"That's an excellent question and one I can answer honestly by saying I don't know."

She nodded. "And the Tools?"

"I'll have to track them down somehow," I said. "I have one piece of the Stone and know where the other two are, sort of. Then we have to go after the Spear and Sword."

"Okay," she said, raising her head and smiling.

Her smile reached all the way up to her eyes. Warmth spread through me.

"Okay?" I asked. "We're okay?"

"We'll get there," she said softly, leaning towards me. Her bright brown eyes met my green ones.

I could get lost in those eyes, I thought. I could look at her forever.

I raised my hand to brush a strand of hair behind her ear. How I longed to touch her, to cup her cheek in my palm, to lean closer and feel her breath on my skin, then press my lips to hers.

My hand hovered in the air for a moment, inches from her face.

Then, slowly, I let it fall back to the couch.

We'll get there, I thought.

CHAPTER TWENTY-NINE
Zemila

"Okay," Zemila said, reluctantly lifting her head from Lochlan's arm. She'd liked touching him.

"Okay?" he asked. "We're okay?"

"We'll get there," Zemila said. Then she leaned forward. She hadn't meant to. She stopped herself and a few strands of hair fell into her face. But she didn't move. She just stared into his impossibly-green eyes.

What a life you've led, she thought. What secrets you've kept.

She understood now. Or at least, she understood better than she had before.

Zemila felt Lochlan move his arm from the back of the couch. She didn't know what she wanted to happen. She didn't know how far she would let things go if they started.

He took a breath.

Timed stopped.

Then she felt his arm fall back to the couch.

Disappointment and relief warred inside her.

They stayed like that, looking at each other. For seconds or hours, she didn't know. Eventually, she closed her eyes and let her head rest on his arm again.

Zemila must have fallen asleep like that. She had a vague memory of soft lips on her temple. Then a growl and an accented voice saying 'Aye, good dog. You watch over your master.' But maybe she'd dreamt it.

She'd dreamed of him many times. Nothing solid though. Just feelings. Warmth. Safety. Trust. Maybe that's why she was so mad at him. It was hard for her to believe those feelings now. How could she after her life had been thrown into such chaos?

Zemila felt something hot and wet on her cheek.

"Ori," she said without opening her eyes. "That's gross."

The thunk-thunk-thunk of a heavy tail meeting carpet made her smile. She opened her eyes.

"Time for a walk?"

Oriole yipped happily in reply and went to sit at the top of the stairs.

It'll be light for a little while, she thought, looking at the clock on her wall. Zemila didn't want to be out alone. There'll be people at the dog park, she assured herself.

"Just let me get a glass of water," Zemila said to her dog.

She walked to the kitchen and around the granite countertop. Taking a glass from the cupboard and filling it, she thought back to everything Lochlan had told her.

She'd gotten lost in it. Not just the story, but in his voice. In him. His accent got thicker the longer he talked, like he'd forgotten to hide. Forgotten to blend in.

She liked that and smiled at the memory. She like that he showed her the part of him he tried to hide from everyone else.

She drank the glass dry in one go before placing it in the sink.

"Damnit," she whispered to no one. She wished he'd told her the truth from the beginning.

Would she have believed him? Would she have accepted him? It's easy to say yes, she would have. But who knows what her reaction would have been.

She wished she knew what she wanted. She wished she could either cut him out or let him in. She wished—

"Damnit," she said again, letting her palm fall with a light smack on the granite counter top.

All at once, a loud cracking sound filled the apartment, Zemila gasped and Oriole started barking.

Slowly Zemila lifted her hand. She hadn't meant to use her gift.

She hadn't meant to leave an imprint of her palm in the granite. But then again, she hadn't meant to crack that window in the hotel room in Paris, or the tile in the JACE bathrooms, or the peppershaker at Once More With Feeling.

And she hadn't meant to kill Simmons.

Not really. Not like that.

But she had.

Zemila took in a slow deep breath.

"Damnit."

φ